What Love Remembers

A CLOSED-DOOR SMALL-TOWN WIDOWER SHERIFF ROMANCE

SIERRA FALLS
BOOK ONE

VERONICA WOLFF

What Love Remembers

Sierra Falls, California, is the kind of sleepy mountain town people leave behind. But Sorrow Bailey stayed, trading her own dreams to run the struggling family lodge. Even her name is a family relic—one that's begun to feel like a curse. Everything changes when she uncovers a cache of letters from her three-times-great-grandmother and namesake, revealing a forbidden love affair.

Billy Preston, the new sheriff, is a widower looking to outrun his grief. After an accident at the Bailey lodge, he's drawn to Sorrow's quiet strength, and admiration quickly turns into something more. But when the discovery of the letters brings sudden attention to Sierra Falls, a string of suspicious "accidents" has Billy wondering if someone will go to deadly lengths to keep the town off the map.

With the community rallying around her, Sorrow finds guidance in her ancestor's words: true joy comes from the family you build, the friends who stand by you, and the love you dare to claim.

Cover Design by RomanceNovelCovers
Interior Typesetting by Edward Giordano

Copyright © 2012, 2026 Veronica Wolff

This novel was originally published in 2012 by Berkley Sensation (Penguin Group USA) under the title *Sierra Falls*. This edition has been significantly revised and updated by the author.

ISBN (Paperback): 978-1-941035-23-8
ISBN (eBook): 978-1-941035-24-5

Content Warning

This book contains the death of an elderly parent, a character living with Alzheimer's, past loss of a spouse, and references to motor vehicle accidents, drinking, and the effects of wartime military service.

Chapter One

Sorrow

I SCOOP MY EGG, potato, and bacon creation onto a plate and hold it out to Dad. "Come on, it's called a frittata. All the ingredients you like, just a different shape. See?" I prod it with my fork. "Bacon, eggs, and hash browns, all mixed up."

Bear Bailey gives it a skeptical once-over. "Mangled up, more like. Nothing beats Sully's scrambles." He winks at our fry cook. "Ain't that right, Sully?"

"Yes, sir." Sully nods sharply without looking up, completely focused on the griddle packed with pancakes. Going against his employer isn't in his playbook. You can take the man out of the military, but not the military out of the man.

"More for me, then." I step around Sully, sneak a bit of frittata onto a plate for him anyway, and give him a pointed look.

My father will never change the Thirsty Bear Tavern menu, but life would be dull if I didn't sneak in my quiet rebellions.

Sully just shakes his head. He's witnessed some version of this same father-daughter debate for years.

Speaking of debates... "Where's Mom?" I ask, dropping onto a stool beside Dad. I'd overheard him ranting to her about something earlier, and my mother's silence had said plenty. Not that my father yells. Bear Bailey just likes to... hold court.

"She's at the front desk," he says, dragging a piece of bacon through a puddle of syrup. "We've got two guests coming in this morning. Young couple from Sacramento. Snowshoe types, most likely."

"They'll need more than snowshoes if this keeps up." Sully wipes his hands on his apron and leans against the pass-through.

I follow his gaze. What started as a light dusting of snow this morning has thickened into heavy flurries.

"Really coming down now," Dad says, swiveling to look out the window. "Looks like it'll be a slow day for business."

"Maybe." I feel a little spark of hope. Maybe I'll have time to roast a nice cut of meat for dinner. Maybe even bake a pie. Dad couldn't complain about that.

Helping run the family's lodge and tavern isn't my dream, but with my older sister and brother long since moved away, and Dad still dealing with the aftermath of his stroke, someone had to step up. Mom helps, but she's not strong enough to do it all, and frankly, she lets my father call too many of the shots.

With my siblings out of the picture, family dinners faded away, and Sully's creations took center stage. My aversion to things with names like "Turkey Loaf" sparked my love affair with cooking.

It started small. TV shows taught me pasta dishes that didn't rely on Ragú. Then came soups. It still amazes me what you can make with meat, salt, veggies, and water.

The kitchen became my haven. I love the creativity, the flavors. I may be stuck in a tiny town, living with my parents, running their inn, but in the kitchen, I can escape. Make enchiladas and fly to Mexico. Whip up bruschetta and vanish to Italy.

Alone in the kitchen, everything fades—worries about housekeeping, plumbing, finances. Just me, the food, and the moment.

I could even picture doing it professionally. What a dream that would be. Not that I'll ever get the chance.

"You sure I can't make you a side of bacon?" Sully's voice startles me.

"Hmm?" I look up to find him watching me.

"Bacon. I can make it crispy. You used to like that."

I smile. "Good memory."

Sully rolled into Sierra Falls on a Harley when I was just a kid. Quiet, a little restless, but he fit right in. Stayed on as cook at the Big Bear Lodge. Folks shortened Tom Sullivan to Sully to avoid confusing him with Tom Harlan over at the hardware store. And just like that, Sully became a fixture.

He's not one to share—just that he did a few tours in Afghanistan and has a couple ex-wives. One thing I do know: he's a good man. I think of him as an honorary uncle.

I glance at the clock. It's 8:30, and I'm already on my back foot—my days don't begin so much as explode. "I should be getting started," I tell Sully. "But thanks."

I scrape the last bite to the center of the plate, savoring it. Next time I'll try sun-dried tomatoes—less moisture.

I clear my dishes and glance outside. Snow's piling up. We didn't get much over the holidays, but January arrived with a vengeance. Too much snow becomes a hassle, and this is definitely edging toward hassle territory.

I have a dozen things I should be doing—shoveling the walk, checking the generator, maybe tracking down that weird clanking noise in the boiler room. But someone's got to hold the fort here for a while.

"Duty calls." I sigh.

Sully dings the bell. "Order up."

Dad looks around for our waitress. "Where's Helen?"

"Probably stuck in this mess. She's got three kids at two schools. And if it's a snow day..."

"Someone's gotta cover." He starts to rise.

I press a hand to his shoulder. "Sit, Dad. I've got it."

Ever since the stroke, his movements have slowed. He deserves to enjoy his coffee in peace.

I grab the plates and serve our handful of regulars. Tourists are rare. Sierra Falls is a gold rush town, too remote for Tahoe's resorts, too far from Route 50 for city traffic. We survive on locals, the occasional stranded traveler, and in season, a trickle of hikers, hunters, and anglers passing through.

I serve Sheriff Billy Preston last. He looks up from his paper. "Morning, Sorrow."

"Sheriff." I soften the greeting with a smile.

I like the man. There's something quiet, maybe haunted, in his eyes. I've heard he's a widower. I try to meet his gaze when we speak, give a genuine smile, a little light against the dark.

He hasn't lived here long. Time will tell if that haunted look fades. I hope it does. He earned my goodwill from the start by not making some dumb comment about my name. Sorrow is a family name, but sometimes it feels like a curse.

Dad's obsessed with our ancestors—so many generations of great-aunts named Sorrow. According to him, I'm doomed to repeat their hard-luck lives if I don't marry right, clean the garage, or call the damn plumber.

"I've told you before—it's Billy." His tone is gruff but polite. He takes his plate, easing my load. "Looks good." Then he adds, low, "But I'd have liked to try that frittata."

His conspiratorial tone surprises me. That anyone wants my food is a thrill. I smile, real and wide. Someday, I'd love to cook for more than just my family.

I hold his gaze. Is he truly sad, or does he just have those kinds of eyes? His smile lights his face, but does it reach his heart?

His eyes crinkle slightly at the edges, like he's trying to

puzzle me out. I realize I'm staring and shake it off. "If you want frittatas, take it up with that man." I nod toward Dad, still yammering at Sully. He'll be in that same spot when I swing back for my lunch shift. "Bear Bailey isn't a fan of change."

I don't know Billy well, and I'm not interested—not like that. I've got a boyfriend. But I do enjoy our chats. He used to be a lieutenant in the Oakland PD, and I love his stories about city life. Plus, there's something about his manner that always makes me feel seen.

An idea hits. "Hold on." I dash back into the kitchen. Last night's apple cinnamon bread is too much temptation for me to keep around. I return with a foil-wrapped bundle. "Not a frittata, but it's a close second."

"Sorry," he says, deadpan. "Law enforcement only eats donuts."

I pretend to be offended and pull the bread away. "See if I ever try to feed you again."

"On second thought, it smells too good." He laughs, snatching it from my hands. "Gimme that."

I laugh too, not caring who sees. It feels good. For the first time today, my shoulders begin to relax.

Then a hideous sound locks me up again.

Outside, there's the long whine of bending timber, followed by a loud crash.

The sheriff and I lock eyes.

For a moment, comfort cuts through the fear, and I'm glad I'm not alone. Which is crazy. I don't even know the man.

But the thought vanishes as fast as it came, and I'm dashing out the door, Billy and the rest of our patrons right behind me.

Chapter Two

Billy

MY FIRST THOUGHT is that someone's crashed a car into a tree.

My second is of my wife.

Every other thought is.

But this time, guilt twists in my gut. I've been joking with a pretty woman, pretending for a moment that I'm just a regular guy.

But I'm not.

Three years ago, my wife was hit by a bus on her way to work. She didn't make it—and I wasn't there.

There's no predicting what'll bring me back to that day. No way to know what small, stupid detail will send my mind spinning. I still find myself wondering—what did she eat for breakfast that morning? Did she read the news over coffee, or head straight out the door? The questions come like waves I can't stop.

This time, it's the crash outside that drags me back.

Most days, I keep a shield up. I shove the bad thoughts aside until the middle of the night, where they always seem to find me. But meeting Sorrow's eyes—something in our shared moment cuts straight through my defenses, and for a heartbeat, I'm back in time. Morning light through our bedroom window, Keri telling me to sleep in for once. I'd been up late with paperwork, and she'd insisted I take my Saturday morning to rest.

When the beat cop showed up hours later, I was making lunch. It had taken them that long to identify her. To find me.

While I'd been showering, gulping the last of my cold coffee, debating whether I could skip a shave, my wife had been dying on the side of the road. While I'd been griping about paperwork, she was already gone.

Six months of leave followed. Then a few years of showing up, doing the job, but nothing more. Lifting weights till my arms shook. Eventually, an old buddy called with a lifeline—Sierra Falls needed a new sheriff. Before I could think twice, I was running unopposed, packing up, and heading for the mountains.

Getting away from the city helped—away from all the reminders, the ghosts. Out here, I can almost find peace.

Almost.

But now, sharing that brief, strange connection with Sorrow Bailey, I feel cracked open. For an instant, it's like she can see straight through me—to all the guilt I've buried, all the pain I can't quite let go of.

I shove the thought aside and bolt from my booth. Out the door. Sheriff again.

Sorrow and I stand shoulder to shoulder. One glance tells me what happened—a tree branch has crashed straight through the Big Bear Lodge roof.

A good chunk of it's gone now, nothing but splintered wood, snow, and shingles. If I angle my head just right, I can see daylight through the attic window on the far side.

"Oh, sh—" Sorrow catches herself. "Sugar."

"Go ahead and say it," I tell her. "Sometimes swearing helps."

She folds her arms tight across her chest, like she might come apart if she lets go. "It's the Sorrow thing."

"The what?"

"My luck. The Sorrow luck. Every woman in my family named Sorrow seems to end up cursed—bad luck with men, money, you name it. Why they keep using the name, I'll never understand."

Edith Bailey bursts out of the lodge, clutching a crocheted shawl around her shoulders. "What on earth—?"

"The roof." Sorrow gives her mom a quick glance, then turns back to the wreckage. "How much is this going to cost?"

We move closer. I rest my hand on the trunk, studying the massive tree. "You've got some dead branches up there."

"I knew we needed to trim them." Sorrow shoots her mom a look. "I told him we needed to trim the deadwood."

I can guess "him" means her father, but that's not my business. I brush snow from a low branch. "This is wet snow—heavy stuff, especially after last week's storm. Even this old beauty couldn't take it."

Edith chews her thumbnail, silent.

I don't know the Baileys well, but Sorrow's mom hovering there feels like the last thing her daughter needs. I guide Edith gently toward the door. "You'll catch a chill, ma'am. Go find yourself a proper coat. I'll help your daughter."

Edith stops short. "Oh, good Lord—the hope chests." Panic floods her face. "Your grandmother's trunks. The attic'll get soaked. You've got to save the trunks!"

"We'll take care of it," I promise, steering her inside. Then I turn back to Sorrow. "What trunks?"

"There's a mountain of junk up there," she mutters. "As if I don't have enough going on." She heads for the door.

She looks so drawn, so alone, that I fall into step beside her. "Can I help?"

Before she can answer, the wind gusts hard, a swirl of snow blinding us. Instinct kicks in, and I reach for her. Silly, really—the cars are parked, the branches above are clear—but I can't seem to stop myself.

We freeze there. Sunlight hits the snow, scattering light across her face and hair. The flakes melt against my shirt, cool against my skin.

When the air clears, she's looking at me. Her eyes aren't blue at all, I realize—they're green, like light through bottle glass.

Guilt slices through me, sharp and sudden. I drop my hand fast. It feels like cheating on Keri. I know it's not true, but my heart doesn't get the memo.

Silence stretches between us, then we both speak at once.

"What do—"

"How is—"

We laugh, awkward and humorless. I try to smile, but it doesn't quite land.

"Just my luck, huh?" she says with a shrug.

"It might not be so bad."

We study the wreckage. Snow drifts steadily through the hole, soft but relentless.

"Or maybe not," I admit.

"Yeah." Pain flickers across her face before she smooths it away. "It's kinda bad."

For a moment, her hurt pushes mine aside. "Seriously, Sorrow. You okay?"

She sighs. "Complaining won't fix it."

Practical. Steady. I like that. She's not one for drama. "What can I do to help?"

"Unless you're a roofer, nothing." She bites her lip, thinking. "Damien—he's my... friend. He's got contacts."

Damien. I've seen him around. The guy she has dinner with, rides off with. More than a friend, clearly.

I want to offer more, to stay, to help. But it's not my place. She already has someone. And I've got a job to do.

We say goodbye, and I head back to the tavern to settle my bill. Time to get back to work.

And try to push this strange, stirring moment from my mind.

Chapter Three

I SEND the sheriff on his way, but the look on his face leaves me feeling pitiable, and I hate that. I might need help, but I'm not helpless. Billy Preston might've been a big-shot lieutenant back in the city, but I refuse to be some small-town damsel in his eyes.

Besides, I already have a man who loves to help. Maybe it's because Damien's stuck behind a desk all day at his family's business, but he seems to relish any excuse to play the hero.

He's always eager to roll up his sleeves—make a few calls, find the right guy, smooth things over. Sometimes he's a little *too* eager and swoops in before I can even try.

Still, he means well. And in moments like this—snow blowing through my attic—I have to admit, his brand of take-charge confidence comes in handy.

I sigh and reach for my phone. I might not need saving, but right now, I could use some help. I sit on an old stool, staring at the attic wreckage as I call him.

"Hey, Bailey," Damien says, his smile clear in his voice. Hearing him is a relief, even if that nickname still grates—a holdover from middle school that still haunts me.

"What's up? I told you I'm picking you up at seven. We'll head back to my place for some barbecue. You can bring that potato salad."

He's already describing our evening before I can explain there's a tree in my attic. That's Damien—quick to jump in, quicker to assume he knows what I need.

When I finally tell him about the roof, his voice shifts into problem-solving mode. He'll call someone, fix it, make it right. It's what he does. And even though part of me is grateful, another part bristles. He never stops to ask what I want—only what he can do.

Still, that sharp focus in his voice calms me in spite of myself. Damien will take care of it. He always does. For a second, I wonder if I take him for granted, but I push the thought away. I can handle plenty, but finding a roofer in this weather isn't one of them. And Damien? He can make things happen with a single phone call.

"Unfortunately, we need someone ASAP." I stand in the center of the attic where I don't have to hunch over. Snow blows in, stinging my cheeks. "A branch from that old pine came down and smashed right through."

"Yeah, it was dumping pretty hard this morning," he says, and I hear a car door slam. "I told your dad he needed to cut that tree back."

"I know. But what Bear wants—"

"Bear gets," he finishes with a sigh.

Everyone in Sierra Falls loves my father, but they all know how stubborn he is. As far as Bear Bailey's concerned, there's only one way to run the Big Bear Lodge and the Thirsty Bear Tavern—and it's his way.

"Don't worry," Damien says. "We'll have you patched up by happy hour. What's the damage?"

I spin slowly, assessing. The snow's slowing, and the sun is coming out. Meltwater is already dripping steadily from the hole, plip-plip-plip.

Sometimes I don't want Damien to swoop in and fix everything—but this isn't one of those times.

"It's pretty bad," I admit. "Snow's piled everywhere, and meltwater's seeping through the floorboards. I called Jack Jessup, but he's booked solid till next week."

"I'll call him," he says, and that's that. He's Damien Simmons, son of Dabney Simmons, CEO of Simmons Timber —his family practically owns half the town. If a Simmons wants a roof fixed, it gets fixed.

"Thanks, Damien."

"My pleasure, Bailey. I'll expect my reward later."

He laughs, and the sound is as smooth as ever. It still gets a reaction out of me—old habits die hard—but mostly it just makes me tired. What we have isn't love; we both know that. Whatever spark we once had feels like muscle memory now.

Damien's always had a way with women—he had it in high school, and he's only gotten better. It's nice being the one he's focused on, but deep down, I've never quite trusted it. Maybe that's old insecurity talking. Maybe it's just instinct.

But he's hot, we're both a little lonely, and honestly, everyone in town expects it. Sierra Falls isn't exactly crawling with singles. "The Simmons boy" and "Bear's youngest" is practically local prophecy.

Still, he gets some things—the weight of family expectations, the sense of duty. Like me, he's stuck around, even when so many others didn't.

Even so, sometimes he gets carried away, and I hate the feeling that I'm another item on his to-do list.

"Thanks, Damien. I'll see you later." I rake a hand through my hair, take a breath, and turn back to business.

Knowing him, a roofer will show up any minute. In the meantime, I might as well do what Mom asked—sort through generations of old junk that never earned a spot downstairs before the water ruins everything.

"What a disaster." I nudge an old trunk, its wood already swollen and warped. It's one of the family "hope chests," though judging by the name burned into the lid—Sorrow—it must've belonged to one of my ancestors. Guess her hopes never made it out of the attic.

I drag it from the wall, wincing at how the wood gleams with water. "Sorry, Grandma Sorrow. Or Auntie. Or whoever you were." Kneeling, I wrestle with the rusted hinge.

"Too bad they didn't name Laura after you," I mutter. If my parents had saddled my older sister with the name Sorrow, maybe *she'd* be the one kneeling in an icy puddle right now. "If I'd had a different name, maybe I'd be the one off in Silicon Valley with the fancy job and car."

But no—Laura and the others ran off, leaving me here with the leaking roofs and rotting trunks. "Maybe I'll find treasure in here," I say as I pry the lid open. "Then it'll be my turn."

A wave of mildew and mothballs hits me. "Oh, jeez." I rub my nose and glance up through the hole in the roof just in time to sneeze.

"All right," I mutter. "Gotta start somewhere."

I dig through the trunk—family photos, papers, all of it damp and musty. Most is junk: old ledgers, threadbare quilts, mildewed frames, even a warped guitar. If it were up to me, I'd haul the whole lot to the Silver City recycling center. But with Bear and Mom? Dream on.

"Seriously?" I groan, holding up a shoebox full of ancient receipts. I toss it into a paper bag. "They *cannot* need this stuff."

Something at the bottom catches my eye—a delicate lace shawl, ivory embroidery yellowed with age. I lift it carefully from the trunk, afraid the wood might snag it. Something flutters loose and lands at my feet.

Letters.

They're bound with a strip of faded rickrack, the paper thin and yellowed but intact. The handwriting is graceful—a looping, old-fashioned cursive. A shiver runs through me. These are someone's secrets. Someone from *my* family.

I slide the ribbon off and unfold the first page. The script is dense, but one line at the bottom jumps out:

Sincerely, and ever your Loving, Sorrow.

"Well, what do you know?" I whisper. I always knew my name was passed down, but seeing it in her own hand feels like touching a live wire to the past. "Which Sorrow were you?"

I plop down, not even caring that the icy puddle soaks through my jeans. The date at the top reads 1851.

It had to be the first—and saddest—Sorrow of them all: my three-times great-grandmother, Sorrow Crabtree.

Chapter Four

Marlene

I sɪт behind the wheel of my pickup, shaking. I've skidded off the road straight into a snowbank.

The old truck's light as a feather—at least in the back—and fishtails at the first hint of flurries. By the end of winter, there'll be enough snow in the bed to weigh it down, but these early-season dustings are always the worst.

I'd love a nice car, something sleek and European-sounding —Volvo, maybe, or Audi. But when Frank left, he took half of our already-lean bank account and left me with this pickup.

He and his new squeeze live in Pinole now, in some well-to-do development, probably driving something shiny and new. The hell of it is, she isn't even that much younger. It might sting less if he'd left for a fresh-faced bimbo. But no—Frank left me for a late-fifties professional type. Pharmaceutical sales. Soon they'll retire, buy that boat we always talked about, and sail off into the sunset.

Some other woman is getting my boat.

And I'm left with the old Ford, two elderly aunts, and an ailing mother, haunted by questions about where I went wrong.

Don't go there, as my grandson would say.

I shove the truck into reverse, willing my hands to stop shaking. It isn't even that cold, for heaven's sake. I hit the gas.

A horrible whirring sound answers me as the tires spin uselessly.

Damned pickup. It's got one of those tiny backseats that take forever to wrangle my aunts into. I wanted a sedan, but Frank insisted. I slam my palms on the wheel. What on earth do I need with a pickup?

If I can't get unstuck, I'll be late picking up the ladies. My aunts and mother are a trio—the famous Kidd sisters: Emerald, Pearl, and Ruby, the "baby" at eighty-two.

If I'm late, they'll be late for the historical society meeting, and I'll never hear the end of it. Those women live for their meetings.

And I've got enough trouble there as it is. Somehow I ended up chairwoman, and we're already a day late and a dollar short planning the annual Sierra Falls Festival.

It's one of those quirky small-town events Northern California's known for. Gilroy has garlic, other towns have chili cook-offs and art walks. For Sierra Falls, it's the Spring Fling in May. Except now it's January, and our coffers are empty. We could host bingo nights till we're blue in the face, and it wouldn't fund a pie toss, much less a whole festival.

I stroke the dashboard. "Come on, girl. Back us out of here, and I'll buy you a nice set of snow tires."

I hit the gas again. That same high-pitched whir. With a sigh, I drop my forehead to the steering wheel.

I'll have to call one of my boys—but which one? Jack and Eddie live closest, but I hate to bother them. Jessup Brothers Construction already has them running around like one-armed paperhangers.

There's always Jack's wife, Tina, but she's never around during the day. Or maybe she just keeps odd hours—I can never seem to catch her. Their son's a senior in high school now, so no carpools to blame. Regardless, I'm not calling her.

Mark's out too. He's a doctor in Silver City and on call today.

That leaves Scott. My park ranger boy with the easy smile. Though not so much of a boy anymore—he just turned thirty-four. His truck can surely get me unstuck, I think as I dig through my purse for my phone, wondering where the years have gone.

The cab's growing cold fast, but I pull off my gloves to dial. My fingers fumble over the screen, stiff with cold.

A sharp rapping on the window makes me jump a foot. "Oh!"

I wipe away condensation with my sleeve. There he is, the new sheriff.

He fills the window—broad, solid, calm—and adrenaline surges through me. I glance in the rearview mirror. Sure enough, his SUV looms behind me, lights flashing softly in the snow.

Why does the sight of a police car always make me panic? I tell myself to breathe. I couldn't have been speeding; I wasn't even moving. I roll the window down. "Did I... is there something wrong?"

"Everything all right, Mrs. Jessup?" Billy Preston's voice is warm, his eyes concerned.

I press a hand to my chest, relieved. He's not here to ticket me—he's just worried. The new sheriff really is such a thoughtful man.

"Please," I say. "Call me Marlene. Jessup was my husband's name. There's another Mrs. Jessup now." That last part comes out sharper than I mean it to.

"All right, Marlene," he says slowly. His gaze drops to my hands, still trembling. "You sure you're okay?"

"I think... maybe not." I try to wriggle my fingers back into my gloves. Why won't they cooperate? "It's hell getting old.

Beats the alternative, I suppose." I shake my head. I'm rambling like a fool.

He opens my door and steadies me as I climb out. "Let's get you in the truck. You warm up, I'll shovel you out, and we'll get you on your way."

I glance back at my pickup. The snowbank isn't high, but I've managed to wedge my front wheels in good. "The darn thing was skidding all over."

"We'll get you out. Don't worry."

He helps me into his SUV, where the heat's cranked up.

"You live nearby?" he asks.

"About a mile down the road, near Big Bear Lodge."

"Ah." He nods, like that explains everything. Which it probably does—the whole town knows everyone and everything.

I settle in and watch him shovel. Sheriff Billy Preston is a big man—broad shoulders, strong jaw, a touch of weathering that only makes him more attractive. Handsome, in a rugged sort of way.

Everyone knows his story. His wife died in an accident several years ago, and he recently moved here, looking for a fresh start.

I watch from his SUV as he finishes shoveling, efficient and unhurried. He gives me a thumbs-up, stows the shovel, and climbs into the driver's seat beside me.

"All set," he says, then notices the tremble in my hands. He gives me a reassuring smile. "Maybe we should leave your truck for now? I'll drive you, make sure you get home."

"Oh, I can't go home. I'm headed to my aunts' house. We drive together to the historical society meeting. I suppose we could always take Pearl's Buick."

He gives me a disbelieving look. "Is your aunt okay to drive in this? Does she have snow tires?"

"That old tank's handled more weather than our town snowplow." A little irreverent giggle escapes me, and I can't help adding, "The car's solid too."

Good grief, who am I today?

Billy shakes his head with a smile. "Lead on, fair lady. Where am I headed?"

"Just up ahead. The old Victorian on Maple. But..." I glance at my truck, small and helpless in the snowbank. "Will it be okay parked there?"

"It's not going anywhere." His smile softens. "And it seems like you've had enough of that truck for one day."

I don't argue. The thought of getting back behind the wheel makes me feel jittery.

We ride in silence for a bit, until he says, "I've been meaning to stop by one of those historical society meetings. Learn more about the town."

"Really?" I glance at him, surprised. "We meet every other Tuesday at the community center. You're welcome to join us anytime."

"I might just do that."

He pulls up to the house. Sure enough, my mother and aunts are peering out the window. They'll have a field day with this—the new sheriff driving me to their door.

"Thank you, Sheriff Preston."

"Billy," he says. "And it's no trouble."

I climb out, and he waits till I'm safely on the porch before driving off.

My Aunt Ruby opens the door before I can knock. "Marlene! What happened? Where's your truck?"

"Long story. I'll explain on the way."

My mother appears behind her, eyes bright. "Was that the sheriff?"

"Yes, Ma. That was the sheriff."

"My, my. He's quite a specimen, isn't he?"

"He's a perfect gentleman," I say. "The pickup got stuck in a snowbank, and he helped me."

We pile into Aunt Pearl's ancient car—she's the only one still driving—and I tell them what happened. By the time we reach the community center, they've extracted every last detail and are already plotting how to thank the good sheriff.

"We should invite him to dinner," Ruby declares.

"Absolutely not."

"And why not? The poor man's probably lonely. His wife passed, you know."

"Everyone knows. And I'm sure he has plenty of company without a bunch of old biddies fussing over him."

"Well, someone should invite him," Aunt Pearl says. "It's the neighborly thing to do."

The meeting's already underway when we arrive, and I hurry to my place at the front. Sorrow Bailey gives me a curious look as I slip into my seat, probably wondering why I'm late.

I tap my gavel. "Sorry for the delay. Let's get started on the festival budget."

For the next hour, I manage to focus on tent permits and stage rental fees, but my mind keeps circling back to earlier—the shock of sliding off the road, the concern in the sheriff's voice as he helped me through it.

Stop it, Marlene. Grateful is one thing; making too much of the new sheriff's kindness is another.

But after the meeting, when I find my truck waiting at the community center—with sand under the tires and a note from Billy saying he took care of it—I can't help but smile.

Maybe getting older doesn't have to mean becoming invisible after all.

Chapter Five

Sorrow

I SIT on one of the attic trunks, ignoring the chaos around me. I've been sneaking peeks at the letters all morning while sorting what needs to go downstairs—just reading snippets here and there—and I can't wait to dive in tonight. The one in my hands looks like a love letter... written by someone who left my ancestor behind.

I can relate. My siblings—and practically everyone from school—have left town, abandoning me in Sierra Falls.

I scoot my feet out of the way of a roofer and slide the stack into a Ziploc before anything gets damaged. Are they all love letters? Torture. All I want is to curl up with a pot of tea and read them, but instead I'm stuck with a crew of careless construction guys.

A horrible crash jolts me. I jump, scuttling across the attic and ducking under the low ceiling. "No! I mean... please. Oh! Watch the dollhouse."

Jack Jessup's crew has arrived like bats out of hell, more focused on speed than on Bailey family treasures. I plant myself in front of my childhood dollhouse. "I'd just like to move some things aside, if you don't mind."

Apparently, they do mind. They barrel up and down the stairs, tromping gritty, blackened snow everywhere. They've cut away the damaged part of the roof, and a big wet clump of snow just fell into an open trunk. So much for my careful sorting—between the wind and the commotion, my tidy little piles don't stand a chance.

I tuck the letters into the waistband of my jeans, grab an armful of vintage dresses, and hustle them downstairs. I'm wrestling the last trunk into a corner when Damien's head appears at the top of the stairs.

"Bailey," he says, eyes widening as he takes in the roof. "Holy crap, you weren't lying. The roof caved in."

"It didn't cave in," I snap. "A branch crashed through. And your guys are doing a bang-up job destroying the rest."

"Whoa, whoa." He bounds up the last few steps, closing the distance to pull me into his arms. "Easy, babe. What do you need? Want me to help clear this stuff?"

I let myself sink into him, exhaling a big sigh. I should hold my tongue—Damien is here to help. I nod. "Yes, please."

With one arm still around me, he shouts to the crew to haul the rest of the trunks and boxes downstairs. He pulls me out of the way as they move fast. The place clears before my eyes.

I press a hand to his chest and step back. "Thank you."

He grins and pinches my chin. "Anything for a lovely lady in distress. And they're not my guys—they're Jack's. Doing me a favor. They want to patch it up and get out of here as fast as you do."

He hugs me close, then pulls back again, sliding a hand up under my sweater. "Whatcha hiding?"

I swat him playfully, aware of the crew still working. "Come downstairs. I'll make coffee and show you."

The Bailey kitchen is my favorite room in the house— sunny and warm, heated by the old woodburning stove that probably breaks every environmental law on the books. The yellow walls and gingham curtains need an update, but if anyone tries to touch them, they'll have to go through me first. Good thing Dad hates change.

Still, there have been updates. When we renovated the tavern kitchen to meet new codes, I convinced Dad to upgrade some of our appliances. Out went the avocado-green fridge, in came a shiny GE with ice and water in the door. The ancient stove got replaced too, with a six-burner and a griddle.

This kitchen is my refuge.

I make Damien's coffee the way he likes it—black, with a splash of half-and-half—and bring it to the table. Loud crashing and scraping echo from above. I squeeze his shoulder. "Can I get you something to go with that? I made apple cinnamon bread."

He takes a sip, then stands to pull me close, nestling his face in my neck. His hand slides down to cup my backside. "I know what I need, and it's not food."

"Jeez, Damien." I laugh and push him away. "You don't quit, do you?"

He waggles his brows. "You know it."

That cocky grin sparks an image of the sheriff—steady, quiet, and about as far from arrogant as a man can get.

I step back, unsettled. Needing something to do, I pull the letters from where I tucked them. "I wanted to show you something."

"I'll show you something," he teases, reaching for me again.

I flinch away, irritation bubbling. We've always had chemistry, but lately it's not enough. Something's missing. And that makes me feel guilty, because Damien really is a good guy, always there when I need help.

"Please. I want to tell you about this. For once, I'm thinking about something besides the lodge."

He traces a finger along my collarbone. "You know what I think about?"

"Be serious." I grab a knife and start slicing bread for toast.

"I am serious." He steps behind me. "Hey, no bread. I'm cutting out carbs this week. Feeling a little loose in the cage." He pats his hard stomach.

I roll my eyes. "Loose in the cage? The only thing loose on you are a few screws."

The guy's all discipline... except when it comes to sex. I see the hunger in his eyes and edge away. "Damien." My laugh feels forced. "I really want you to see this. Besides, you can't expect me to get"—I lower my voice—"in the mood, with all this going on." I point to the ceiling.

"What better time?" He picks up a slice of bread, then pushes it away decisively. "All that hammering—you could make all the noise you wanted, and nobody would hear a thing."

"I'm showing you what I found." I sit at the table, ending the conversation, and lay out the letters.

He sighs and sits across from me. "Okay, Bailey. Shoot. What'd you find?"

"Letters." I untie the rickrack ribbon and sift through them.

He squints. "You're turning me down for a bunch of old letters? Come on, Bail." He takes my hand, thumb circling my palm. "I've gotta get back soon. We're wasting time."

Normally that touch would melt me, but not today. I pull my hand free. "They're from my great-great-great-grand-mother, Sorrow Crabtree."

"Poor woman," he says, drumming his fingers.

His tone makes me look up. "What's that supposed to mean?"

"Sorrow Crabtree... that's some name." His phone buzzes, and he checks it before setting it aside.

"No, listen. There's a story. Her father loved his wife so

much that when she died giving birth, he named their baby Sorrow."

"Huh. Is that what's in the letters?" He reaches for them, and something protective flares in me.

"Wait." I scoop them up before he can touch them. "Let me read you a bit. It's dated April 1851—can you imagine?"

"Cool," he says automatically.

"Wait—listen." I find the line I want. "*You may be fancy, Mister Buck Larsen, but my mama told me to stay away from men like you.*"

I glance up. He's sneaking a look at his phone again.

"Buck Larsen," I repeat. "He's practically a legend—frontiersman, explorer, California hero. He lived here in Sierra Falls during the Gold Rush. Before he became *Buck Larsen.*"

"I know who he is."

"Did you know he lived here?"

"Of course. It's in every tourist brochure."

"Well, I didn't." My voice edges sharper. "I've lived here forever, and nobody told me. Did you know my ancestor knew him? She wrote him love letters."

"Huh. Okay." He checks his watch. "That's cool, Sorrow. Maybe you can write your own brochure."

"I'm serious."

The crunch of tires on gravel pulls my attention. I peer out the window. "Who's that?"

Damien joins me, hands sliding around my hips. "Preston," he says flatly.

My pulse kicks up. "What's he doing here?"

"No clue. But I'll go find out." He starts for the door, but I grab his wrist.

"Wait." I don't want a scene—those two aren't exactly fast friends. I paste on a smile. "I'll get it."

I step outside before the sheriff reaches the porch and shut the door behind me. "Sheriff," I say with a polite smile.

He's in jeans, a flannel, and a canvas jacket—no uniform today. I try not to notice how good he looks, or to think too hard about the little flip in my stomach when our eyes meet.

"Ms. Bailey." He tips the brim of his cap. "Figured I'd check in, see how you're holding up after yesterday."

"Everything's fine. Jack Jessup's crew is patching the roof."

"Good." He glances up at the hammering overhead. "Mind if I take a look? Just want to make sure it's safe."

"That's not necessary—"

The front door opens behind me. Damien steps out, arm sliding possessively around my waist. "Preston," he says curtly.

"Simmons." The sheriff's jaw tightens.

"We've got it handled," Damien says. "My guy's taking care of it."

"Your guy?" He arches a brow.

"Jack Jessup. Doing me a favor, getting it patched fast."

"Appreciate you checking in, Sheriff," I say quickly, trying to break the tension. "But really, we're fine."

His gaze shifts from Damien to me, something unreadable flickering in his eyes. "All right then. You know where to find me if you need anything."

He turns and heads for his truck, and I watch him go, ignoring the little twist in my chest as he walks away.

Damien squeezes my hip. "Guy's got nerve."

"He was just checking on us. It's his job."

"Right." His tone says he doesn't buy it. "I really do need to get back to work. You gonna be okay?"

I nod, suddenly tired. "Yeah. Thanks for getting Jack's crew here so fast."

He kisses my forehead. "Anytime, babe. I'll call you later."

I watch him drive off, then turn back inside. Through the kitchen window, I spot the letters waiting on the table.

I pour a cup of coffee and sit, tuning out the steady hammering above. I pick up another letter, unfold it carefully, and read.

Dear Buck,

You say I am cruel to refuse you, but what choice have you left me? You speak of love yet never of staying. You paint pictures of places I shall never see, adventures that will never be mine, but not once do you ask if I might want to go with you. You've already decided I won't. You've already decided I am content to remain here, waiting, while you chase your fortune.

You are wrong.

I may be a woman bound by expectations you will never trouble yourself to understand, but I am not without dreams. Not without desires that reach beyond these mountains. Still, I know my duty, and I know my heart. And both keep me here, even as you prepare to leave.

Do not mistake my refusal for a lack of feeling. I refuse you because I feel too much, not too little. I refuse you because I know that loving you would break me, and I have no wish to spend my life mourning what might have been.

If you truly cared for me, you would understand this. But I suspect your freedom matters more than I ever could.

Yours in sorrow,
Sorrow Crabtree

THE LETTER TREMBLES in my hands. My ancestor wrote these words almost two hundred years ago, but they could've been written yesterday. The ache in them feels fresh, immediate.

She loved a man who wouldn't stay. A man who wanted adventure more than her.

Buck didn't truly *see* my ancestor. Didn't see that she might want more than to wait by the hearth while he chased gold in the distant hills.

Damien's always there for the practical stuff but checks his phone when I share something that matters. He tries, but he doesn't really *see* me either.

The sheriff's gaze was different. Like I matter. Like what I want matters. And then there was that flicker of disappointment when Damien appeared.

I shake my head, irritated at myself. What am I even thinking? Billy Preston is just doing his job. That's all.

I fold the letter and set it atop the stack. Above me, the hammering continues a steady rhythm through the old beams. I wonder if my ancestor heard the same sounds when they built this place, back when Sierra Falls was new and the future felt uncertain.

Some things, I think, never really change.

Chapter Six

Sully

UNLOADING meat in this slushy parking lot is killing my lower back.

I haul another side of beef from the Jeep's trunk. The monthly drive to Carson City for supplies is a pain, but I can manage it. Bear sure can't, not with that bum leg after his stroke.

Still, sometimes I want to get back on my bike and ride off. I wandered for years, chasing something that never appeared. Maybe I'll spend my whole life waiting for it.

Damien breezes out the tavern door with Edith on his heels. They spot me at the same time, calling hellos.

Edith stops short and turns to tell Damien, "I didn't know Sully was back. I'm sure he can give my car a jump. I don't want to trouble you."

I've got plenty on my plate but keep my mouth shut. We both know her offer's pure formality. Lately, Damien takes every chance to help anyone remotely connected to Sorrow. The kid's worse than a rent collector, always coming around. I'm starting to wonder how much the girl even wants his help.

Sure enough, he says smoothly, "Edith, you know helping you is never any trouble."

Smooth operator. I'm happy to be left out of it. I hide a grin, grab a pallet of bread and buns, and haul it inside.

Don't get me wrong—I appreciate anyone looking out for Sorrow. But something about their fling doesn't sit quite right. The way women look at Damien, you'd think things would be perfect between them.

I guess a girl doesn't have a lot of dating options in a small town like Sierra Falls. Especially someone like Sorrow, too busy to make it to Silver City for any nightlife.

I glance back at Damien. I like the kid well enough, but he's a smidge too slick for my taste. Maybe that's why, when I see them together, I just don't get it.

Damien pops Edith's hood. "Did you leave the lights on? That'll burn out the battery in no time."

"I never do. It beeps if I try."

"Even the interior lights," he says. "They'll drain the juice if they're left on all night."

Bear's heavy step sounds behind me. I turn to see him watching Damien and Edith.

His cheek jumps with an old tic. "That boy's got the town charmed."

"And your women seem to be at the top of the list," I say. Bear scowls, so I add, "Sorrow could do worse. It's nice for a woman to have a man around—buy her dinner, tell her she's pretty."

Bear's face doesn't change. "My fool daughter is set on cooking her own dinner."

"You know what I mean. A girl likes to feel appreciated." I sober. "She's special. Good on Damien that he noticed."

"That sheriff's been doing some noticing too. He's been coming around more than usual."

I think on that. "Yeah, I've seen his eyes on her once or twice."

"Don't know if I should encourage it or punch the man," Bear mutters.

I laugh. "It's never wise to hit a lawman."

Edith's engine roars to life, and Damien gives the gas a few sharp revs.

"Looks like Superman saved the day," Bear says, his voice edged with bitterness. Maybe still wanting to be Edith's Superman, if you ask me.

"No surprise there," I say. Whatever I think about Damien Simmons, the guy's helpful.

Bear eyes the Jeep. "Hey, Sergeant, these groceries aren't going to unload themselves."

"That's Captain to you." I shoulder past him, hauling out a couple of tenderloins. When he bends to help, his hands tremble. I shoot him a look. "And I'm ordering you to keep your hands off my ground round."

A cloud darkens his face. "Seems to me I paid for it, and I'm perfectly able to carry it, too."

I count to ten. Bear hasn't been the same since the stroke—no man would be—but he fights his weaknesses, and anyone who notices.

Edith hurries over. "Bear, I need you."

That gets his attention. The woman knows her husband.

Bear raises his brows. "What is it?"

"Damien says we need to keep the car running for half an hour to recharge the battery."

He narrows his eyes. "And?"

"And would you do it, honey? Sit in the car for me? I'm so chilly, and these gloves aren't doing a thing." She flexes her fingers. "I need to go in and find my good driving gloves. The lined ones make all the difference."

I see what she's doing and wonder if Bear does, too.

He scowls. "Can't we just let the damn thing run?"

"I'm afraid to leave it on with nobody in it. Come on, I turned on the radio so you can listen to the game while you wait. I'll just be a second." She pauses, smiling sweetly. "Unless you're cold too?"

That seals it. "I don't get cold easy, you know that."

Bear shuffles to the car. Edith catches my eye and winks. She's good, keeping him busy, making him feel needed.

Back to unloading the Jeep. I've wasted too much time jawing, and now wet spots are blooming on the cardboard as the food starts to thaw.

Tucking a couple tenderloins under one arm and a case of corn dogs in the other, I think how I don't really mind the work. Physical labor's good for a man. Clears the mind. And with three tours in Afghanistan under my belt, I've got plenty of memories to clear.

Besides, I like helping the Baileys. Truth is, I've come to love them. Been around long enough—I'd have to be a hard-hearted son of a bitch not to love someone like Sorrow as my own kid.

There's Bear Junior too, away on his second deployment. I felt as proud as Bear Senior when the boy went ROTC, and even more so when he made the Corps after graduation. Though, as an Army man, I never resist ribbing him during the annual Army–Navy game. Hooah.

Laura's a great kid, too. The oldest Bailey girl is all piss and vinegar. Her apartment in San Francisco's only four hours away, but she doesn't visit often. When she does, she wakes up after a few days with eyes like a trapped animal, itching to run back to city life.

But running's something I understand. *Just passing through* was my motto when I first rolled into Sierra Falls a couple decades ago—aimless, exhausted, roaming the country on my bike, trying to make sense of what happened over there, or maybe just what happened to me. When it came time for the "coming back" part of hell and back, the world waiting for me wasn't the same.

A couple of wives. A couple of motorcycles. A couple dozen jobs and a couple thousand miles later, I ended up here. And something about Sierra Falls made it hard to leave.

I slam the Jeep doors shut. Bear's in his car, squinting at the radio like he might change the fate of the Forty-Niners by sheer will. The Baileys have become like family to me, up to and including that grumpy old bastard.

As I head back into the tavern, I suck in a deep breath. The mountain air's so pure it scrubs a man clean down to his soul.

I used to think I'd leave Sierra Falls. Kept putting it off until one day I realized I had a job, a place to live. A *place*.

After I left the service, I cut myself off from the world. But here I am, caught up in life again, and it feels good. Somewhere along the way, I found friends. Family.

I hope some good comes of those letters that have Sorrow so worked up. The girl needs something to shake her out of that rut she's digging for herself.

And then there's Bear Junior. I owe the kid an email. He's heard about Damien and wants to make sure the guy's intentions are good. Wonder what he'd think if he knew the sheriff's been sniffing around too.

Someone else has been coming by the lodge lately—Marlene Jessup.

Pausing at the door, I shake my head, smiling to myself. Sassy eyes, soft curves, and a mouth that could bring a man to his knees. Now there's a woman I wouldn't mind getting friendly with.

Chapter Seven

Billy

I CLICK off my phone and sit in the SUV, parked on the gravel strip that passes for the tavern lot. Scott Jessup just canceled— no after-work beers for us tonight.

Scott's a mix of thoughtful and boisterous, a good man with an easy laugh. We met months ago on a missing person call that turned out to be a stoned hiker. Afterward, we grabbed a beer. He was one of the few with the guts to ask about Keri. Most people tiptoe around the subject of my late wife, like I might've forgotten about her. But Scott listened, steady and sincere, and I've respected him ever since.

Friday beers became our thing. Except tonight he's dealing with a bear break-in—someone's garage freezer got raided.

I glance toward the main lodge. Can't see the roof from here. Has it been fixed? I keep pushing the thought aside, but something about Sorrow Bailey keeps dragging it back. Yesterday she looked so lost. Did her boyfriend help her patch things up? If not, the house must be freezing by now.

There's something about her that doesn't quite line up with the rest of this place. Like she's seeing something everyone else is missing. I can't put my finger on it.

I slam my hand against the steering wheel. "What the hell," I mutter. Thinking about some woman.

I had my woman. I married her. She's gone.

I buckle my seatbelt. With Scott bailing, I might as well head home. Get in a workout, burn through the ghosts. A hard lift in the garage, maybe a beer in front of the TV till I'm too tired to think.

Still, I wonder if the Baileys can sleep with the wind howling through that hole in their roof.

"Dammit." I unbuckle and climb out, slamming the door.

It's just a friendly visit. A quick check to make sure everyone's safe. Something a sheriff does. And I like being sheriff. Being useful.

Leaving Oakland for Sierra Falls was the right call. There's peace here, purpose in small things—helping folks like Marlene or the Baileys.

I pocket my keys. I'll just pop in, say hi, maybe grab a club soda. With all the work going on, Sorrow probably won't even be around. And if she is, I'll keep it professional.

A group of twenty-somethings spills out of the tavern, laughing too loud. I pause to give them a look. Most people after burgers and beer hit the Thirsty Bear, but the younger crowd prefers Chances across town.

My eyes narrow on the kid sliding into the driver's seat. I've got zero tolerance for drunk driving. The cell at the office is empty, and my deputy, McGinn, would love a DUI collar. But the kid calls out a polite good evening, clear-eyed and steady. I nod and let them go.

Inside, a blast of warm air and classic rock hits me. I scan the room, taking in all the familiar faces. Jack Jessup's with his crew. Helen's behind the bar. Sully's off the clock, sitting with Bear Bailey, who looks like he hasn't moved since yesterday.

No sign of Sorrow. The small tug of disappointment catches me off guard. Guilt follows close behind, and I push it down. Just a friendly visit.

Helen pauses her wiping, leaning on the bar. "Evening, handsome. What's a man like you drink after a hard day?"

I look anywhere but at her. "Club soda, thanks."

Helen's a flirt. Harmless, really, but a little much for me. She's married, got kids, and still loves to pour it on thick. The other guys lap it up. I just smile and stay out of her way. I'm not built for that kind of attention.

I turn to Bear. "How's that roof coming along?"

He swivels on his stool, raising his Bud toward Jack. "Fixed up, nice and tight. Marlene's boys know their stuff. Too bad the other Jessups didn't join the family crew—they'd be rich."

I can't picture Scott anywhere but outdoors, and Mark's doing fine as a doctor in Silver City, but I don't say any of that. Instead, I say, "Getting anyone to patch a roof in this weather's a miracle."

Bear puffs up. "Damien—Sorrow's boyfriend—he's got his fingers on the pulse. You'll learn."

So that's what appeals to Sorrow? Damien's pull in town? "Where is she tonight?" I ask, casual.

Bear scowls. "Where she always is. The kitchen. Where she doesn't belong."

That catches me. "That's a twist. You a modern man now, Bear? Thought the saying was a woman's place is in the kitchen."

He doesn't laugh. "The girl's got her mind on things. She always cooks when that happens."

"As someone living on too many frozen dinners, I gotta ask—how's that a bad thing?"

"If she made *real* food, maybe it wouldn't be," he grumbles. "God knows what I'll walk into later. She bought a bunch of something called leeks. Don't we have enough of those already around here?"

I study him. The man's pride seems to begin and end with

Sorrow landing Damien. "You should be proud," I say carefully. "She's got talent and she enjoys using it. Not everyone can say the same."

He stiffens. "When'd she cook for you? Sully handles food here. Sorrow just puts weird sauces and mushrooms on everything. You know they grow those things in manure?"

I laugh. "It wasn't like that. She gave me a few slices of her apple cinnamon bread before patrol."

"I thought cops only liked donuts."

The jab's gruff, not mean, and it makes me smile. "I like donuts, too. But I like that bread better. You put it on the menu, you'd make a fortune."

Bear grunts, about to fire back, when his foot slips off the stool.

I grab his elbow. "Easy there."

He jerks free, bristling. "I had a stroke. I'm not an invalid."

I nod, backing off. Pride's a hard thing to lose. Still, he wobbled. Could be the beer, could be something more. I keep him talking, just in case. "So what's on her mind?"

He blinks. "Huh?"

"You said Sorrow's got things on her mind. What's got her holed up in the kitchen?"

He sniffs. "Found some letters. Thinks we're related to Buck Larsen."

It takes a beat to process. "*The* Buck Larsen?"

"Who knows with that girl?" His face softens, a ghost of pride there. "She found old letters in the attic. Says my great-granddad was his natural son."

He spins his beer bottle, smiling faintly. "She's at the house, stirring and chopping. Go see for yourself."

Chapter Eight

Sorrow

I DRY my prized butcher knife till it gleams. German-made, professional-grade, worth every penny. Tilting it toward the light, I check the edge. A chef is only as good as her sharpest blade.

"Remind me not to cross you."

The voice from the doorway startles me. My knife stills midair.

Sheriff Preston fills the frame, all broad shoulders and quiet authority, and my heart gives a ridiculous skip.

I snap my gaze back to my task. The sauce simmers on the stove, and I've taken a moment to clean up—I can't abide a messy kitchen. "You know better than to surprise a woman holding a big knife."

"It's safer than a woman who..." He glances toward the tavern, pulling a mock-terrified face. "Well, never mind that."

I smirk. "Been at the bar, have you?"

"How'd you guess?"

I shrug, sliding my tools back into the block. I know exactly what he almost said. Helen's part-time waitress, full-time flirt, and probably all over Billy like white on rice. Most men run toward Helen. Except her husband, and that's exactly the problem. But it's not my place to gossip.

Still, good to know Billy seems like the sort of man who'd run *from* a Helen.

He wanders closer, giving my knives an appreciative nod. "Nice."

I tamp down the silly thrill that gives me. "Thanks."

He looks around the kitchen. "Your mother let me in. Hope you don't mind me showing up so late."

"On the contrary." The sudden hiss of rapid boiling makes me jump, and I rush to turn down the heat. I stir the sauce—thankfully not burned—and swipe hair off my forehead with my arm. "You're just in time to clean out that dish for me."

He gamely shrugs out of his coat and rolls up his sleeves. "What are we making?"

"Beef Bourguignon."

He scrapes onion bits and bacon fat into the compost. "Don't you mean *boeuf*?"

I laugh, tapping my spoon clean. "Impressive."

"Hey, I saw that Julia Child movie."

I wipe my hands on my apron and grab a sieve. "So you won't complain if I ask you to hold this?" Straining the sauce always gives my arms a workout.

"I'll do you one better." He takes both sieve and saucepan with easy confidence. "You scrape."

I can't help thinking of Damien—so competent everywhere else, magically useless near a stove.

He adds, "I'll only complain if you don't let me eat it when it's done."

I raise a brow, surprised. "Sorry, Sheriff. If you saw that movie, you know it won't hit the oven till tomorrow."

"I told you, it's Billy."

The correction lands warm in my chest, and I turn back to the stove, smiling to myself.

He inhales deeply. Straining the sauce has only intensified

the aroma. "And I'll definitely take a rain check. I'd cross an ocean for good Beef Bourguignon."

I pause. "Would you really?"

He nods, saying, "I love Sierra Falls, but good restaurants? Only thing I miss about the city. No offense to your tavern."

I laugh. "None taken. I'd rather... I don't know... mop the garage than eat Sully's 'Prospector's Pie' again."

Billy's laugh booms. "What on earth is that?"

"Meat pie," I say, grimacing.

"Sounds... maybe not so bad. What kind of meat?"

"All kinds." I shudder.

He laughs again. "Just how many kinds can there be?"

"Oh, you'd be surprised." I head for the fridge, and he opens the door for me.

"Is that why you learned to cook? An aversion to mystery meats?"

I slide the casserole inside. "Necessity is the mother of invention." As I wash the sieve, a better truth slips out. "If I can't whisk myself off to another country, cooking lets me travel in my head."

I dry my hands and turn, only to find him much closer than before. His presence fills the kitchen, warm and quietly commanding.

The silence stretches.

I grasp for normalcy. "Can I get you something to eat?"

"I... I think..." His stomach growls, and we both laugh, the moment breaking.

"I'll take that as a yes."

"If your apple bread and that sauce are any indication, I'd love a taste of what you're serving."

We hear the double meaning at the same moment, and a flush crawls up his neck. I pretend I don't notice.

"I mean... if you don't mind. I don't want to be trouble."

"Not at all. I have to eat, too." I duck into the fridge, letting the cool air soothe my own warm cheeks. What is wrong with me? "How do you feel about pasta?"

"I feel great about pasta."

Finally—a man who doesn't fear carbs. "I can pull together an Aglio e Olio."

"Sounds fancy."

I grab the olive oil and check my garlic. "Just Italian for 'garlic and oil.' Easy."

Billy reaches up and grabs the colander and the big pasta pot, lifting them in a silent question.

"Perfect," I say, honestly impressed. "Thanks."

He starts filling the pot. "While the pasta's boiling, you can tell me about those letters."

I freeze for a second. "You know about the letters?"

"Your dad told me."

And he's *interested*? I blink, thrown. I pour olive oil into a saucepan and add a glug of Pinot Grigio from the fridge. Then I hesitate and hold up the bottle. "Want a glass?"

"Why not." He sounds surprised at himself, a little off-balance.

I pour generously, because same. I'm all buzzy and nervous —apparently, I kind of like having the sheriff in my kitchen.

We sit at the table to wait for the sauce to reduce and the water to heat. He sets a fingertip on the small stack of letters. "These the ones?"

"They are. From the 1850s. My three-times-great-grandmother."

He shakes his head in awe. "When I see something this old, I can't help imagining the person holding it. Paper was expensive then. The pen and nib, the ink—it was a whole thing."

He's voicing thoughts I've had for years. I burn to know who that first Sorrow was. A mystery woman, rumored to have borne a child out of wedlock, which was unthinkable back then. The family's woven the tale over generations, but did Sorrow Crabtree really lead such a hard-luck life?

There are no photos, nothing to picture her by. Just a couple of old dresses in the attic that I like to imagine were hers—curvy-bodice, low-neckline dresses. Not stagecoach dresses. Dresses for dancing. For whiskey shots, bawdy jokes, and poker hands.

He traces a careful finger along the stack. "Are they really written to Buck Larsen? Did he write back?"

"That's the thing." I grab a few from the top. "She never sent them. Buck lived here, then left for the capital, and... well, you know the story."

"Me and every fifth grader in California." His eyes meet mine, warm with wonder. "What they don't teach is how he left his pregnant lover behind..."

Heat flares low in my belly hearing him say the word *lover*. I clear my throat. "Looks that way. I'm working through them, but the handwriting's tricky."

"May I?" He reaches out, and I hand him a letter. He studies it. "Handwriting is a lost art."

I lean in, and he instinctively shifts the page so I can see. I scoot closer without thinking. Our shoulders touch. Suddenly I can't focus on the words.

But he can. He laughs, pointing at a line.

"She really gives him what for. Listen: *I am nothin but a Grass Widow, left for dead. Folk been sayin how grand you are now, livin in Sacramenno. I say yer nothin but a coward, Buck Larsen, runnin off like you did.*" He leans back. "Hoo-boy. She must've been something. Them's fightin' words."

"Wow. 'Grass widow?' No idea what that even means."

He picks through a few more letters. "This is remarkable. Have you read all of them?"

"Not yet." Excitement hums under my skin—finally, someone who cares. "So... you think they're interesting?"

"What, the letters?" He gives me a look. "Who wouldn't?"

Damien. My dad. My whole family probably. Pretty much everyone, except maybe the historical society, and for some reason I'm not ready to share with them yet.

"I'm wondering if they could help bring in more business to the lodge," I say. "I just don't know how yet."

"You should take them to the historical society."

I laugh. "You read my mind. But what do *you* know about the historical society?" Only the Kidd ladies talk about it, usually while trying to rope me in.

He turns his chair toward me, earnest. "Seriously. They could look into the Buck Larsen connection. And answer your questions—about pens, grass widows, all that. I was talking to Marlene yesterday—"

I blink. "You were talking to Marlene?"

"Yes, I was talking to Marlene." His eyes twinkle—are we flirting? "They're having financial trouble. This would be huge for them. You're not a member, I take it?"

"Me? No way. Too many older women in one room, all trying to set me up with their grandson or grandnephew or paperboy."

"Paperboy?"

"They've known me forever." I wave that off and sip my wine. "But you might be onto something. I'll have Mom bring it to the Kidd sisters." At his confused look I add, "Marlene's maiden name was Kidd."

"Marlene has sisters?"

"No, no." I shake my head. "Marlene has aunts. Two. And her mother's still alive. All in their eighties."

"Oh, right. I dropped her at her aunts' house." Billy frowns. "But I don't think I've met them yet."

"Oh, you'd know if you had. Emerald, Ruby, and Pearl. The grande dames of Sierra Falls. They don't get out much anymore."

"Oh, my."

"Oh, yes." I smile at him—and suddenly the room feels intimate. Suddenly I'm imagining what it'd be like if he leaned in and kissed me.

And he looks like maybe he's imagining it, too.

My heart thumps hard. *Whoa.* I recite Damien's name in my head, because what is wrong with me?

But then the pot boils over with a furious hiss. I shoot to my feet and rush to the stove, tossing in linguini.

"That's a lot of pasta," he says.

I smile at the pot. "You seem like a man with an appetite."

"How'd you guess?" He lifts his wine and joins me, looking over my shoulder. "That might be too much even for me. Still, leftover pasta in the morning? Nothing better."

I nod—and God help me, I find myself wondering what it'd be like to serve this man breakfast.

Chapter Nine

Marlene

I SNEAK a quick sniff of my wrist. Did I overdo the perfume? Walking into the tavern—all beer and fried things—I start worrying my Estée Lauder sticks out.

Ridiculous, really. You'd think a sixty-three-year-old woman would have more confidence. But the divorce rattled me. And here I am, on a blind date.

My eyes adjust to the dim room. Conversation dips as people glance over to see who's come in. Cheeks heating, I head for the first table that's neither too close to the door nor tucked away like I'm hiding.

Normally, I'd never choose the Thirsty Bear—meeting a prospective beau in front of everyone and their cousin? No thanks. But I'm hoping to catch Edith. And there are no secrets in Sierra Falls, anyway. I could drive to Sacramento and folks would still hear about it.

I unwind my scarf and pat my hair into place. I dye it and get regular blowouts, but gray has a mind of its own. I hate that almost as much as the new lines that seem to appear overnight.

"Marlene!" Edith waves from across the room.

I wave back with a smile. She looks effortlessly lovely—she always does. I hope the dim lighting is treating me just as kindly.

She murmurs something to Helen behind the bar, then

hurries over. "I ordered us a couple glasses of wine. Sauvignon blanc for you, right?"

I half rise for an air-kiss. "Perfect." Of course it is—Edith remembers everything.

She's been a puzzle since we were girls: quiet, watchful, absorbing every detail, then suddenly roaring like a lion when it mattered. Not that she needs to roar much—Bear's been doing that for decades.

Helen arrives with our wine, looking put out she had to step from behind the bar. Edith and I share a little chuckle once she's gone.

"She's a piece of work," I whisper. "Flirts with anything in pants, then turns into a witch with a capital B for the rest of us."

Edith sighs. "I know."

"So why keep her?" Anyone in town would leap at the extra hours.

"We all have our troubles," she says, vague as ever.

"Ain't it the truth." I toast her wisdom and take a sip, but the wine suddenly tastes too tart. Edith's forgiving nature always makes me feel a little small. I try to soften it. "To women with troubles."

She sips, then shakes her head. "How can you say you have troubles when you're looking so pretty?"

I blink at the compliment. "Oh, Edith, it's you who's pretty. As always."

Her blond looks have aged well, and it seems her daughters' will too. Isn't fair skin supposed to be more delicate?

I touch my forehead, wondering if I should try Botox. Plenty of doctors in Reno or Silver City. Maybe it's time.

"Enough about me." Edith leans in. "So, you're meeting a man tonight? How exciting."

Hardly. I paste on a smile. Exciting would be having

already met him and discovering he was a gentlemanly widower judge or a retired doctor. Someone kind, respectable, mortgage paid, and a nice sedan with leather seats in a color named something like ebony or champagne. Then I could quit this dating-app nonsense.

Next time Frank comes to town, he'd see how well I'm doing. How spoiled I am. And he'd regret everything.

"But aren't you worried about this online stuff?" Edith asks. "I've heard stories."

I've heard them too, and part of me is terrified. But I force breezy confidence. "Oh no, it's perfectly safe. They screen everyone." I hope. "Besides, what choice do I have? I've lived here all my life, and I haven't seen many retirees zipping around Sierra Falls in sports cars looking for wives."

Edith deflates. "Forget men, then. How are you?"

I swirl my wine, thinking. How am I?

I'm a sixty-three-year-old woman on a blind date, trying to hold onto my dignity. Last time I dated, I didn't need reading glasses to put on mascara. Last time I dated, it was boys I grew up with—boys my parents vetted—not strangers who could be kooks for all I know.

I went from raising four boys to caring for two elderly aunts and a mother in the early stages of Alzheimer's. I shouldn't be sitting in a bar drinking Bear Bailey's crappy sauvignon blanc.

That's how I am.

What I say is, "I'm plugging along, Edith. You?"

She glances around, then leans in, conspiratorial. "I have news."

I perk up. Gossip is the best cure for malaise. She looks pleased—good news, then.

A smile creeps in as I guess. "It's Sorrow, isn't it? She and the Simmons boy finally got engaged."

"Oh…" Edith looks puzzled. "No, not that. But it does have to do with Sorrow. She found letters."

I sag a bit. Letters aren't nearly as exciting. "Letters?"

When Edith gets to the word *affair*, I perk right back up. Turns out, Bear's great-great-grandmother had a child out of wedlock with Buck Larsen. She wrote a stack of unsent letters full of juicy details.

Edith's eyes are glowing. "It's just what the town needs."

I hate to be the wet blanket—why is it always me?—but I can't help asking, "How do you know they're real? They must be over a hundred years old."

"Over one hundred seventy years old," she corrects, beaming. "And the woman had no reason to lie."

I'm unconvinced. Some woman connived Frank out of a forty-year marriage—who knows what people did back then? "All the more reason she could've made something up."

"Why would she? She never even sent them." Edith waves that off. "Don't you see? We can turn Spring Fling into a Buck Larsen Festival. Get publicity. Tourists."

I pause. She has a point. The town could use a boost—financially and otherwise. Maybe this will attract new people… maybe even older, single men. Tweedy historical types drift through my mind.

Finally convinced, I smile. "Wait till I tell them."

Them meaning my mother, Emerald, and my aunts Ruby and Pearl—three preacher's daughters, with a father who scared off every suitor until the girls aged into spinsters together. My mother was the wild one, ran off young, came back pregnant and secretive, and never left again. They're the backbone of the historical society.

"I'll get them started on a special gold rush quilt," I say.

"We could have a raffle!"

"We could put together a book of old California recipes."

Edith brightens. "We could put on a show. The dresses we found? Sorrow—Bear's ancestor—was a dance-hall girl. We could do a performance. Maybe an exhibit."

She bustles off to start her list, leaving me alone with my nerves.

I check my watch for the umpteenth time. I arrived a little early, but now he's officially late. I nurse my wine—I don't want to be empty-handed, but I definitely don't want another. This one's hitting hard.

Still, Edith's news has stirred a little optimism. Maybe the date will go well. Maybe he'll be The One.

I adjust my shirt. Should've worn a sweater—it's chilly by the door. But moving now would look strange.

I rub warmth into my arms, annoyed at myself. I didn't wear a sweater because all mine are old hand-knit cardigans, suddenly too frumpy for dating. Too fusty.

And I resent that feeling. I love those sweaters. Why aren't they good enough? Why am *I* not good enough? Which leads me straight back to Frank. This is all his fault.

My optimism leaks away. My nerves buzz. Where *is* this man?

"A woman like you..." a male voice says behind me.

I turn to find Sully. A devilish glint in his eyes brings a smile to my face. Sully's always had a word for me, and my ego likes the attention more every year. "A woman like me what, Tom Sullivan?"

He sets a sparkling drink on the table. "A woman like you shouldn't be kept waiting."

"A woman like me should do lots of things. Like this—" I push the glass away. "I definitely shouldn't."

"I know." He nudges it back. "That's why it's just club soda with a twist."

Relief loosens something in my chest. "How'd you guess?"

"You were wearing a hole in the table, spinning your wineglass. Thought you could shift that nervous energy to a cocktail straw instead."

"I'm not nervous." *Am I that obvious? How does he know?*

"You're the boss." He smiles, but doesn't leave or sit.

Why doesn't he sit? I narrow my eyes. "If anything's making me nervous, it's you hovering."

"If I'm hovering, it's because you haven't invited me to join you."

Would he really sit if I asked? Do I want him to? Why is he being friendly? He can't be interested in me.

I dismiss the thought immediately. A man like Tom Sullivan would want someone sassier, wilder. An older, bustier version of that bartender. Not me.

Not that I know who he dates—no one gossips about him. Only about his past, coming home from Afghanistan a changed man, wandering for years like someone out of *Easy Rider.* Probably all romantic myth.

"I'm meeting somebody," I say, subtly checking my watch. I need a wealthy retiree with a sedan, not someone who rides a motorcycle and still looks too muscular for his age.

Tom doesn't take the hint. "Seems he's late."

I bristle. It's true, but presumptuous. His tight white cook's T-shirt, the Army infantry tattoo on his forearm—he looks strong, vital. Maybe not a distinguished gentleman, but something else for sure. And when did I start calling him Tom?

I sip my bubbly water.

His tattoo sparks a thought. I'm eager to change the subject anyway. "They say you went to war."

"So I did," he says, guarded.

The pain in his eyes warns me to tread carefully. "Would

you talk to my grandson?" His expression turns skeptical, so I rush on. "He wants to enlist after high school."

His eyes tighten. They're a startling blue—dark, like indigo. It throws me off balance.

"Don't you get that look with me, Tom Sullivan. Hear me out." My voice trembles—probably the wine. "I had an uncle on my grandmother's side who served. You were here when we buried him at Arlington. And if you don't remember, listen to Ruby and Pearl for half a minute—they invoke him every chance they get." I press on. "There's nothing I'd love more than seeing Craig serve his country. But he doesn't understand how serious it is. How hard he'll have to work. I worry he thinks it's like one of his video games."

Sully stays silent long enough to make me nervous. Finally, he nods. "I understand. Bring him by, Marlene. I'll talk to him."

I exhale a tension I hadn't realized I was holding. "Thank you, Tom."

A gust of wind blows in as the door opens. Sully looks up, jaw tightening again.

"It's not right," he mutters. His blue eyes lock on mine. "This date of yours better pay up. If he tries any nonsense like splitting the check, I might have to come back over."

Heat floods my cheeks—and good Lord, when was the last time I blushed?

Chapter Ten

Sorrow

Mom's voice echoes down the hallway a second before she appears in the laundry room doorway.

I know that tone—another duty I don't want. Still, anything beats ironing linens.

"Did you hear me, Sorrow?" Her white-knuckled grip on her purse makes me set down the iron. Mom never looks this tense. "I need you to call your friend again."

"Who? Damien?"

She nods. "The road is closed. I thought he could make some calls. Get it cleared."

"Wait—our road is closed?" Irish Camp Road isn't a major thoroughfare, but it's not a backroad either. "I'm sure it was plowed hours ago. Why would Caltrans close it?" They handle weather like this in their sleep.

"It's not the snow," Mom says. "There's something blocking the road."

What exactly am I supposed to do about that? Why does everything fall on my shoulders? And where are my siblings when there's indentured servitude to go around?

Guilt cuts through me. BJ's stationed in Djibouti. Ironing hardly compares.

I sigh. "Fine. I'll call Caltrans."

"Maybe you should call Damien."

I hesitate—partly because of the inappropriate thoughts I've been having about someone else, partly because of the guilt tied up in all of it. "Caltrans will take care of it."

"Please." Her tone softens into a plea. "I think Damien could call someone in charge and get it cleared faster."

Mom rarely gets this worked up. I flip off the iron, defeated. "Okay, sure. I'll call Damien." I unplug it just in case —my luck, the whole lodge would burn down otherwise—and edge past her, searching for my phone.

She follows right on my heels. "This is very important, Sorrow."

I let out a small laugh at her intensity. "I said I'm on it, Mom."

"I'm going to present your letters to the historical society. Marlene thinks they might breathe some life into this town."

A few days ago, the thought of sharing them made me antsy. But after Billy's reaction... maybe I'm even a little excited.

"Good." I lift a hand for quiet as I call him.

But I don't need quiet for long. Damien is in a meeting and not to be disturbed. I can guess why—Simmons Timber is ready to thin several acres for fire prevention, and his father keeps trying to expand the cut. Damien's pushing environmental responsibility; Dabney's worried about keeping people employed. They've been butting heads more than usual.

"He's unavailable and... oh, crap." I close my eyes and tip my head back, breathing deep. A closure on our road doesn't just mean Mom missing her meeting. It means no one can reach the lodge or tavern. A whole day's business gone. "Crap," I repeat. "We've got two groups of hunters coming tonight, and I already bought salmon for the tavern."

"Well, Sully can't cook it," Mom says. "He hasn't even

come in yet. That fool man insists on riding a motorcycle at his age."

"He drives the Jeep in this weather, Mom."

"Well, what are we going to do?" There's an edge in her voice I rarely hear. "I don't want your father getting upset. And I especially don't want him going out to check on it himself."

I grab my coat and scarf from the mudroom hook. "Don't borrow trouble. I'll check it out. Dad's glued to the news—he won't even know I'm gone." His TV addiction is aggravating, but at least I know he's safely tucked away from the public areas.

I'm pulling on my snow boots when the main entry door creaks open, followed by a tentative knock—someone polite enough to remember a family actually lives here.

"Anybody home?" a man calls.

Billy. My hand flies to my hair. I'd yanked it into a messy ponytail this morning—not exactly my best look.

Why do I care? He's just a man.

But he isn't just a man. He's Billy.

Ridiculous. But still... I pull out the elastic, shake my hair loose, finger-comb some life into it, and head out to greet him. "Hi, Billy."

Something in his face softens. "Hey, Sorrow." His gaze drops to my boots. "You know your road—" He stops when he sees my expression. "You do know."

"Yup. It's closed."

He nods, frowning. "There are signs posted, but somehow nobody notified Caltrans. I called it in—they should have it cleared by this evening."

"This evening?" So much for our guests.

"But I need to get to my meeting," Mom says.

That meeting again. Meanwhile, I'm thinking about a

couple hundred dollars' worth of salmon that won't freeze well.

"I told Marlene I'd drive her and the Kidd sisters," Mom goes on. "All she has is that pickup. You know the women hate climbing into that. And I don't like the thought of Pearl's Buick in this weather."

"Mom, I'm sorry. You're going to have to miss the m—"

Billy cuts in. "I'll take you in the truck, ma'am."

I shoot him a look, waiting for an explanation.

He jingles his keys. "How do you ladies think I got here?"

I shake my head—he must've gone offroad to get here. "You're nuts."

He shrugs. "I had to see if today was the day Sully finally put his Prospector's Pie on the menu."

A laugh startles out of me. "Now I really know you're nuts."

"Hey, a little four-wheeling is good for the soul."

"You mean driving off the road?" Mom asks. "Is that allowed?"

"Are you suggesting I give myself a ticket?" the sheriff teases, slipping an arm around her and guiding her toward the door. "Button up that coat and let's go. I guess I'll just have to wait for that Prospector's Pie." He shoots me a wink.

A zing of excitement hits my chest. Before I can stop myself, I say, "I can do you one better. You like salmon, Billy?"

Chapter Eleven

Marlene

THIS DATE IS GOING SOUTH fast. I've had plenty of time to sit here contemplating that sad fact while this total stranger talks at me. Not a single question about me. He just drones on about fishing—and corrects me every time I dare call it that. *"Angling, Marlene. It's called angling."*

When he starts in on something called "bite indicators," I tune out completely. I've already had a man chew my ear off about fishing, and look how that turned out. I don't need a new one.

But it does get me thinking. Men have all these hobbies—sports, fishing, golf—while some days it feels like I've gone straight from raising four boys to caring for three elderly women. Unless I count dusting and laundry, I have a sad lack of interests that are mine alone.

Somewhere in the middle of the bite-indicator monologue, I make my decision: forget men for a while. I'll pour my heart into the historical society instead.

Which is how I end up early, prepared, and waiting for our ride to the town hall. Getting my aunts and mother ready ahead of schedule was a feat.

Now that we have these letters, the meeting promises to be rip-roaring. I haven't told the ladies yet about Buck Larsen spending time in Sierra Falls, and I'm making a grand show of having a secret to reveal. With the promise of high drama, I wrangle Ruby, Pearl, and Ma into their coats.

But the drama starts before we even get outside. An unfamiliar car rumbles up the drive, and when I open the door, Billy Preston is parking in front of our house.

"Oh, good heavens," Ruby whispers, eyes wide at the big sheriff's SUV. "The law is here."

Pearl edges into the doorway, gripping my arm. "What do you think happened?"

Ma pipes up, "Did he find out about that lipstick I took?"

"Oh hush, Emerald. That was back in the fifties."

I spot Edith in the front seat and pat Pearl's hand. "I think Edith had car trouble again."

Billy hops out. "You're all looking lovely today. I've heard nothing but good things about you ladies." He bounds up the steps, taking an aunt on each arm. "Your chariot awaits."

I lock the house and take my mother's arm, following him to the SUV. "Sheriff, you probably have a dozen more important things to do."

"Maybe so, but this was at the top of my list." My aunts positively preen at the attention. He smiles and helps me climb into the extra row of seats. "You going to be okay back there?"

"Yes." I ease in, though my mind won't settle. Now here's a considerate man. I sensed it when he helped free my car from that snowbank. This is a man who wouldn't chew a woman's ear off about bait lines. I'm not used to getting help—twice in a row from the same person, no less—and it makes me feel guilty. "You don't need to drive us old biddies to our meeting."

"I don't see any biddies here." He winks at Pearl.

The moment I'm buckled in, Ruby leans forward to investigate the control panel between the front seats. The police radio crackles to life with distant, unintelligible chatter.

The ladies gasp. I chuckle. They'll be talking about this for weeks.

They're talking about it now, in fact—seated in the Sierra Falls Town Hall as we wait for the meeting to begin. Edith and I sit up front. She's dying to gossip about the sheriff, but I silence her with a look. We're the heads of the historical society; we have to project at least a little dignity.

As chairwoman and de facto treasurer, I get the gavel. I give it a firm bang. "Time to get this meeting to order. First item of business: our budget."

We address our dwindling bank account, and as usual, the money talk dissolves into grumbling.

Edith shushes them. My head snaps toward her—this is new. "Marlene and I think we have a solution," she says. "We found letters."

I give her hand a quick pat. It isn't like Edith to step up like that. Looks good on her.

"Letters?" someone in the back calls. "How are a bunch of letters going to help us?"

"They're historical letters," Edith says.

"What kind of historical?"

"Maybe they're just old."

June Harlan speaks louder than the rest. "How do you know they're real? You can't date things with the naked eye."

Pearl turns in her seat. "You listen up, June, and let her tell it. If Edith and Marlene say they have letters, they have letters."

"Well, where'd they find them?"

I bang the gavel again. "The Bailey family found them."

Edith beams. "And we think our next festival should be a Buck Larsen festival."

June throws up her hands. She turns to Pearl, asking loudly, "Did she say Buck Larsen?"

Ruby frowns. "Buck Larsen's dead. He can't come to the festival."

"No." Pearl pats her sister's arm. "He wrote the letters. Isn't that what you're saying, Marlene?"

"No." I wince. I should've told my aunts and mother ahead of time. I thought it'd be a fun surprise. Instead, the meeting is unraveling. "The letters were written by Sorrow Crabtree."

My mother turns to Ruby. "Isn't that Edith's child?"

Ruby nods. "What's that about Sorrow?"

"Sorrow wrote letters," Pearl repeats, her 'whisper' booming down the aisle.

"Not our Sorrow," Edith says, exasperated. "*Our* Sorrow found the letters, written by her great-great-great-grandmother."

Understanding ripples across the room. "Ahh."

I set the gavel down. "Turns out Buck Larsen was one of Sierra Falls' early pioneers. If we theme our next festival around Buck Larsen and the Gold Rush, we might draw more tourists."

Edith leans in. "More tourists means more money for Sierra Falls."

Ruby lights up. "So you're saying Buck Larsen is Bear's kin."

My mother stiffens. "Bear skin?"

Pearl pats her hand. "Bear Bailey. They mean his ancestors."

I can't take it anymore. This crowd needs a spectacle. I clear my throat. "Sorrow Crabtree was one of the early residents of Sierra Falls. It appears she had... an affair. With Buck Larsen. She had his baby."

A wave of *oohs* sweeps the room.

The meeting falls apart after that. The excitement is too

much. I spot Billy Preston waiting at the back and quickly wrap things up.

As I stand to put on my coat, I turn to Edith. "You never did tell me why the sheriff was driving you today." The chatter is loud, so I lean close. "Seems Billy Preston has an awful lot of business at that tavern of yours."

Edith puffs up. "He just happened to be there."

"Mm-hm." I button my coat. "Lucky you. Or should I say, your lucky daughter."

Edith freezes mid-scarf-wrap. "Sorrow, you mean?"

"Yes," I say, impatient. "Sorrow." First the apple bread, now this. "Seems to me I've seen the two of them together a lot lately."

"Not him," Edith says. "The sheriff's a widower."

"Well, that's a silly thing to say. It's his wife who died, not him." We both look at Billy. He stands straight and tall, that sheriff's jacket broadening his already broad shoulders. "Seems to me he's still a young man. Not hard on the eyes, neither."

Edith makes a thoughtful little *hmm*. "No, he's not hard on the eyes, is he?"

I squint. "He reminds me of... I don't know... a cowboy from a TV movie."

"Not as handsome as Damien, though," she says.

"Maybe not. But he makes Damien look like a kid in comparison."

"Damien isn't a boy. He's Sorrow's age. Old enough to start thinking about settling down." Her gaze drifts back to the sheriff. "Are you saying he's looking to remarry?"

"I didn't say marriage." I abruptly start gathering my papers.

All this talk of spouses makes my stomach twist. If I'd been a widow, would I have remarried? Would the pain have been this sharp? Sometimes, when I'm feeling small-hearted, I wish I were a widow—wish my husband had died instead of divorcing me. Some days it seems like burying him would've been easier than the shame of him disposing of me.

Pearl approaches the table with a contented smile—the meeting has been as dramatic as promised. "Are we leaving now?"

Ruby and my mother trail behind her, still bundling up. Ma struggles with her sleeves, but before I can help, Billy appears.

"Let me get this for you," he says, guiding her arms into the coat. "You got all turned inside out."

"What a gentleman," Ruby says.

I study him. Widower or not, whether it's Sorrow or someone else, someday some lucky woman will find herself turned inside out by this sheriff.

Chapter Twelve

Billy

I FEEL AWKWARD. I've gone home to change—nobody wants their dinner guest showing up wearing a sidearm—but now I worry I look like I'm trying too hard. And I refuse to admit that worrying about it is the definition of trying too hard.

Am I trying?

Of course not. The last time I tried with a woman was with Keri. We spent years as colleagues, then friends, our courtship slow and steady. Flowers, symphony tickets, dinners at places I didn't care about but thought she would. Sitting through a three-hour avant-garde opera? Now *that* was trying.

No, this is just a friendly visit, classic small-town living. Sorrow's mother leads me into the lodge's private quarters. I've never eaten back here—tourists dine in the tavern—and I'm curious to see how the family interacts.

"You're looking handsome this evening," Edith says as we join Sorrow's father in the den. Bear sits in his recliner, watching a muted college basketball game.

I've gone with jeans and a sweater, but catching Bear's scowl, I regret ditching the sidearm.

"Bear," Edith prompts, nudging him, "say hello to Billy. If it weren't for him, I'd have missed my meeting."

He nods once, then turns back to the game.

"Evening, sir." I settle onto the giant sectional, eyes drifting to the TV. The old brown leather is as comfortable as it looks. "Kentucky came out strong this year."

Bear's eyes narrow. "You a Kentucky fan?"

Feels like a trap. For all I know, Kentucky fans aren't allowed in Big Bear Lodge.

"I went to Colorado State," I deflect. Time for a safer subject. "That's where I discovered my love of the mountains."

"Why go all the way there?" he asks, suspicious, like travel is a character flaw.

"Football scholarship."

That gets his attention. He looks me over. "Really now?"

I straighten. "Running back."

"Ahh." He nods, satisfied. "Yeah, I see it. You've got that stocky look. I played ball, too, once upon a time. Different era. We didn't bother with nonsense like pads."

"You play in college?"

He hesitates, then says, "Nah. Didn't need it. Played high school, then played around here. Town stuff."

We watch in silence for a few minutes before he surprises me. "I appreciate you driving Edith. I'm sure you got better sheriff duties to tend to."

"Not a problem," I say, and I mean it. It was a nice break. Small favors like that keep me upright these days—being relentlessly friendly, staying busy, keeping the ghosts at bay.

When I circled back to drive the women home, they invited me in for coffee and Danishes, but asked surprisingly few questions. I could tell they wanted to. And I can't blame them—a young widower like me probably feels like a community project. Oddly, I find it touching.

"I don't know what it is with women and meetings," Bear grumbles. "You meet the Kidd sisters yet? Driving my wife saved me from dealing with those old birds. They're gonna use our letters, though. It'll turn this town around, you'll see."

"Thanks to Sorrow," I say. At his look, I add, "Your daughter found them in the first place, saw their worth. Most folks would've tossed them."

He shrugs. "I guess."

"Can I get you a beer?" a voice asks behind me.

I turn. Sorrow stands in the doorway, blond hair loose and wavy around her shoulders, the firelight catching her eyes.

The world stills. Sorrow has the kind of beauty that demands attention. Curvy, in a sweater that hugs the dip of her waist and swell of her hip. My mind goes straight to my hand resting there.

I swallow. "Yes, ma'am, I think I could use a beer."

I haven't been with a woman in a long time. A couple mindless hookups—out of town, of course—just enough to remind me I'm human.

But this is Sorrow. There's no such thing as "mindless" with her, and anything deeper than that would feel like cheating.

I drag my gaze to her hair instead. She usually wears it back. Not that I don't like it that way. She's a natural beauty, the sort that looks just as good with makeup as without. But tonight, in this warm light, hair loose and sweater snug, she's stunning.

She gives me a puzzled little smile. "Is there a problem, Sheriff?"

I realize I've been staring. "You look..." *Edible.* My eyes land on the oven mitt in her hand. "Like you could use some help."

A flicker crosses her face—disappointment?

I stand abruptly. Get a grip. "Tell you what. Let's get that beer, and I'll give you a hand in the kitchen."

Bear shoots me a look. Probably never occurred to him to help with dinner prep.

We step into the kitchen, and she hands me a Bud from the fridge.

"Sounds like a good trade," she says.

"Give me a job," I tell her, cracking it open. Because if I just stand here staring at her, I might start wondering how soft that sweater—and what's under it—feels.

She glances around, choosing. "We'll ease you in slow. Want to set the table?"

"Table setting? Child's play." I pull out plates and cutlery. "What's on the menu? I strained that sauce of yours and didn't even get to taste it."

"You'll have to settle for my salmon. It's better for you anyway."

I inhale. "Wow, that's like no salmon I've ever smelled."

"It's with bamboo shoots and green curry."

"I love green curry," I say, genuinely impressed. I head into the dining room to set the table. She follows, taking the napkins from my hand to spread them out. From across the table, I catch her eye. "One question, though. Is Bear going to go for that?"

She laughs. "He'll go for it, or go hungry."

"A rebel, huh?"

"I'm making up for my teen years."

We end up side by side at the head of the table.

"Well, I'm just happy I get to benefit," I say.

She opens her mouth like she wants to say something but isn't sure how. I wait, curious.

"Did your wife like to cook?" she asks, then quickly adds, "I hope you don't mind me asking."

"I don't mind." Oddly, it's always a relief when people ask about Keri. Most tiptoe, not realizing I long to talk about her.

Grief set me apart for so long; talking brings me back to the living.

I lean against the table. "Keri—my wife—was a lawyer. That's how we met, in court. Between her long hours at the DA's office and me being on the force, we ate more sushi than anything else. When she did cook, it was always some fancy salad. Good, sure—goat cheese, blood oranges—but they never filled me up."

I laugh at the memory, and it feels good. It feels *right* to smile about her.

Sorrow holds my gaze with a warm, open look. No platitudes. No scrambling for condolences. I'm grateful.

Talking about Keri makes it impossible not to note the differences between the two women. Keri with her sharp black bob and courtroom polish. Sorrow with her wavy hair and soft edges. Keri in power suits; Sorrow in something soft and comfortable. Opposites.

I adored my wife. She was a force—manicured nails, quick retorts, a stride that owned the room. The memory hits hard. Such a loss.

I realize I'm staring again. Sorrow's eyes are kind. Gentle where Keri was fierce. The sort of woman who might twine her fingers in my hair and pull me close, just to give me a moment's comfort.

A bark cuts through the moment. I'm grateful for the interruption. I've put women out of my mind. Best to keep them there.

"I didn't know you had a dog," I say.

She stiffens, glancing toward the den. "We don't."

Strange reaction. "Not a fan?"

"What?" She looks back at me. "I love dogs. I just... I think I know who that is."

A dog bursts into the kitchen—friendly, high-energy, white

with brown spots. Looks straight out of a Hollywood casting call.

"Hey, little guy. Who do you belong to?" I crouch as he bounds toward me. When I look up, Sorrow is rigid.

A man strolls in, and the dog races to his side.

Damien Simmons.

The boyfriend.

Chapter Thirteen

Sorrow

"Hey, Bailey. You look great." Damien steps in close.

I fight the urge to flinch, hyper-aware of Billy beside me. Damien and I have a thing—he's my boyfriend—so why am I stressed? I tip my head so he can brush a kiss across my cheek. No way am I giving him a full-on mouth kiss with the sheriff standing there.

Billy steps forward, offering his hand. "Damien, good to see you."

They shake, white-knuckled, each trying to out-grip the other.

"Hey, Sheriff." Damien flashes that easy Sierra Falls poster-boy smile. "Thanks for taking care of our Edith today. The woman does love her meetings."

Our Edith. My spine snaps straight. Helping around the lodge is one thing; laying claim to my mother is another. I bite my tongue—boundaries, Damien.

"My pleasure," Billy says. He gestures toward the dog. "That's a cute dog. What kind is he?"

"Just a bird dog. Aren't ya, Coop?" Damien scratches behind Cooper's ears, then smooths a hand down his side. "He was a rescue mutt—pointer, most likely. Loves to hunt, don't you, boy?"

Cooper wags like Damien hung the moon. He can get in line with the rest of the town.

I finally register Damien's clothes: top-of-the-line gray-and-white camo. "You went hunting?"

"You were out hunting in this weather?" Billy asks at the same time.

"I did and I was." Damien directs that smile at me. "Quail season doesn't end till February."

"Oh." So that was the "important" meeting that couldn't be interrupted earlier? "You held all your calls so you could hunt?"

The sheriff laughs. At least someone finds it funny.

Damien taps my chin. "Don't look so bummed. I brought you a few quail in the cooler—you can cook us up one of your gourmet feasts."

He wanders into the den, and we follow. His sudden presence makes me feel smothered. I tell myself I'm glad he had a good day, but it would've been nice if he'd answered my call instead of ignoring me and then showing up unannounced for dinner.

Billy pulls the curtain back to check outside. It's full dark, snow glowing like a white sheet under the moon. "I still can't get over you wanting to hunt in this."

"Not a hunter, Sheriff?" Damien sinks onto the couch. I perch stiffly at the end, and he shifts closer.

Billy watches us a little too closely, sending heat up my neck. "Sure, I've hunted," he says. "Still have venison from the fall. And I love the snow—skiing, snowshoeing. But sitting in it all day? Not my thing."

"Me neither," Mom calls out.

I silently agree—not that anyone's asking.

"Don't knock it till you've tried it," Damien says. "We hike around. It's good exercise. I'll take you sometime."

The whole exchange rubs at me. "You never offered to take me."

Damien turns to me, earnest. "Would you like to go hunting with me tomorrow?"

"No," I admit.

"A-ha! There you go." He addresses the room. "I tell you, it's more fun in the snow. More of a challenge."

Billy asks, "What do you hunt with?"

"Twenty-eight gauge."

"That's big for quail," Dad grunts.

Damien turns to him, unfazed. "Mister Bailey, when it comes to shooting, Rhett Akins gets it right." He sings, "'A gun's like a woman... it's all how you hold her.'"

Dad laughs loud and warm.

Maybe Dad should be the one dating Damien. I stand. "Boy talk. I'm outta here."

But Damien hooks a hand in my jeans pocket, tugging me back. Heat hits my cheeks.

He pulls me down beside him. "What's eating at you, babe?"

I ease out of his grip. Truth is, I'm not sure. "I thought you were supposed to have a big meeting with your dad today."

Damien exhales hard and flops back. "Oh, that. Yeah, we tabled it. The old man convinced me to hunt instead. What was I supposed to do? He's the boss."

Classic Dabney—he could ditch work for the apocalypse if it meant a day outdoors. The Simmons men have been clashing over environmental issues, and Damien's been gaining support. Dabney probably wants time to remind everyone who runs the show.

"He's just trying to distract you," I say.

Looking at Billy, Damien adds, "My dad and I go rounds over how much we should cut. He always says"—he drops into a booming voice—"'People need paper, son.' But there's a way to be mindful of the native habitat. It's good PR. And good for the wildlife."

The men drift into logging talk, and I seize my chance to escape.

Mom follows me into the kitchen, her whisper sharp. "Sorrow Ann Bailey."

Uh-oh. Full name. "What is it, Mom?"

"You be a good hostess and ask that boyfriend of yours to eat with us."

"He knows he can."

"I didn't hear you invite him. A man needs to hear you say it."

I roll my eyes. "What is this, 1950?"

"Hey, Bailey." Damien appears in the doorway. "Got enough food for one more?"

Mom shoots me a look and slips out. Something in me pinches tight. I turn to Damien. "Do you have to call me Bailey?"

"I've been calling you Bailey since junior high." He twirls a piece of my hair. "Sorrow's just such a... I don't know... mopey name."

Mopey. "Yeah, and it's all mine."

He pulls me close, body warm and solid. "C'mon, mopey. Give me a proper hello."

It's nice having a man who cares. Nice not to be alone. And he's helped me out of so many jams. I *should* want him around even when I don't need help.

I try to relax into it. His body feels good, and he looks good. So why do I feel... put upon? Shouldn't I be melting? Shouldn't there be fireworks?

Voices drift in from the den—Billy's low rumble, Mom's

chatter, Dad's occasional *hmph*. They sound absorbed. Nobody's coming in.

I rise onto my toes. I tell myself I'm being polite—just not wanting to kiss my boyfriend in front of a guest.

Damien's hands glide down my back and cup my bottom. "Shorty," he teases. "I need to pull you up to reach me."

He lifts me higher, and I loop my arms around his neck for a slow kiss. I try to focus on him, but the voices in the next room buzz in my ears. I can't tune them out.

He senses it and shifts to kiss along my jaw, nuzzling behind my ear. "C'mon, gorgeous," he murmurs.

A shiver runs down my skin. The man definitely has moves.

"Sorrow," Mom calls, "do I smell something burning?"

Nothing is burning—unfortunately. I pull away, and we both sigh.

"Mom won't want to keep hungry men waiting," I say.

He rests his forehead against mine. "Are you saying you're blowing me off again?"

"Me cooking dinner is hardly blowing you off." Even if, yes, I'm eager to get back to it—for more reasons than one.

He squeezes my shoulders. "It's okay. I'm a patient man."

Mom bustles in, tossing bottles into the recycling. "I set another place, Damien. You'll be sitting right across from the sheriff."

A knot twists in my belly.

Not what I pictured for tonight. Though why that bothers me so much, I can't say.

Chapter Fourteen

Billy

I STUDY the man across from me. Truth is, I'm a little jealous of Damien Simmons. Not his looks—which are good—and not his sizable bank account. It's his ease, that nonchalant way he moves through the world.

I lost my ease when I lost my wife.

But Damien is young and eager, the kind of guy who flirts with waitresses and jokes with strangers like he's everyone's buddy. It makes me wonder how much anybody really knows him.

"So, this is actual bamboo?" he asks, eyeing the food on his fork. "Does that make me a panda?" He flashes a grin and takes a big bite.

Bear chews and swallows, frowning. "Why you didn't just toss the fish on the grill is beyond me. Some butter, some salt. Good meal, less time."

"You seem to be enjoying it," Sorrow says without looking up.

I agree. The man gripes plenty, but he's clearing his plate. I jump in before the tension can settle. "Well, I'm impressed."

"Me too," Damien chimes in. "Totally."

The compliment sounds rote, so I add, "I used to eat a lot of Thai. This is as good as anything I had in the Bay Area."

"Thank you, Sheriff." Sorrow puts her fork down, genuinely touched.

I lean back, washed with contentment—good food, cold beer, fine company. And Sorrow. When she asked about Keri earlier, something shifted. My grief sets me apart from people, but her openness offered me a bridge back. I wait for the guilt to hit, but it doesn't.

Cooper explodes into frantic barking.

"I'll go check," Damien says, sliding from his chair. "Hey, quiet, Coop," drifts from the foyer. When he returns, a pretty blonde walks beside him. "Look who I found."

Edith jumps up with a squeal. Bear's face cracks into a rare smile. Sorrow, though—she tenses. Barely, but enough for me to catch.

Edith hugs the woman over and over. "What are you doing here? Why didn't you call? You didn't drive all the way from San Francisco in this weather? Billy! You have to meet our Laura."

I stand.

"My older sister," Sorrow says quietly, and I notice she doesn't rush toward her.

Laura slips a small hand into mine, bright smile in place. "Ooh, you're much cuter than the last sheriff."

The comment startles me. The sisters aren't just different —they're *extremely* different—and women like Laura put me on alert. I aim for friendly but not receptive. "Glad to oblige. I hear your last sheriff was a good man."

Laura shrugs and wanders to the table. She pokes the curried salmon with the serving spoon. "Is that hard-ass deputy still there?"

I chuckle. "McGinn? He's a lamb once you know him."

"No thanks." She drops the spoon with a wet plop.

Yep. A handful. Makes me appreciate Sorrow all the more. I steal a look at her, watching Laura with guarded eyes.

"Sit down, sit down," Edith says, helping her daughter out of a stylish, fuzzy coat.

"You can eat bamboo with us," Damien adds, emerging with a plate and cutlery. Boyfriend-of-the-Year material, that one.

Everyone settles again. Damien starts to spoon food onto Laura's plate, but she holds up a hand. "I ate already."

"You're missing out," I say, studying her. Under the chandelier, the family resemblance shows—same blond hair, same fine features—but the similarities stop there. Her designer boots, skinny jeans, and faux-fur collar scream urban snow-bunny. She's gym-trim, all taut lines.

Not like Sorrow, who looks like she's built for real life, not magazine shoots. Something I prefer.

I catch myself. Damn. I swig my beer. I barely know these people, and here I am sitting in their home, cataloguing them, for God's sake.

"So I guess this means the road is open again," Bear says.

"Thanks to Billy and his efforts," Sorrow says, and Bear grunts in acknowledgment.

Laura perks up, looking between us. Something calculating shifts behind her eyes, and a queasiness hits me. Is whatever spark Sorrow and I share so obvious?

Not that it matters. She has a boyfriend—right there—and even if she didn't, I've sworn off relationships. Love hurts. I learned that the hard way.

"You're making friends already, Sheriff," Laura says. "I'm impressed."

"A man tries," I say lightly.

"Tries and succeeds." She reaches over and tweaks Bear's

ear. "It takes a lot to get a compliment out of grumpy old Bear Bailey."

Bear's mouth twitches. Apparently a grunt counts as praise.

Laura continues her inspection. I finish my beer too fast under her scrutiny. "I see you're not just strapping," she adds, "you're a can-do man." She flicks teasing eyes toward Sorrow. "I'll bet Helen at the bar is all over him."

Sorrow looks as uncomfortable as I feel. She pivots the conversation. "What brings you back to Sierra Falls?"

Laura's shift is instant—a quick dimming. "I thought I'd take a vacation."

Sorrow sips her beer, tight around the edges. "What about your job?"

Laura shrugs. "It's like a... sabbatical."

"Sounds like a nun thing," Bear mutters.

Sorrow ignores him. "Isn't that for professors?"

"It's a very high-stress job," Laura says. "You have no idea how cutthroat Silicon Valley is. Especially in Marketing."

"Laura is vice president of her department," Edith adds proudly.

Laura twists her napkin. The change from bubbly to cagey is stark. I wonder if she lost the job and can't admit it.

"Good you can take a vacation, then," Sorrow says, though she won't meet her sister's eyes. "I don't suppose you'll be able to help around the lodge. You were too busy last visit. Reno, Tahoe... vacations are busy things."

"Oh, that won't be necessary," Edith says quickly. "We've got everything under control, don't we, Sorrow?"

If this is *under control,* I'd hate to see chaos.

"On the contrary, Mom," Laura says brightly. "I'd love to pitch in."

Sorrow abruptly stands. "I made a pie."

I stare. Laura offered help—exactly what Sorrow needs—yet she's upset. Curiosity pushes me up to help.

Damien moves to stand, but I stop him. "I got this one."

He raises his beer in salute. "Works for me. I hate the kitchen."

I follow Sorrow with dishes in hand. "What was that about?"

"Nothing." Her voice is tight as she turns to the sink.

"Didn't seem like nothing."

She stills. "Every once in a while, my sister breezes in."

There's more here. "Seems like you could use the help."

She puts down the plates and faces me. "Trust me, next time something goes wrong around here, Laura will claim some personal drama and hightail it back to San Francisco faster than you can say Miss Fancy-Pants Vice President."

I chuckle. "That so? Maybe that's a good thing."

Bear's laugh booms from the dining room. Sorrow flinches. "Stick around long enough, Billy, and you'll see. There's a favorite daughter, and it's not me." She says it lightly, but the hurt is clear.

Laura might breeze in with charm and shine, but Sorrow feels like the backbone here. I meet her eyes. "I don't have siblings, but I've lived enough to know favorite and most valued aren't always the same thing."

"And besides," I add, "maybe she'll distract Bear long enough for you to get that frittata on the tavern menu."

"Yeah, maybe." She softens, giving me a shy, grateful smile. Up close, she's so pretty she almost glows.

A dangerous thought. I'm not looking for a woman. I had one, and I lost her. And this one already has a man. Still, it's hard not to notice she outshines her sister without trying.

"C'mon," she says, pulling a pie from the fridge. "You ever had Butter Pie?"

My eyes go wide. "There's such a thing as Butter Pie?"

"My specialty. Made this morning."

"Is it really what it sounds like?" I lean in, inhaling. "My life has been incomplete."

"It's exactly what it sounds like. Butter, sugar, vanilla, eggs. Whipped cream. Some people add cranberries, but—"

"Cranberries?" I interrupt. "Why mess with beige perfection?"

She laughs. "Should we go for broke?"

"Hell, yeah."

"Grab ice cream. A little more beige never hurt anyone." She nods at a drawer. "Scooper's in there."

I get the ice cream, scoop, and plates, practically salivating as we return to the dining room.

Laura frowns at the pie. "Is that what I think it is?"

"Yup," Sorrow says, her mood lifting.

Laura folds her napkin. "You know I can't eat that."

Sorrow stiffens as she sets the pie down. "If you'd told me you were coming, I'd have baked my famous Splenda and Air Pie instead."

I choke back a laugh and take my seat, cheering inside. "I say you're crazy."

"Crazy, huh?" Laura's eyes spark. "Why am I crazy?"

"To pass this up? Your sister's cooking is some of the best I've had."

Laura gives me a coy smile. "So you're saying I don't need to watch my weight?"

What the hell am I saying? She's baiting me. Flirting. Land mines everywhere. "I'm saying... I'm gonna shut up and eat some Butter Pie." I take a giant bite to prove it.

Everyone laughs—except Sorrow.

I glance at her. If I have a real friend in this town, it's her, and I instinctively look to her to share the moment. But her eyes are flat, fixed on her sister.

I know women. I've been married. Worked with plenty. I've listened. Paid attention.

And I recognize that look.

It's jealousy.

Chapter Fifteen

Sorrow

I GRAB the remote and turn up the volume. "I can't hear over your talking."

My sister leans across the sectional and snatches it from my hand. "Let's watch that reality show I told you about. This woman's just cooking—how is that interesting?"

"Please." I yank the remote back. "I just want one break. I worked all morning, and I'll be working in the tavern all night. What have *you* been doing? I have this tiny window to relax, and this is what I want to watch. If you're bored, go do something."

"I don't know what to do," Laura moans.

"You sound twelve. Finish unpacking—you brought enough clothes to dress an army."

She slumps deeper into the cushions, ignoring me. "Do we have to watch cooking shows?"

"The host is discussing techniques for velveting tofu."

"Exciting." She lets out a grumpy *hmph*. "Do you really need to know this? You should just be a chef."

The offhand comment makes my chest tight. Old resentments bubble up. "Gee, Laura, I'd love to be a chef. But I'm stuck here."

"It was just a suggestion. No need to bite my head off." She shrugs. "Maybe if you spruced this place up, it'd be more interesting for you."

"Maybe if you hadn't fled Sierra Falls, this place wouldn't need sprucing." I crank the volume. "Of course it needs sprucing. Duh."

"Easy, cowgirl. I'm just saying, if you livened it up, maybe you'd get more visitors. Keep you busy. I don't know how you survive out here in the woods."

I mute the TV and glare at her. "Busy? You don't know the meaning of busy. You cut and ran after graduation, leaving me holding the bag."

When she left, our brother BJ was already in college on an ROTC scholarship, committed to serve after graduation. By the time it was my turn to make choices, Dad had his stroke, and someone needed to run the place. Mom couldn't handle the physical stuff—shoveling snow, unloading groceries, making beds. So I gave up my dreams and stayed.

"I'm not having this conversation again," Laura says.

"So now you're telling me what I can and can't talk about?" All I wanted was to watch my stupid show in peace. My feet ache, and something about Laura's pouting pushes me over the edge. "You can tell your fancy coworkers what to do, but you're not vice president of me. Don't breeze in here and think you can boss me around. You haven't earned the right to tell me how I should do things."

"Jeez." She looks away at the screen. "Relax. I'm not bossing. Just making friendly suggestions."

I ignore that and barrel on. "You left for bigger horizons, leaving me here doing work I don't want to do."

She rolls her eyes. "Don't do me any favors. Nobody said you had to stay home with Mom and Dad. If you don't like it, make a change."

"Seriously?" I turn off the TV and face her. "So I was

supposed to leave after Dad's stroke?" I was a junior in high school. He was laid up for months. I kept taking on more until I was basically running the place.

"I don't know." She levels a look at me. "You seem pretty happy. You're like queen of the castle."

"Hardly." The word comes out sharp. "It's not unicorns and rainbows around here. I do the best I can. Unlike some people who visit their family so they have a fresh audience to complain to."

"Well, you should feel free to complain to me anytime." Her tone goes bland. "You hold things in forever, then explode when it's too late to do anything about it. How's anyone supposed to know how you feel if you don't let them in? Even Damien—you keep him at arm's length. And I don't know what's up with that sheriff. I saw you giving him googly eyes. He's too old for you. Stick with Damien. You want help around the lodge, you need to go for the hot, rich one."

My vision goes red. "Let's clarify something. Your version of letting you in actually means letting you tell me what to do? Like I need your advice."

She gives me an evil look. "If the shoe fits."

"Thanks for being there for me. This has been awesome."

"Fine, forget the Damien–Billy thing. If you're so in over your head, I see things you could do better. My life hasn't been a fairy tale either, but I've got experience. You could try listening to me for once."

I glare at her. "Oh, so I should let you take over? Just the easy things, like having Big Ideas. Meanwhile I'll stick to shoveling snow. Dad would love that. He and Mom adore you. Laura, Laura, Laura—she can do no wrong. Vice President Laura, so experienced."

She sits bolt upright. "What? You're the one Dad has running the show."

"I'm hardly running the show. He has his nose in everything. Second-guesses everything. Unlike you, who can do no wrong."

The home phone rings, and I answer with a clipped, "Hello?" It's Helen from the tavern. The water heater has sprung a leak. "Of course it did," I mutter.

"Well?" Laura asks when I hang up.

"The water heater is leaking. It's a commercial model. That means a very big leak." I cradle my head in my hands, trying to think.

"What can I do?"

"There's nothing you can do."

"You should let me help. You're being stubborn." She gets up from the couch. "When you're done butting heads, let me know. I'm here."

I give her a tired look. "I appreciate the offer. But unless you live here, you can't really help."

"Fine. Whatever. Damien knows the place. You should call him."

I stare at the phone, wishing everyone would stop pushing me toward Damien. "It seems like all I do lately is lean on him."

She shrugs. "Guys love swooping in on white horses to help a lady out."

Laura might not be reliable when it comes to the lodge, but she knows men better than I do. I hate that she's right. Damien does seem to like helping. And he genuinely cares about my family. Still, I hedge. "It's taking advantage, calling this much."

"Damien Simmons is not the kind of man who gets taken advantage of." She waggles her eyebrows. "If any advantage is taken, it'll be when he cashes in on your gratitude later tonight."

Heat floods my face. "Laura."

"Seriously. Call him."

Maybe I'm being stubborn. Finally, I pick up the phone, hating the feel of her eyes on me as I make the call.

We have a quick conversation, and, as always, he rises to the occasion. My boyfriend loves saving the day. He's great at it. He does it all day long at Simmons Timber. A broken water heater is just one more thing for Damien to conquer.

I hang up. "He said we should get a tankless heater. His plumber is coming out today. The guy owes Damien a favor, so he's comping the labor."

Laura gives me a wicked smile. "Like I said. Hot and rich."

But I just scowl, unable to shake the feeling that my problems are nothing more than another item on Damien's list to triumph over.

I exhale, tired clear through.

Chapter Sixteen

Sully

I swipe my sleeve across my forehead, and the stink of fry grease hits me all over again. I could boil this shirt in bleach and it'd still reek. I'm damn tired of smelling like burgers every day.

I peek through the pass window into the dining room. Folks are drifting in for lunch—burgers and fries, two hours straight.

But I've got a job, and I do it. A man doesn't serve in the Army without learning duty.

An irritated voice rises above the lunch chatter. Edith and Sorrow are showing Laura those old letters, and instead of it being a sweet moment, the tension is thick as the grease on my grill.

Edith plays clueless, like always, pretending everything's fine. But I know better—she notices everything in this lodge. Acting oblivious is her way of making people work things out for themselves. Genius, if you ask me.

They've pulled up extra chairs. Maybe Marlene will join them. I angle an ear toward their table.

"Listen to this part." Laura waves a letter, practically vibrating. *"Sierra Falls is like a bit of gold sparkling in a dry creek bed."* She slaps the table. "See? We're the ones who've struck gold. We make a website, pull some of these Buck Larsen quotes—"

"That's not a Buck Larsen quote," Sorrow cuts in, voice sharp. "That's a Sorrow Crabtree quote. If you read further"—she snatches the letter—"she writes, *I don't understand how you don't see the beauty... how you could ever leave such a place. How you could leave me.* If anything, sounds like he couldn't get out of here fast enough." She gives Laura a pointed look. "Sounds like some people I know."

Laura waves her off. "Doesn't matter. People will get the gist."

"It doesn't matter? We can't rewrite history. It's enough that Buck Larsen lived here for a time and left an illegitimate child behind. We don't need some misty-eyed version. The truth is interesting enough."

Laura snatches the letter back. "It's not *as* interesting."

"Be careful with that," Sorrow snaps.

Laura rolls her eyes. "This is called marketing, Sorrow. People love a love story."

"I know what marketing is. I'm not an idiot."

The pop of grease snaps me back to the grill. I duck into the kitchen. Tempers out there are hotter than this grill.

Growing up, the Bailey girls were close enough in age to annoy each other but too far apart for their worlds to overlap. By the time Laura hit high school, she wanted nothing to do with her kid sister. Then came college, then the big San Francisco job. They never really got to know each other.

Now they're adults, but the surface differences keep them at odds. Deep down, they're more alike than they think. If only they'd give each other the chance.

I flip the burgers and wander back to the window just in time to see Laura yank the letters again. I smirk. Both women are strong as hell, but right now they're bickering like children.

Still, it's more entertaining than flipping burgers, so I keep an ear peeled to the pass-through.

"Mom, tell her," Laura says. "I majored in marketing. I have a degree."

"Honey," Edith says gently, "Laura is vice president of her company's marketing department."

Sorrow sounds ready to blow. "Well, I have a degree in running this lodge, which is just as real as her experience."

Silly, the whole lot of them. The lodge is falling down around their ears, and these letters are a real find. Why they can't just talk it out is beyond me.

The door opens, and I brace myself. Marlene's entourage—Emerald, Pearl, and Ruby Kidd—shuffle in, a slow-moving barge of white hair, bright clip-on earrings, and powdery perfume. And where they go, Marlene isn't far behind.

I check the grill and dart out to usher them inside. A gust of icy air swirls past, and I angle myself to block it—putting me face-to-face with Marlene.

Hell, she's a fine-looking woman. Winter's set in for good, but she doesn't frump up like everyone else. Sleek, white down coat, big sunglasses—pure Jackie O. The woman is class.

"Thank you, Tom," she says, my first name husky on her tongue.

Marlene pulls off her sunglasses, and the smile she gives me knocks me flat. She hasn't done any nonsense to her face, unlike plenty of women our age. Time's written across her features, and she's all the prettier for it.

"Looking lovely, Marlene. As ever." I frown at the thought, because she deserves better than that chump she met for drinks last week. I'd know how to treat her right. Why shouldn't I meet a woman like Marlene for drinks? Hell, why not Marlene? Yet here I am, stuck flipping Bear's burgers.

"If you're sweet-talking me, why do you look like you just sucked a lemon?"

I've got nothing, though I'm sure a dozen good comebacks will hit me at midnight. Instead, I just grin like a fool.

She folds her sunglasses, tucks them into her bag, and with a polite smile, glides over to join the Bailey women.

I head back to the kitchen, but when Edith stands to get drinks, I say, "You sit. I'll get the teas."

Laura twists in her chair. "Where's Helen?"

Bear grumbles, "Yeah, where is that woman? Bar won't tend itself."

"Don't know," I say, "and not my business." I've spent too many years trying to find some inner peace; drama isn't on my agenda.

A man at the bar mutters, "Give the woman a break. I hear her husband's a real son of a bitch."

Deputy Marshall McGinn stands from the end of the bar, pulling on his jacket. "Pour your own coffee, Bear. Or let Sully do it."

I shoot him a glare. "Aren't you on duty?"

"Watch out," Sorrow calls. "Marshall might give you a ticket next time he sees you."

"Just look at him funny and he'll fine you," someone adds. "Ain't that right, Deputy?"

Marshall only shakes his head, and laughter follows him out. He's by the book—former military, honorably discharged after getting wounded in Iraq—and he takes his badge more seriously than most folks in Sierra Falls like.

I turn to the bar to pour the women's drinks. No need to ask—the older ones want iced tea, the younger ones their diet colas. Their chatter picks up again, and I listen with half an ear.

But my mind keeps going back to one thing: Marlene Jessup's perfume.

Beats the smell of fry grease any day.

Chapter Seventeen

Marlene

I can't help myself—I watch Tom walk to the bar. The way he's been looking at me... it's been a *look*. I haven't gotten one of those in years.

I've sworn off men. So why am I sneaking a peek at him?

Ruby leans in. "If you ask me, it's not right, not showing up for work. That Helen's a fast woman. Lord knows where she's off to." Her conspiratorial whisper isn't a whisper at all.

"You hush." I nudge her arm. "That's not our concern."

Pearl ignores me. "Doesn't pay to be a fast woman."

"Our Emerald was a fast woman," Ruby adds.

Heat floods my cheeks. I look at my mother. "Good on Mama for getting out of Sierra Falls and living a little."

My grandfather, Frederick Bose Kidd, was a pinched, tough-as-nails preacher who raised the Kidd sisters with a heavy hand and a hefty dose of brimstone. No wonder they're all spinsters.

My aunt presses on with a definitive nod. "Fast living is what gave our Emerald the Alzheimer's."

"Whoa," Laura mutters.

Sorrow sighs. "Not this again."

Laura laughs quietly. "So... having sex before marriage gives you Alzheimer's in your later years?"

I want to hush such inappropriate talk, but freeze when Laura's comment triggers a matching smile from Sorrow. That sisterly goodwill is too rare to interrupt.

"I love their scientific theories," Laura says.

"Some things never change," Sorrow agrees.

"Emerald's the one who frittered away her youth." Pearl and Ruby shake their heads like matching bookends.

Laura looks from the others to my mother, who's sitting with her usual pleasantly blank expression. "You guys, she's sitting *right* here."

Little does Laura know she and Sorrow sound just as callous when they fight. Every generation of sisters has its share of trouble.

"Emerald doesn't hear us anymore," Ruby says. "Fast living took its toll."

I can't hold back. "Good heavens, that's your sister you're talking about. My *mother*."

"What's that, dear?" Ma asks, a smile in her voice. She's spent a lifetime bearing her sisters' judgment with mischievous good humor. Even now, even as the dementia creeps in, that smile never fades.

I fight the urge to hop up and hug her. Instead, I slide a napkin under her sweating glass. One day soon I'll have to put her in a home—a place that can give her the care she needs. It's the hardest decision I've ever faced. Some days she's her usual, playful self. But other days, it's like pieces of her are missing. The mind is a funny thing—solid, but with blank spots, like Swiss cheese.

Edith finally chimes in, her voice edged. "Pearl, Ruby, you're sounding like your father."

Ruby sits primly. "Emerald was the one who ran off. Not us."

"Met that man. In Los An-ge-lees," Pearl drawls, stretching out every syllable.

Laura leans toward Sorrow. "Seriously? Emerald went to LA?"

Sorrow nods. "Word is, she used to party with Raquel Welch."

"True enough," Pearl says. "Till she got herself in trouble."

My jaw drops. That 'trouble' was *me*. "You ladies are just jealous."

I put up with a lot, but this is too much. I used my tiny nest egg to wall off the porch so the women can have a TV room. I've put off vacations, lunches, trips with friends— always taking a backseat to what my aunts and mother might need.

It's wearing me down.

Tom hustles over with a tray. "How 'bout some iced tea for you ladies?" He catches my eye, holding it. An earnest look crosses his face, like he's trying to save me from the conversation.

I pull my shoulders back, suddenly self-aware. Earlier he said I looked lovely. With his gaze still on me, I wish I'd slipped off to the restroom to touch up my makeup.

What am I doing? Flirting? The man's nickname is Sully, for goodness sake.

"Sully!" Bear's bellow cuts through the chatter. "What the hell are you doing? I don't pay you to pour drinks. Is that something burning? Get on those burgers, man. Beef ain't cheap."

"On it." Sully disappears into the kitchen, muttering, "I never burned a damned burger in my life."

He returns carrying baskets stacked high with burgers, fries, chicken clubs, and one grilled cheese.

I can't resist teasing him. "Look at you, Tom. Serving the women. What will Bear say?"

"I don't give a good goddamn what the man says." The deadpan delivery, paired with that wicked look, makes me giggle.

I cover my mouth. When was the last time I giggled? Trying for poise, I say, "Cooking, tending bar, and now this? Seems to me you need a day off."

Mama looks up as he sets down her club. Her face powder has settled into her deep wrinkles, but her smile is bright. "Aren't you a gentleman?"

He tips his chin. "A table of gentle ladies requires no less."

"Tom Sullivan," I exclaim. "You surprise me."

Apparently, I *am* flirting. I'm out of practice, but it feels good.

He sets my grilled cheese in front of me. "More tea for you, Marlene?"

"Any more and I'll float away." I flash him a confident smile, eager to show Sully—and the world—that my ex-husband is a fool.

He sets Laura's lunch in front of her. "Eat up," he tells her, giving her shoulder a squeeze. "I'm watching you, kid. You need more than Diet Coke and carrot sticks to fuel you."

The man is considerate. He notices things.

He gives me one last look, and I return my most pleasant smile. Maybe I can have a man in my life and my own interests, too.

When he heads back to the kitchen, I make myself refocus. "Sorrow, did you bring the letters?"

"I did." She proudly hands a small stack to each woman.

"Those letters belong to the family," Bear calls from the bar.

Sorrow deflates, her shoulders sinking.

Sully pokes his head through the pass-through. "Bear Bailey. Give the girl a break."

I silently agree. Sorrow has always had that wise, burdened look, like she's responsible for everyone. Girls like her end up taking on too much and forgetting their own hearts.

Laura rolls her eyes. "Why does Sorrow need a break? Just because she has the same name doesn't mean the letters belong to her." She turns back to the table. "It's time to plan. And you ladies need to forget your past festivals. The Buck Larsen Fair is going to be big."

"Yes," Sorrow says, patience thinning. "A Buck Larsen festival is exactly what we were talking about. Before you came."

"I think we should get the lodge involved," Laura says. "Run a special rate. Include discount festival tickets."

Sorrow glares. "You let me worry about the lodge."

"I thought you hated the lodge."

"You are totally twisting my words."

The sniping starts again, and I sag. I've had enough sniping for a lifetime. I catch a glimpse of Sully through the pass-through. What would he do if I just marched in there and joined him—leaned against the counter and sipped my tea?

I drag my gaze away. The last thing I need is to start batting my eyelashes at Tom Sullivan. Best to stick to my plan: pouring my heart into the historical society. Which means planning the best festival Sierra Falls has ever seen.

"Maybe we should advertise this year," I say. "What do you girls think?" I make sure to include both Bailey sisters.

"I have all kinds of ideas," Laura says. "I'll do a press release, of course. Maybe partner us with a celebrity."

The ladies coo. Laura is a handful—not like Edith at all— and when she's in charge, she's something else. Ambitious. Always has been. Even in high school she'd sneak out after curfew but still make honor roll. No wonder she's so successful.

"How do you know all this?" Pearl asks, awed.

"I have tons of marketing experience," Laura says, brightening.

"So we've heard," Sorrow mutters. "Five thousand times."

"That's wonderful," Ruby says.

"Edith, you must be so proud," Pearl adds.

Edith smiles and pats her daughter's hand.

The gesture hits me. I love my boys, but I've always wondered what it might've been like to have a daughter.

"I'd be thrilled to take over publicity," Laura says. "We could do online promotions."

"That sounds fantastic," I tell her.

"With what money?" Sorrow asks, her voice flat. Steam practically rises off her.

Laura waves her off. "We won't need much. We'll use social media. Guerrilla marketing."

"Gorillas?" Mama looks alarmed.

Pearl gives Ruby an uneasy look. "I don't think we have a permit for those."

"I don't think the fairgrounds will allow wild animals," Ruby agrees.

I choke back a laugh. "She meant guerrilla, like in warfare."

Pearl shakes her head primly. "I think Buck Larsen is enough of a theme."

"Yes, dear," Ruby says soothingly. "We don't need to include things about wars."

I let out a sigh. This isn't going as planned.

Sorrow scoots her stool back with a scrape. "You know what? You ladies have at it. My fearless sister seems to have this under control." She heads to the bar, calling into the kitchen,

"Sully, I'd love you forever if you made me one of your cookie sundaes."

He peeks out, smiling warmly. "You got it, kid."

The last time I had a sundae, I was a kid myself. Sully is so good with the Bailey girls. It's too bad he doesn't have children of his own.

My heart stutters. Maybe he does. Maybe he has two dozen kids. How should I know?

The conversation at the table fades as I strain to hear Sully and Sorrow. I study his profile as he scoops ice cream, his jaw strong and clean-shaven.

He peeks out of the pass-through. "You still like whipped cream?"

Sorrow makes a face. "Duh. It's not a sundae without whipped cream. And please do that thing with the chocolate sauce."

I hold my breath, waiting. He just grins knowingly. Take off that apron, put him in a collared shirt, and he'd be downright dashing.

That's it. I need an excuse to go over there.

He slides Sorrow's sundae toward her just as I step up to the bar.

"You make desserts, too?" I manage, aiming for breezy. But I catch sight of his special chocolate flourish—an elegant cursive S across the top—and my voice cracks. "Adorable."

"S for Sorrow." She plucks the cherry and pops it into her mouth. "Sully's cookie sundaes are to die for."

"Cookie sundae?" I ask.

"Yup. Cookies all along the bottom. He bakes them himself." She takes a huge bite, sighing in bliss. "I make a mean crème brûlée, and it still couldn't compete with Sully's chocolate chip peanut butter cookie sundae."

"Hell, woman. I'll make you one," Sully says, leaning on

the pass-through counter. His biceps are unreal for a man his age.

"I couldn't," I say, considering both the ice cream and those arms.

He narrows his eyes. "You can't eat ice cream?"

"Well, I can. I just... shouldn't."

He's having none of it. "If it's your figure you're worried about, you can toss that concern right out the door." Something assessing flickers in his gaze. The intensity warms my blood. "I say you need some ice cream."

He grabs a spoon, and my mouth goes dry. My ex-husband never cared what I needed. Never paid attention.

"Try this." Sully scoops a perfect mix of ice cream, cookie, and whipped cream. "The secret is mixing the dough into the ice cream."

"Be sure to break off enough cookie from the bottom," Sorrow says.

I approach the pass-through and reach for the spoon, stunned. My husband never offered me ice cream. He used to think I needed to watch my waistline.

But Sully doesn't hand me the spoon. He lifts it toward my mouth. "Have a taste." His voice is gravel.

My heart kicks. The last time a man fed me anything, I must've been in my twenties. I hesitate, then open my mouth. His eyes lock on mine.

And then I taste it. I shut my eyes, sighing in bliss. When I open them, I can't stop my grin. "You've got a way with food, Tom."

The moment stretches, and when I glance back toward the others, a quiet has settled over the tavern. The women read their letters and Bear sips his beer.

Sully's voice cuts through the calm. "I want a day off." There's an intensity in it.

Bear looks up. "What's that?"

I watch closely.

"I said I need a day off, Bear."

What does Sully do on his days off? Does he date women he meets online? Take them out for drinks? Would he ever take me out?

"I'm taking a night off." Tom Sullivan meets my eyes, and it's like he's read my thoughts. "A man needs to live his life."

Chapter Eighteen

Sorrow

"OH, GOD... WHAT NOW?" I'm tugging at the bodice of the old dress I dug out of the attic when a loud thud shakes the house. How did pioneer women even breathe in these things? I gather the heavy skirt and race downstairs, half expecting to find the walls caved in.

I tear through rooms until I stop short in the den. My sister. Of course.

"What the—?" My eyes widen at the giant black workout contraption dominating the space. Two men in blue uniforms shove furniture aside to make room. "What on earth is that?"

Laura smirks and points at my dress. "The question is, what on earth is *that*?"

I tug the neckline up and the bodice out. "I asked you first."

"It's an elliptical trainer." She gives me a maddeningly innocent smile. "You're looking pretty saucy, baby sister. Is that one of Sorrow Crabtree's dresses?" Her eyes light. "Hey, I know. We should have people dress up for the festival."

As if Laura really cares about the festival. Costumes are just another way for my sister to soak up the spotlight. "You just want to play dress-up." I point at the machine. "What's that doing here?" The shifted furniture exposes carpet five shades darker and the baseboards are caked with dust. Great—more for me to deal with.

"Cardio," she chirps.

"Put it in your room."

"It won't fit."

"Obviously. It's ginormous. Careful!" I dart in front of Dad's recliner as the movers haul it dangerously close to the TV. If anything gets damaged, *I'll* be the one who pays. I swing back to my sister. "Laura, this cannot go in here."

"I thought Dad could work out in front of his shows. It'll be good for him."

I cross my arms, partly for emphasis, partly to keep my overexposed chest from spilling out of this bodice. "You mean *you* could work out. Dad's not using a treadmill."

"I told you, it's an elliptical trainer. It's better for your knees." She keeps that cheerleader tone, and it's infuriating.

"Try walking. Works for the rest of us."

She shakes her head. "It's not the same as cardio. You could use it, too—you need to get your heart rate up."

This conversation is accomplishing that just fine. "Chasing down problems is all the cardio I need."

Her expression says she disagrees. "If you say so."

Is she sizing me up? I straighten the bodice, irritated. This snug saloon-girl dress isn't helping. "What are you really doing here?"

"I told you. I'm rearranging the den. Since when is that a federal offense?"

"No, Laura. I mean why are you here? Home. Don't your minions need you back in San Francisco? And if this is just a visit, why are you installing an elliptical?"

A flicker of doubt flashes in her eyes. A-ha. She dodges, as expected. "Speaking of rearranging furniture, I can't believe you all still have that stuffed bear."

I groan. The black bear's been in the foyer since we were kids—yes, it's disgusting, but I pick my battles, and Dad's bear isn't one. "It's a hunting lodge."

"It's hideous, is what it is."

"Of course it's hideous, but Dad's never letting us deep-six his bear. His name is *Bear*, for crying out loud." I fold my arms again. My sister's a master at derailing conversations, but I won't let her off the hook. "Would you please stay on topic?"

"You tell me. What's the topic?"

"Maybe if you took a break from reorganizing the entire world, you wouldn't have trouble paying attention."

"Maybe if you—"

"The *topic*," I cut in, not wanting to know what my sister has queued up, "is why you're here."

"To visit." Her answer is too quick. "What's wrong with a simple visit?"

Laura fled Sierra Falls the minute she graduated. There's no such thing as a "simple visit" with her. "You never just visit. So tell me—why is the big-shot VP taking a sabbatical? What do you want?"

Her eyes narrow. "I don't want anything from you. Jeez, Sorrow. Why do you always feel so put-upon? No wonder Damien hasn't sealed the deal with you yet."

I practically shriek. "What? What is that supposed to mean?"

"You know exactly what it means. It's time for Damien to put a ring on it, but why would he when you're always on him about everything?" She delivers it with that cool, infuriating calm.

I know that look—battle mode. Fine. I can play that game. Arms crossed, fingers curled tight against my biceps, I hold my ground. "Who says I want Damien to put a ring on it?"

Even saying the word *ring* gives me a jolt—more panic than anticipation.

Laura must see it. I watch the cogs turning as she tips the movers and shoos them out. She turns back to me and says evenly, "Don't tell me you've got a thing for the sheriff."

"I'm not into anybody." I start straightening the den, snapping out a throw blanket and smoothing it way more than necessary. But my stomach flips. Am I... into the sheriff?

"Oh, God." Laura gapes. "You *are* into him. He's kind of old for you, isn't he?"

How does she always read my mind? I turn to face her head-on. "Billy is not old. He's, like, late thirties. Since when is that old?"

Her slow smile spreads. "Want some sisterly advice?"

"No."

She offers it anyway. "Go for someone your own age."

"I told you, I'm not going for anybody."

"Damien is cute and rich," she insists. "Keep your head in the game, kid. Eyes on the target."

"I'm not a kid." I feel boxed in. I don't want to talk about either man. How does she always get the upper hand? "And what's with all the bad sports metaphors? Some people aren't trying to win something. We're not all as mercenary as you."

She studies me with a smirk. "If nothing's going on, why so defensive?"

A knock at the back door cuts her off. We trade a look.

"Saved by the bell." I hurry out, wondering who on earth it could be. Folks usually come through the front and walk right in.

But Laura's right behind me. I whisper over my shoulder, "Nothing is going on with Billy. Damien and I are just dating. I'm not marrying anyone, not now, not anytime soon. Thank you for your interest." That ought to shut her down. I open the door.

Billy.

Laura stops beside me and snickers. "Speak of the devil."

Evil. She is actual evil. Sent to torment me.

Billy's eyes drop straight to my breasts—which, thanks to this ridiculous neckline, are practically gasping for air. I try to gather my dignity. "Hi, Bill—"

But Laura steamrolls in. "Sheriff! What can we do for you? You here to see Sorrow?"

He looks instantly wary. He's intuitive; he can probably feel the sibling warfare radiating off us. "I'm always happy to see Sorrow," he says slowly, choosing his words with care, "but I'm here because your father sent me."

Laura leans against the wall, giving him a playful, flirty look. "Aren't you happy to see me, too?"

I would kick her if I could get away with it in this skirt. Instead, I glare.

She's always so effortless with him, and it irks me. Am I jealous she's so at ease with men? Or that she's at ease around *Billy*?

The realization hits: I'm craving his attention myself. I shoulder in front of her. "What's up?"

"I just got off duty and was grabbing a coffee when all hell broke loose." His eyes stay on me. "They need you at the tavern."

Of course they do. "Give me a sec to change."

I hustle to my room and pull on my jeans in record time. What now? Explosion? Locusts? I shrug on my fleece and jog back down the stairs, asking, "What is it this time?"

"The freezer died."

"Oh. Okay." Not what I expected. Could be worse. My

mind ticks through contacts. "Can't Sully just move the food to the garage freezer?"

"No. That one's down, too."

"Both freezers?"

He nods.

"Weird," Laura says, utterly missing the point.

I shoot her a look—surprised and irritated she's still trailing us. "Thanks, Sherlock."

I can feel her eagle eyes on me and Billy, tracking every move. Why is she tagging along? She's a varsity-level flirt, and her presence makes me intensely uncomfortable.

"There's more," Billy says. "The food's spoiled. The units must've been down a while."

I stop cold. "Crap." Hundreds of dollars in patties, chicken tenders, corn dogs... all the junk Dad insists Sully cook. Not much of it fresh.

A heavy rock forms in my stomach. "All that food... that'll cost us a fortune." And with so few lodgers at the inn lately, the restaurant is our lifeline. We can't turn people away. "What are we going to feed people?"

"Can you call your distributor?" Billy asks. "Get an emergency delivery?"

"We don't really have one."

He frowns. "What do you mean you don't have a distributor?"

"Well, bread gets delivered. But Dad doesn't trust the other guys. He likes me and Sully to buy the meat ourselves."

"Wow," Laura says. "That sucks."

"Yeah, thanks," I mutter, rubbing my temples. Either help or go away.

Having her here for this mess—while she watches every nuance between me and Billy—puts me on edge, makes me feel exposed.

He leans in a little, voice low just for me. "Don't worry. We'll handle it one problem at a time. I've got business in Silver City tomorrow—come with me. We'll hit one of those warehouse stores, you can stock up, maybe grab a small freezer to tide you over. I'll be driving the SUV—it's plenty big."

Relief washes over me. "Okay."

A plan. Thank God. Plans mean control. I manage a smile, using humor the way I always do to keep from spiraling. "The Sheriffmobile, huh? Does that mean we can speed?"

"I won't tell if you won't."

I look up to thank him—and freeze. He's staring down at me, warm brown eyes steady on mine, his presence so solid and sure it steals my breath.

Oh, crap.

I *do* have a thing for him.

Chapter Nineteen

Billy

Had I seriously just told this woman I'd speed to the store for her? In an official vehicle, no less. What the hell is wrong with me?

I jog to catch up to Sorrow as she strides toward the tavern. My gaze skims down her back, and… yeah, that's what's gotten into me. Her fleece jacket and jeans hug every curve, and I can't help imagining giving that perfect ass a good squeeze.

I scrub a hand over my eyes. Get it together, Billy.

Since Keri died, I've had a few flings—hookups that served a need, nothing more. But I've never been this drawn to a woman. All day, I find myself wondering how Sorrow's doing, if she's holding up, what elaborate dish she's dreaming up next.

And every time, guilt follows fast. Why should I get to want things, feel things, live my life, when Keri never got half a chance at hers?

Yelling spills from inside—Sully and Bear going at it. Sorrow's face falls. "Sully never shouts," she says, sounding lost.

As if she needs more drama today. I get the sense Sully's like an uncle to her.

Laura appears behind us—I hadn't even realized she was following. "Wow, check it out," she says. "Sully actually has a voice."

I shoot her a look. Big sister seems too wrapped up in her own issues to register anything beyond herself.

She catches my expression. "Seriously. If you Googled 'strong silent type,' you'd find a picture of Sully."

We step into the kitchen just as Sully tells Bear, "Your daughter didn't touch your freezer."

Bear scowls. "Freez-ers." Then he spots her. "Sorrow. What the hell happened? Why're the freezers busted?"

My hand curls into a fist. I'm not a violent guy, but right now I wish I weren't an officer of the law. Just one good punch. Instead, I step forward. "Calm down, Mister Bailey. I'm sure your daughter knows nothing about it." Why her boyfriend hasn't told Bear to cut the crap is beyond me. Damien might help around here, but he sure doesn't stand up for her.

Sully growls, "Neither of us knows about it."

"Well, it can't be coincidence." Bear kicks the industrial freezer. "They're both dead, and the food's spoiled. Somebody must've done something to overheat 'em."

Laura opens the door and slams it shut, nose wrinkling. "Did you take a look, like, under the hood or whatever?"

First reasonable thing she's said all day.

"Good idea." I nod at Sully. "You get that side." We pull the unit from the wall. Dust coats the baseboard in thick clumps, and a dark puddle glistens on the floor.

"Is that melted ice?" Laura asks.

I dip a finger into it. "Freon."

"I can't look." Sorrow boosts herself onto the counter with a sigh. "I wish BJ were here."

I peek from behind the stainless steel panel, eyebrows raised. Because that's a... peculiar choice for a name.

"My brother," she explains.

Laura clarifies, "It stands for Bear Junior. He's got the magic touch with machines."

"He's stationed in Djibouti," Sorrow says softly. "Flying copters."

"My boy knows his way around a motor," Bear says proudly.

I turn to ask Sorrow something, but she's unzipping her fleece, and my mind blanks.

Damn. When did thermal underwear get this sexy?

I force my attention back to the freezer. "You got a screwdriver? I'm no BJ, but I can take a look."

Everyone stares, except Sorrow, who hops down and digs one out of a junk drawer. Is she really the only one around here who knows what's what?

Our hands touch as she hands me the tool, and something tightens low in my gut—something I haven't felt in years. I focus hard on the back panel.

I don't need to be an electrician to see the problem. Condenser tubes snake along the back, and Freon beads off them in a slow, shiny drip.

Bear sees it too. "What the hell?"

Sorrow steps closer. "What is it?" She smells like shampoo or lotion—some flowery, distracting thing.

"The condenser," Sully says.

"Yup." I lean in, wishing for better light. "It must be cracked or..." My words trail off as I run a finger along the tubes. Then I find it—an edge too sharp to be a simple crack.

"Regular wear and tear?" Laura asks.

Sorrow counters, "That wouldn't explain both freezers dying at once."

"Not wear and tear." I stand and wipe my hands. "I think it was sliced."

"Someone cut it?" the sisters echo.

I nod at Bear. "Looks like you've got a vandal on your hands."

Bear laughs. "Vandal? There are no vandals in Sierra Falls. Everyone knows everyone. This is just how things go around here." He looks at Sorrow. "Right, girl? All hell breaking loose on the regular."

I don't buy a word of it. Those wires were cut, and it makes everything else that's gone wrong lately feel connected. I'd stake my badge the Baileys are up against more than everyday chaos.

Bear may not want to hear it, but Sorrow does. She gets it, eyes wide. "Who would want to destroy our freezers?"

"Nobody destroyed our damned freezers," Bear snaps. "You're not in the big city anymore, Sheriff. There's no crime out here. You can be as suspicious as you want, but that won't make criminals appear."

"Not to interrupt," Sully says, "but what are we going to feed people?"

Sorrow squares her shoulders. "Billy said he'd drive me to Silver City for supplies." Something in her voice, like resolve—maybe even trust—hits me hard.

"We can stock up," I add. "Get a small replacement freezer till you can get a bigger one delivered."

"That doesn't feed people right now." Bear checks his watch. "Hell's bells, girl. It's 4:30. People are gonna start showing up for Sully's early bird any minute."

Silence settles, tight and tense, until Sorrow says, "I could cook."

Bear shakes his head. "Ain't you been paying attention? All our food's spoiled."

"Just the frozen stuff. I can make pasta."

I love how she stands up to him. The way she snaps back defuses his temper, turning him into a harmless grump. "She makes a good pasta," I say with a smile.

Her sister pins me with a wicked look. "When have you

had her pasta?" Something in her tone makes heat crawl up my neck.

Thankfully, Sorrow jumps in. "I've got everything in the pantry—garlic, olive oil, olives, capers. I can make a puttanesca."

Bear hoots. "What the hell's that?"

"Give the girl a shot," Sully says, solemn as a preacher.

"You, too?" Bear looks between his cook and his daughter, then stiffens, like a lightbulb's gone off. "You're serious."

Sorrow folds her arms, and I have to fight the urge to uncross them myself and rub her shoulders... maybe skim my hands down her back to that curve of her waist. Hell, I need to stop thinking like that.

"I've been meaning to tell you," she says. "I want to start cooking one night a week."

"You'll do no such thing," Bear fires back.

Sully shrugs. "Told you the other day—I could use a night off."

Bear looks downright betrayed. "What the hell? It's a conspiracy, that's what this is."

"Your daughter can cook," Sully insists—which, from him, is basically a speech.

"If it weren't for Sorrow's cooking," Laura adds, "I'd have lived on cereal."

Sorrow gives a small, shy smile, and it hits me how long she's been cooking in the background without a scrap of thanks.

Sully bristles. "Wait a minute. My food's not that bad."

Laura shakes her head, amused. "We love your cooking, Sully. But sometimes a person wants soup and salad instead of cheesy chili fries."

"I can cook," Sorrow says, chin high. I feel a surge of pride. "People like my cooking, Dad."

Bear grumbles, "So everyone tells me."

"Who else has told you?" she asks, honestly curious. Too modest for her own good.

"Him, for one." Bear jerks his thumb at me.

I blink. "What?" I feel my face go hot. "I—"

Sorrow gives me the cutest confused smile. "You told my dad I could cook?"

The way she asks tugs somewhere deep. I try to come up with something smooth, but Bear barrels on.

"I don't know what you fed our sheriff, but he's been crowing about... I dunno... bread or something. All that time in the city, maybe he forgot how to eat meat."

I laugh. "I love meat. For the record."

Sully adds, "Sorrow does a fine brisket, sir. Her secret is Coca-Cola, if you can believe it."

"Fine, fine." Bear waves him off. "Sorrow can cook. One night a week—Tuesdays. We'll call it Ladies' Night."

"Ladies' Night?" Sorrow rolls her eyes. "Should I feel insulted?"

I can't help it. I reach out and squeeze her shoulders, murmuring, "Hey. This is good. He's saying you can cook."

"You start tonight," Bear says, moving to the window and yanking aside the lace curtain. "And you better get moving. Jack Jessup's truck just pulled into the lot."

Chapter Twenty

Marlene

I PEEK into the kitchen and feel an unexpected wash of relief when I spot Sully. Which is silly—the man is always here. But I want him to talk to my grandson, Craig. That's all.

Still, I catch myself wondering what he does when he leaves the tavern on that loud motorcycle of his. Where does he go? Is there a woman waiting for him somewhere?

How is it I know positively nothing about a man I've seen —and greeted—for over two decades?

There's a commotion in the kitchen, so I linger, fussing with my hair as I watch. I pull off my scarf and slide a hand under my bob to make sure it still curls under.

Looks like the Baileys are having appliance trouble. Bear wears his usual crotchety face, though his girls—for once— aren't bickering.

The door swings open and I jump aside. "Oh!"

Laura skids to a halt before barreling into me, a hand to her chest. "Sorry, Marlene. Gotta run and get some ingredients from the house kitchen."

The door swings shut behind her. Through the gap, I glimpse Sorrow and the new sheriff speaking quietly.

I bite back a smile, pleased I insisted my family dine here tonight. If something's afoot, I'm not missing a second of it.

I head to the table where my son, Jack, and his family wait.

My daughter-in-law, Tina, wears her familiar sour expression—she'd wanted to go somewhere fancier, naturally. We've never managed to see eye to eye, especially on money. She loves the upscale places in Silver City, and though my boys do well with Jessup Brothers Construction, I sometimes wish she remembered not everyone was raised that way.

Jack stands to scoot in my chair, and I give him a warm smile. "Thank you, dear." My ex-husband might be a son of a bitch, but we raised ourselves some gentlemen.

"I'll go grab us some menus," he says.

"No need for that," Bear calls as he bursts into the dining room.

Sully's right behind him. "Freezer's down."

I make myself avoid looking at the cook, focusing instead on smoothing my napkin in my lap. I raised four gentlemen, and I can be genteel, too.

Jack stops mid-stride, menus in hand. "Want me to take a look?"

"No need," Bear says. "They're both dead."

I finally glance at Sully. His eyes are already on me—riveted, like he can see straight through me. I clear my throat. "So... you're not cooking tonight?"

"Sorrow's trying her hand at it," he says, his expression softening.

It gives me pause. What else puts that warmth on his face? Does some other woman get that look? A small pang hits me, foolish and unexpected.

"Sorrow's cooking?" Jack asks.

"And pigs must be flying," Tina mutters.

I shoot my eyes to her. That woman's manners come and go as they please.

Bear shrugs. "She's making some putanleska pasta. You don't have to eat it."

"Oh!" I say, delighted. "A puttanesca. That sounds wonderful. Of course we'll eat it, Bear. Good heavens."

I feel Sully walk over and wish I had a drink to busy myself with. There's only so much fussing one can do with a napkin.

Why am I acting like this? The divorce has thrown me more than I care to admit. What happened to my confidence?

"Evening," Sully says to the table. "How are you folks doing? It's Craig, right? Didn't recognize you at first. You're growing like a weed."

I forget myself for a moment, all attention zeroing in on my grandson. "Yes, this is Craig. And I think you already know my son Jack and his wife, Tina."

Jack gives me a look. "Seriously, Mom? Of course I know Sully. Join us," he says, gesturing to the empty chair.

"It'd be an honor," Sully replies.

I watch him, mesmerized by this different side of him. I've seen him for most of my life, but somehow never really *seen* him. Something's different tonight. He's not wearing his apron —just khakis and a snug navy polo. And his eyes... deep blue, almost purple, like lapis.

He turns to Craig. "I hear you want to join the service, son."

Craig beams. "Yes sir."

"Good for you."

Silence settles over the table. Tina's eyes go icy as she darts a glare from me to Sully to Craig. "I thought this discussion was over. My son is doing no such thing."

Sully suddenly feels a million miles away, separated by a gulf of cold wariness.

Have I made a mistake asking him to talk to Craig? Crossed a line? But the boy will be eighteen soon. Pretending he's still a child won't help him.

Someone needs to speak, so I do. "I thought Tom—Sully—could tell Craig about his experience."

Tina stiffens, but this isn't about her. Craig is stubborn, and he needs information, not emotion.

"We don't want him to go," Tina says sharply. "He's got a job waiting for him at Jessup Brothers."

Jack reaches across the table and takes his wife's hand, then meets my eyes. "The boy's too young, Mom."

I appreciate the effort, but I have the wisdom of years. The boy will do what the boy will do. And if they dig in their heels too deep, Craig might go and do the opposite just to be contrary.

I turn to Sully. "How old were you when you enlisted?"

"I didn't enlist. I was a West Point man."

"You were?" My eyes widen. It sounds so masculine, like something from a movie.

He looks amused. "Yes, ma'am."

I touch his arm without thinking. "Good Lord, don't call me ma'am. Makes me feel ancient." His arm tenses—hard ropes of muscle. Tom Sullivan is in shape.

I draw my hand back, touching my neck. Why does Bear keep this place so warm?

"Fine... *Marlene*," he says with a rare smile, and it's like the sun breaks through and warms something in my chest.

What is wrong with me? I haven't had a hot flash in years.

Sully turns back to Craig. "Have you thought about college? It's a good path."

Craig slumps, scowling at his parents. "Not if there's no money."

"First thing you'll learn in the service is not to talk to your parents that way." Sully's tone shifts—commanding without raising it. An officer's voice.

Craig's eyes widen.

"You'll sit up like a gentleman, too," he adds. "Elbows off the table."

The boy straightens instantly, hands in his lap.

Jack and Tina gape. I bite my cheek not to laugh.

"If money's tight," Sully continues, "you could do ROTC, like Bear Junior."

Tina looks like she swallowed a lemon. "Only kids with good grades get scholarships."

Jack gives her a calming look before turning back to his son. "You can always join the construction business with me and your uncle. Nothing wrong with that."

"I'd rather enlist," Craig mutters, staring at the table.

Tina sits rigid, ready to snap. "I don't want my boy to get killed."

"He doesn't have to see combat," Sully says gently. "There are plenty of jobs where—"

"I want to see combat," Craig says, defiant.

Tina flushes red. My heart softens—this is clearly a frequent fight.

She turns to me, eyes shining with pain. "You raised boys. Don't you understand what I'm going through?"

"Craig is your son," I say quietly, "but he's my grandson. Don't think for a minute I don't understand." I take her hand. "I might seem like a dried-up old prune, but age brings wisdom. I know what it is to be protective. But a mother has to let go sometime. The boy needs to decide the man he wants to be. We can only help him understand his choices. Arguing won't change his mind—it might even push him further."

I squeeze her hand. She hangs on like it's a life raft. My throat tightens. Motherhood is learning to swallow the ache.

"Why don't you let us talk?" Sully suggests softly. "You and Jack go grab a glass of wine."

I nod toward the bar. "I see Edith back there. Ask her

about those letters—you still haven't heard the whole story. Don't worry, you can trust Tom—Sully—to talk to the boy."

Tina bites her lip, chin trembling, and quickly pulls away from my touch, as though just then realizing how we were sitting. I brace for a fight, but she only nods and lets Jack guide her to the bar.

I have faith in my son—something in Tina speaks to him on a deep level. Maybe she'll let me in someday.

As they settle at the bar, Craig eyes Sully warily.

"College is still an option," Sully says, "if you want that. If you enlist now, you get free schooling later. Which branch are you considering?"

Craig fidgets with his napkin. "Huh?"

"What branch of the military?" Sully repeats.

"I kind of want to be a Marine. Like BJ."

Sully nods, gears turning. The boy hasn't thought this through. I decide humor might help. "Seems you've had trouble convincing any of these boys to go Army, Tom."

His sternness cracks, giving me a half smile. "I suppose I have." Then he turns back to Craig, intensity returning. "This is a big commitment. You're not enlisting just because you don't want construction, or think big guns are cool, or it'll be like a video game, right?"

"No sir." Craig grins. "Though I hear they give a sweet enlistment bonus." He stretches out the word sweet.

Sully stiffens. "That's not what I wanted to hear."

Craig tenses, looking younger than seventeen. "They think it's a joke. Like I'm a joke. The whole family. They'll take me seriously when I bring home a fat check."

"The family thinks no such thing," I start to say, then stop. He's still a boy; boys say thoughtless things.

Sully stays steady. "People take you seriously when you make decisions like an informed adult. Money doesn't make you a man. Serving your country isn't something you choose for a paycheck."

At *adult* and *man*, Craig snaps to attention.

"You don't join because you're good at shoot-'em-up games," Sully continues. "Whatever branch you pick, they'll chew you up and spit you out. Break you down and build you back up. So be serious. I'm listening. Why do you want to join?"

Craig pauses. When he speaks, the boyishness is gone. "Because I want to be part of something bigger than myself. Because I believe in this country. Men before me fought and died so I could play those games, and now it's my turn to serve."

His answer is more articulate than anything I've heard from him. I sit quietly, picturing Sully in uniform. In fatigues, in dress blues. I imagine him at West Point, then in Afghanistan, walking past rows of boys no older than Craig, barking orders.

I watch Tom Sullivan—really watch him—in a new light.

Chapter Twenty-One

Sorrow

"No, I said I'm cooking." I wedge the phone against my ear, trying to talk to Damien, chop olives, and sauté garlic all at once. "The freezers went down and everything spoiled, so I'm making pasta for everyone."

"We've got reservations," he says, voice glitching through a weak connection. "I'm taking you to Silver City."

"We need to cancel. That's what I'm trying to tell you." The relief that hits me feels wrong. Not because I'm excited to cook for a crowd with limited ingredients—far from it—but because I need to have a conversation with Damien I've been dreading. A breakup conversation.

The kitchen door swings open. Laura and Billy come in carrying canned olives, a big jar of capers, and a few bottles of red.

I whisper an overjoyed "Thank you!" and nod toward the counter. "Right there. Can you open the olives?"

"What's that, babe?" Damien asks.

The phone slips. I hike it back up, neck cricked at an impossible angle. A sharp stitch zings up my shoulder. "Sorry, I need to make this quick. Dinner and a movie isn't happening —I'm cooking for a restaurant full of people."

"Can't you just get it started? Laura can dish it out."

"No, I can't." I frown. After everything—after begging for

years to get this chance—he wants me to hand it off? "It's not that simple, Damien." These days, not much is.

I've been thinking about that sheriff a few too many times a day. When he's around, I can let it all hang loose. Be myself. Be understood.

I grit my teeth, making a face no one can see. I need to break things off with Damien. Tonight. "Why don't you come here instead? I'm making pasta." My cheek hits a button, and the phone makes a clicking sound.

"What?"

"Sorry, sorry—this thing is driving me nuts."

Billy comes up behind me, silently showing me the opened olives. He's helping. He knows tonight matters. He gets it.

He lifts a can, eyebrows raised in a wordless, *Drain these?* His cuffs are rolled up, exposing strong forearms, muscles flexing as he moves. He's so solid and capable... and dangerous.

Nope. I cannot think about him like that. Or wonder what else about me he'd understand. What his hands would feel like on my skin. How he'd hold me.

I snap myself back and find him watching. He repeats the silent question. I nod, cheeks heating. I cover the mouthpiece and whisper, "Save some of the juice."

"I'm losing you, Sorrow. What was that?"

That's it—this isn't fair to Damien. I need to end things. "Come over, you can try my puttanesca. It's a tangy pasta." Maybe we can talk over dinner.

"You know I avoid carbs."

"Of course you do." I exhale hard and chop with renewed, frantic purpose—my knife slamming into the board like it can steady me. "I really should go. Ow—" I slice my thumb and stick it in my mouth. "Damn." Sloppy chopping. I need to calm down. I'm the one who wants to do this.

Damien sounds concerned. "You all right, babe?"

"Yeah, I just cut myself."

The sheriff sets down the can opener and takes my shoulders, his touch gentle and sure. My breath catches. He leads me to the sink, holding the phone so I can rinse the cut.

"Is it bad?" Damien asks. "Can't your sister help?"

"It's no biggie." I dig in the junk drawer for the first-aid kit. Billy takes it from me, and I give him a weak smile while he applies antiseptic and Band-Aids with careful, deft hands.

Back at the cutting board, I clear my throat. "So... you coming over for dinner?"

"You know, it sounds crazy there. And honestly, it's crazy here. I'm buried. Rain check? I think I'll work late. Let you have your moment in the sun. Save me some leftovers, okay?"

I hang up, feeling a messy mix of disappointed, unsurprised, and relieved. Now that I've decided we need to talk, I need it to happen. The waiting feels like an axe hanging over my head.

The rest of the night blurs in kitchen madness. Word spreads through Sierra Falls that I'm cooking, and suddenly the place is packed.

I cobble together a salad with beets, goat cheese, and candied walnuts from my pantry. A handful of random veggies, a couple cans of white beans, and chicken stock turn into soup. Billy cores apples, and I bake them for dessert. Portions are tiny because supplies are low, which everyone seems to think is some fancy, big-city thing.

Mom comes in with the last plates. "Have you eaten anything?"

I ignore that. I eye the teetering stack of dishes. "I don't have to do those too, do I?"

Billy appears, taking them from her and loading the giant stainless sink. "I got these, Edith."

"Hey, Sheriff." I say the title playfully, and instead of

formal it feels intimate. I'm giddy on adrenaline, thrilled someone outside my family is here to see me shine. "I didn't know you were still around. It must be midnight."

Mom checks her ancient Timex. "It's 10:30, and Sheriff Preston has been helping all night. You'd think the town ran out of food."

I watch him pour a glass of wine. "You were here all night?" Now that I think about it, I did catch glimpses—opening wine, clearing dishes. Yeah, he's been here.

He hands me the glass. "And miss your grand debut?"

The gesture warms me. I sip and let out a blissed-out sigh. "Thanks. I'm ready to drop."

Mom scrapes the last of the pasta. "Eat before the Jessup boys come in for fourths." She hands me a plate. "Your dad's trying to start a poker game. I'm sure it breaks every gambling law." She shoots Billy a panicked look.

Billy winks. "Did you say something, Mrs. Bailey? I didn't hear a thing."

Mom bustles out. I hop onto the counter and dig in. "I didn't realize how starved I was."

Billy pokes around for leftovers, coming up with a cup of soup and half a baked apple. "Not much left."

He plates it for me, then resumes the dishes, loading the industrial washer with practiced efficiency.

"It's perfect." Only a serving of pasta remains, the sauce reduced to thick, tangy clumps of capers and olives. I hold up my fork. "This bit is my favorite."

A memory hits hard, thickening my throat.

Billy notices. "You all right?"

"Yeah. Just thinking about my brother. BJ loves my puttanesca." I laugh. "Drives me batty, though. I buy these great Italian reds, but he insists on drinking Budweiser with everything."

Billy shakes his head. "An abomination."

"Totally."

"Everyone knows Miller goes best with Italian."

I hop down and bump him with my shoulder as I put my plate in the dishwasher. "Heathens. All of you."

I'm distracted. Billy hears it instantly.

He wipes his hands and hooks a finger under my chin, tipping my face up. "Uh-oh. I see those cogs turning."

His touch sends a charge straight to my belly. I'm wrung out, raw, and suddenly aching to lean into him. To let someone —*him*—take care of me for once.

But Damien. I can't sink into another man before ending things with him. I step back. "I'm just tired."

Billy loads the soap, starts the dishwasher, then turns back to me, serious. "This is more than tired."

"Jeez, Sheriff. Remind me not to get pulled over by you."

"Don't make me break out the tough-guy act." His voice dips into mock-stern, but there's a dark glint beneath it— something that makes me think of being pulled over and pinned against a cruiser, frisked by Billy Preston.

Heat floods my cheeks. What is wrong with me? Damien and I had chemistry—good times, even. But I never felt this sharp, breathless, skin-tightening awareness. This urge to step closer, to spill everything, to be known.

I have to break up with Damien. Like, *yesterday*.

"You're not distracting me," Billy says. "So you might as well spill it."

"What?" My eyes widen. Did he read my mind?

"Your eyes give everything away."

Something in his tone, in the quiet kitchen after a long night, pulls me toward him. He wants to listen. To understand.

I'm surrounded by people but still so alone. Always

paddling to stay afloat, dreaming of different things, different places—and no one sees. Except Billy.

"Tell me," he says softly.

And I can't help it. I exhale, and it all spills out. "I told you about my brother. He always knows how to handle Dad." Guilt pricks me. "Dad's a good man. His stroke... it was hard. But he drives me nuts. He's so old school. Take the whole ladies' night thing. Should I be offended that I can only cook if it's ladies' night?"

I glance up, expecting him to brush it off the way Damien would. But Billy's brow is thoughtful.

"It's hard," he says. "He's from a different generation. But that doesn't change the fact that this is a chance for you to cook. Taking it doesn't mean you agree with him. Let me guess, it's been his way or the highway for years?"

"Yeah, that one's not hard to figure out."

"And his dad ran this place before him?"

I sigh. "I get where you're going."

"Do you?" His voice is gentle. "Think about it from his perspective. I bet what he's able to do—what your mom even lets him do—changed after his stroke. He was the master of his universe. Now your mom won't let him out of her sight without a phone in his pocket."

It hits me hard. "Yeah. That's the whole of it." The shame comes hot. I've only been thinking about my side. Dad's stroke changed everything, just slowly enough that I stopped seeing the shift. "He worked timber when he was younger. He used to be really physical."

"I know the type. Change is hard for him. But aging happens to every man—if they're lucky." Billy brushes a strand of hair behind my ear, and the light sweep of his finger sends my pulse soaring. "Besides, he'll come around. Once he sees ladies' night pulls in every man in Sierra Falls just to taste your cooking, he'll get it. I've never seen this place so full."

His hand lingers by my cheek, and I fight the instinct to turn into it. How does he do this—make me feel both softer toward Dad and better about myself with just a few words?

What else could a man like that make me feel?

One turn of my head, one step closer, and everything would change. What would he do if I leaned in?

The door swings open. Laura stops dead at the sight of us standing so close. Heat blasts across my face.

She waggles her brows. "Kudos, kiddo. Your pasta was a hit. Even I loved it."

I turn away, rinsing a sponge that doesn't need rinsing, trying to breathe normally. "I thought you didn't do carbs."

"Shut. Up." She bumps me, placing a few final dishes into the sink. "I don't eat a lot of pasta. But I'll eat what you make. Duh."

I grin despite myself. "I'm honored."

"No, seriously." Laura's tone softens. "It was fantastic. Better than anything I ever had in North Beach." She cuts a look at Billy. "Right, Sheriff?"

Billy smiles. "I've been to North Beach a time or two. She's right."

"Wow." I set down the sponge, genuinely floored. "Thank you. Both of you."

Laura's eyes gleam. "And someone else has arrived to taste it."

I know that look. It's trouble. "Who?"

"Damien's here." Her voice goes sing-song. "He's starting a pool game with Eddie. I told him you'd be right out."

My shoulders tighten.

Billy reaches out, and my heart leaps—then plummets

when he gives my arm a goodbye squeeze. "I'll leave you to it, then."

I wish—ridiculously—for jealousy. Competition. *Something.* But he only looks slightly amused, the way a man does when he's not threatened by boys. Meanwhile, I've got to face a boy who only makes my chest feel jangly and wrong.

Damien's voice booms from the bar. I feel embarrassed. Which makes no sense; he's hot, athletic, from the wealthiest family around. So why the tight, uncomfortable feeling?

I try not to look crestfallen. Damien's here, but I want to play pool with Billy. I want *him* to walk me home.

Billy's hand had felt so sure. So right.

I shake myself. Time to talk to Damien.

But what if this connection with Billy is all in my head? He's older, a widower. He lived a whole life before he met me. Maybe he'll never move on from it. And if he *is* ready—does that mean he didn't mourn enough? I'm way out of my depth.

Billy's voice cuts through. "See you tomorrow?"

"Tomorrow?" I study him. His gaze is steady, warm. Faint lines at his eyes and brow speak to years outdoors. Hard on a lawbreaker, but soft on me.

He's nothing like Damien. Not technically as handsome, not as young. But he radiates calm, strength, wisdom—things I suddenly crave more than anything I share with Damien.

"You remember." A hint of amusement. "Silver City?"

Our shopping trip. I'd forgotten. Excitement sparks. "Right. Of course. Totally. Tomorrow."

Across the kitchen, Laura snorts.

I blush. That was maybe a little too enthusiastic.

Billy doesn't notice. "Good news. A buddy in the restaurant business talked to his supplier. They'll open the warehouse for us tomorrow morning. He'll give you a new industrial freezer at cost."

My jaw drops. Appliances cost a fortune. I've been in denial about it. "At cost? Really?"

"One that won't break down." He winks, managing to be cute, rugged, and thoughtful all at once.

I want to fling myself at him.

"Rack 'em up!" Damien shouts from the bar, making the men laugh.

And suddenly I know.

I don't want Damien.

I want Billy.

Billy

WHEN I SHOW up early the next morning, Sorrow's already in the tavern. I spot her right away—tousled blond hair down her back, flannel shirt tied around her waist. From behind she looks relaxed, perched on a barstool, chatting with her father. Sully's frying up hash browns, and the smell hits me as soon as I step in.

Bear nods. "Sheriff."

"Bear." I nod back. Keeping my tone casual, I ask, "Everything okay up at the lodge?"

"Smooth as silk. Why wouldn't it be?" Bear's grin is easy, dismissive. "You still worrying about our troubles? Downed trees, faulty lines... that's just mountain living. Comes with the territory. Stay in Sierra Falls long enough, you'll see."

The way he says it—like I'm being paranoid—makes me drop it.

Sorrow turns to me with a bright smile. "Hey, Billy."

My pulse jumps.

She might be dressed casually, but Sorrow's no slouch. She's all woman—confident, capable, at ease in her skin. The kind who'd be as sure of herself in the bedroom as she is on that barstool.

I need to stop going there in my head.

Last night, I went there repeatedly. I'd spent half the

evening imagining touching her hair, wondering how those waves would feel under my fingers. But the thing about her— the thing that really wrecks me—is the spark she carries without even knowing it. That quiet courage I can't seem to look away from.

Every time I see her, something in me wakes up, something I told myself was gone for good. She radiates light, alive and hopeful in a way that knocks me off balance.

And then I caved and touched her. It was just a brush of her hair, then her chin, her arm... I hadn't wanted to stop. I had to turn to the sink, splash cold water on my face just to get myself under control.

I force a casual look, like I'm not walking around with a fist squeezed around my heart—wanting her and feeling guilty for it. Guilty because of Keri. And because of Damien.

I clear my throat. "Morning, folks. Sorrow, you ready?"

She lounges there, leg swinging, shirt pulling tight as she leans back, and suddenly I'm a self-conscious teenager again— aware of every step, where to look, how to smile.

It hadn't been like that with my wife. Keri and I had known each other for years before we ever hooked up. Coffee, posttrial drinks—we'd eased into things. By the time we realized there was something between us, being with her felt as natural as breathing.

Sorrow... is different.

I'm not sure I deserve someone like her, not with the kind of ghosts I'm carrying. She's built for beginnings, and I'm still living in the aftershocks of an ending. But I keep coming back to her. She's radiant, yes—but there's a calm to her, too, a quiet ease I didn't realize I'd been starving for. Sorrow's dependable in a way most people aren't anymore. She shows up for the people she loves, and keeps showing up, no matter what's been thrown at her. That kind of depth and promise scares me... and at the same time, draws me with a pull stronger than I've ever known.

I lean on the bar beside her, ignoring the floral scent of her shampoo. The smell of Sorrow in the morning.

"Good news," she says around a mouthful of pancakes.

Her eyes are bright, her mood contagious. It burns through that cloud sitting heavy over me, just for a moment.

"Sock it to me," I say, stealing a triangle of her toast. I've always appreciated a woman with appetites.

"Our cupboards are full, or they will be. We don't need to get groceries after all."

Disappointment pricks at me, and I tell myself I should be grateful for the reprieve. I'm only hanging around to keep an eye on things. That's all.

"That is good news," I say, hoping I sound sincere.

My day off is back on the table. I should probably feel relieved. If only I could remember what I'm supposed to do with my time.

She swallows and nods. "So I won't need to bother you with that this morning."

"It wouldn't have been a bother." If anything, the little twist in my chest tells me spending the morning with Sorrow would've been the highlight of my week. I take another piece of toast, too dry in my mouth. "What happened?"

"Damien heard about our troubles last night." She glances at me, quick. "He didn't hang around, though. Pretty much left right after he found out."

Is she trying to tell me something? No. Women like Sorrow don't send hidden messages to men like me.

"Damien has some friends," she continues.

Bear smirks. "*Some* friends?"

"Yeah, okay." She shoots him a look. "He has a lot of friends. He knows restaurant owners—"

"Some as far away as Reno," Bear adds.

I keep my expression pleasant. How do I compete with that? I've got a buddy who knows a guy.

Her smile tightens. "Yes, Dad, even in Reno. Anyway, apparently any minute now, men will start showing up with food. Enough to tide us over, but not too much for our regular fridge."

"Well, that's wonderful." Funny how I don't feel wonderful.

"It is, isn't it?" She crumples her napkin. Is she disappointed too? "Though I can't imagine what Damien offered to get them to sell food from their own kitchens."

Bear's coffee hits the counter with a thud. "He offered not to kick their asses."

"Easy there, cowboy," she says, patting his shoulder. Then she looks at me. "I may not need groceries, but if that other offer still stands...?"

"The freezer?" Something eases in my chest. "You bet."

She grabs her purse. "Good a day as any to spend a ridiculous amount of money on appliances."

"Stick with her, Preston," Bear instructs. "Make sure she picks out a good one."

I help her into her coat. "I'm sure she can pick her own appliances, but I'm happy to weigh in if she wants it."

She throws me a glance that feels... mischievous. I resist the urge to put an arm around her as we head to my SUV.

It's a long, forty-five-minute drive to Silver City. Forty-five minutes of not noticing the line of her thigh beside me. Not breathing in the soft scent of her hair, not staring at how the sunlight sparks those waves to gold.

My mind slips to Keri, and the familiar ache settles in. But today, it isn't quite as sharp.

Is this what moving on feels like?

I glance at Sorrow again. My heart's heavy, but something else feels lighter. Open.

She's like that morning light cutting through the windshield, and I'm blinking awake after a long dark stretch.

Sorrow is nothing like my wife—Keri avoided the sun, swore by her fancy creams and designer hats. But Sorrow sits with her face tipped toward the light, freckles dusting her nose, jeans and a purple flannel making her look cozy and vibrant. And there I go, imagining her in my old red plaid shirt. Just that shirt. And panties.

Damn.

I need to stop thinking.

Talking. Talking will help. "We should be in Silver City by ten. Lucky Damien knows so many people. Good thing I'm not competing with him—money, charm, powerful friends..." I shrug. "A guy could get outmatched real quick."

She gives me a blank look.

The joke dies in my throat. I flip on the radio, and classic rock fills the cab.

"Yeah," she mutters. "Damien's something else." She leans forward, hair slipping from behind her ear, sending another wave of scent my way.

I stare at the road. Maybe silence is safer.

I keep insisting I'm not interested. That I can't be. I barely survived losing Keri—I can't lose someone again. But going on like I have been? Closed off? That's its own kind of dying.

I came to Sierra Falls looking for peace. Lately, the only time I feel anything close to it is when I'm with Sorrow. She's grounded. Rooted. Real in a way that anchors me. I've spent so much time drifting in my grief, but being around her reminds me what solid ground feels like.

I glance over again. She's so different. So refreshing. So damn beautiful.

And it hits me like a bolt. I want her. For real. Not just in my head—right here in my life.

I shift in my seat, panicked for something neutral to say. This is ridiculous. She has a boyfriend.

The radio rolls into a commercial, and she reaches for the console. "May I?"

I nod, grasping for small talk. "You like music?" God, what am I even asking?

"I like a little of everything." She flips through stations, leaning over, her elbow resting dangerously close to my thigh.

I crack the window.

Cooking. Safe topic. "Why do you cook?"

She's quiet a moment. "The kitchen is my solace," she says softly. "A place for me to go... in my head. There's not much else to do at the lodge. Usually it's just me behind the desk, or cleaning rooms—"

"You clean the rooms?" I shoot her a glance. "When do you sleep?"

She sighs. "It's not that much. We don't have so many guests. Planning menus, doing prep—it's my way of traveling. Tasting Indian curries or Chinese stir-fries... it's like visiting those places."

"You've never left Sierra Falls?" I ask before I can stop myself. I wince. Damn. That sounded patronizing.

"Well, sure," she says quickly. "I took some class trips. Sacramento, San Francisco. But real traveling..." She shrugs. "Guess that's not in the cards."

I want to tell her she gets to decide her cards. That someone should help loosen Bear's grip on her. Why Damien doesn't push for her, I have no clue. Hell, I've been pushing Bear since their roof collapsed. But I keep that to myself.

She shifts, studying me. "How about you?"

I blink. "How about me?"

When I look over, I wish I hadn't. She's studying me like she can see things I don't even know how to admit.

I wish she'd look out the window.

I also want to reach over, take her hand and hold it.

"You were a high-ranking police officer," she says. "In Oakland. Must've been exciting."

I lock onto the road. That was another life. "Exciting is one word for it."

"Must pale in comparison to Sierra Falls."

I shoot her a look. I'm good at controlling conversations—my whole job used to be about coaxing secrets. Yet Sorrow always catches me off guard. "Hey, we were talking about you. How'd the tables turn?"

She gives me a wicked smile. "I'm not done with my questions yet, Sheriff. So you left gangs for grandmas?"

"Thank God."

"You don't miss it?"

Miss it. Hate it. Both. It's complicated.

I dodge. "I'm happy putting myself out to pasture."

She laughs. "You're hardly ancient."

Some days I feel it. But today—Sorrow's sneakers on my dash, sunlight on her skin—it doesn't hit me the same way.

For once, the weariness doesn't come.

Chapter Twenty-Three

Sully

I KEEP one eye on things from outside the kitchen as the men haul out the old freezer and roll in the new. They work fast, hooking up the water line and electricity, easing that big beast into place.

I busy myself with pointless tasks—I don't need to be here. Not with Billy Preston supervising. I lean against the pass-through to get a better look.

Billy and Sorrow stand together, but it's Billy telling the guys to sweep up their mess. He catches the worry on her face and warns them not to ding the door. Finally, someone else is looking out for her.

I eye the sheriff. He's been hanging around a whole hell of a lot lately. I've got to admit, I like the guy. As former military, I understand a man who chooses a uniform. I respect that.

It makes me think of Damien, who has yet to earn mine. His uniform is khakis and pricey sunglasses—not my thing. But Sorrow likes him, so I guess that's something.

The door swings, catching my attention. The installation guys head out. "You're all set," one says. "Give us a call if there's any trouble."

I nod my thanks. Curious about the new freezer—and, I hate to admit, a little excited too—I head into the kitchen.

But Sorrow and Billy are already there, standing close. Not about-to-kiss close, but close enough. Talking in quiet voices like two people who've definitely thought about it.

I clear my throat. "Excuse me."

They jump apart like I'd caught them red-handed.

Unsure what to do, I snag a rag off the counter, turn on my heel, and head right back out. An adolescent move, sure, but better to look like an idiot than walk in on them mid-lip-lock. Especially since one of them still has a boyfriend.

I'm surprised they haven't broken up yet. Damien's been scarce lately—like he knows something's up. The sheriff, meanwhile, seems to be around every time I turn around. And from what I just saw, where there's smoke, there's fire.

Well, hot damn. I let that notion sit. Billy's older than Sorrow, and he'd better not be taking advantage—but no. I dismiss the thought. Billy's a good man. A widower. Not the type to toy with a girl's affections. If anything, he's the serious type, with serious intentions.

And what exactly are those intentions? Sorrow deserves someone who has them. Bear wouldn't know subtle if it bit him, so it falls to me to ask.

I get my chance soon enough. The phone rings, and a moment later Sorrow hurries out of the tavern. Billy stands at the door, shrugging into his coat.

"Hey, Sheriff," I call. "Got a second?"

He pauses, hangs the coat back up, and gives me a curious look. "Sure thing." He joins me in a booth.

"Sorrow head out?" I ask, unsure how to begin.

"Something at the lodge. Nothing big. Sounds like a light's out and Bear can't find the bulbs."

I shake my head with a smile. "Good thing he's got Sorrow. Otherwise he'd just sit in the dark and complain."

Billy chuckles. "Probably blame her for it, too."

"Something like that." The banter breaks the ice, and a comfortable silence settles.

I take a breath. Now or never. "I've known Sorrow since she was barely tall enough to see over the counter. She was a good kid, and she's grown into a good woman." I meet his eyes. "You're a lawman, and I respect you, but I've got to ask..."

I falter. I can command a battalion, but this overprotective-uncle routine? Not my wheelhouse.

"What my intentions are?" he asks.

I let out the breath. "Yeah. That's the one."

Billy hesitates. "She has a boyfriend," he says at last, words saying one thing, eyes saying another.

"Doesn't mean you don't like her."

He shrugs. "Sorrow is special."

"You've got feelings for her."

His chin goes up in a nod. Then he looks down, something weighing on him.

"But there's something else, isn't there?" I prompt.

He looks up, gaze distant. "It's more than the boyfriend." A humorless laugh. "I'm a broken man, Sully."

"Don't seem broken to me."

"Not broken, but... my wife. Keri. I can't seem to forget her."

I know something about that—maybe not about wives, but about ghosts. Young men who died while I lived. "I should hope not. I don't think we ever forget the past. We just keep going."

He sits with that for a moment, then continues. "Keri cast a long shadow. She was powerful—a lawyer in the DA's office. She could make hardened felons quake." He smiles. "She was something else. I never would've cheated on her, never dreamed I'd be thinking of another woman."

The smile fades. He leans forward. "That's the thing. I wouldn't just be moving on. It feels like breaking my vows even to look at another woman. And I'm no longer the man I was when I married her. That feels like a betrayal, too."

"Men change." I think maybe it's time I changed, too, but I push it aside. "You've got to keep living. That's how you honor her. Otherwise you might as well have died with her. Losing your wife so young? Of course it makes you different. You'll live different. You'll love different, too."

"I am different," Billy says quietly. "There's a quiet in me now. A peace I didn't know I was missing. Not till I came here and met Sorrow."

I nod. "Some folks call that wisdom."

"Maybe." He shrugs. "All I know is, for the first time in a long time, I feel like there might be things worth looking forward to. Because of her. When I'm with her, I feel... happy." He says the word like it's foreign. Then a darker glint sparks in his eyes. "And I feel a whole hell of a lot more than that."

I know that look. I growl, "I'll have to caution you there, son."

Billy laughs. "Understood." He sits back, looking lighter. "You ever lost anyone, Tom?"

I sigh. Should've poured drinks before this talk. "I've known loss. Not a wife, but it was loss all the same. I felt a lot of guilt stepping off that plane back onto American soil. Coming home when a lot didn't. But those boys—they'd have wanted me to live. They'd have kicked my ass if I gave up on my life. I bet your Keri would do the same."

"Kick my ass from the great beyond?"

"You bet." Then it's my turn to go quiet. Maybe I should take my own advice, maybe ask Marlene out properly.

"It's time to let go and give in to your feelings," I tell him— and realize the words apply to me, too. "You'll never lose the grief, but you're young yet. You move through it. You can't let yourself feel guilty. It's no dishonor to Keri if you have real feelings for another woman."

Billy holds my gaze, something unspoken passing between us. Respect.

He's good people. Solid. I can see him and Sorrow working. Which means she needs to do something about that boyfriend of hers, and soon. I'd love to warn her the way I'm warning Billy, but if I brought up her love life, she'd look at me like I'd sprouted horns.

An evil smile curls onto Billy's face. "I could always arrest Damien for something."

I bark a laugh. "No need for that. I've seen how she is with you. If I know Sorrow, that boy will get his walking papers any day now."

She returns and slides in beside Billy. "Let there be light."

Talk about lightbulbs—Billy's eyes blaze when he looks at her. "All good?"

"All good." She leans against him. "But I'm beat."

I watch in silence. They have no idea how obvious the sparks are. I just hope she can handle Damien. Sorrow's a bit innocent with men, not realizing the effect she has.

Damien, though—he's a pro. Smooth talker. I've tried to like him, but the guy seems to earn a living mostly by wearing expensive clothes and talking on his cell. Born into the richest family in Sierra Falls, treated like royalty.

The front door opens, letting in a blast of winter air. Speak of the devil.

Sorrow stiffens. "Damien, hi," she chirps, too bright.

He nods. "Bailey. Sheriff." Then, toward the back, "Sully, congrats. Heard you got a new freezer."

Sorrow pastes on a huge smile. "What a surprise. I thought you had to work."

Damien takes in the scene. "I like to keep you on your toes." He shoots Billy a pointed look. "Wanted to check out the new setup. See if you need anything."

Looks like things might come to a head sooner rather than later. I suppress a grin. Best entertainment I've had in a while. Youth really is wasted on the young.

Sorrow stands, brittle. Damien wraps an arm around her waist, holding her a beat longer than necessary.

She pulls away. "Well, come see."

He strides to the kitchen—of course he does—and I follow, Billy at my back. Guarded is the word that comes to mind.

Damien inspects the freezer. "She's a beauty."

"A friend of mine is in the restaurant business," Billy says evenly.

I frown. "Nobody better tamper with this one."

Billy meets my eyes, and we share a look. "I'm talking to Bear about installing a security system," he says.

"Good luck," Damien mutters. "This already cost him a fortune."

Sorrow nods like a bobblehead. "Billy's friend got it for me at cost."

"I'll bet he did," Damien murmurs.

Sorrow and Billy are focused on the freezer, so I'm the only one who catches the smirk on Damien's face. Hard to tell if the kid's about to laugh or take a swing.

"Well, Sheriff, nice work," Damien says. "It's big. Reminds me of those Transformer movies. Like it might come to life."

"Yeah, right?" Sorrow tries for playful, but tension threads her voice.

Damien shoves his hands in his pockets. "So I guess you don't need me."

"No—" She stops herself, gives a defeated laugh. "I mean, of course we need you, but this is handled."

I note the "we," not "I."

I back away. Seems like a perfect time to run an errand. Maybe swing by the house—Marlene's grandkid wants to see my Army medals.

Folks say all's fair in love and war, but right now, war sounds easier.

Chapter Twenty-Four

BILLY'S FRIEND moved heaven and earth to deliver the freezer early, and I eye the big, whirring beast while I clean the kitchen, scrubbing away grease and dust. Counters, stovetop, floor—wipe, scrub, mop.

Cleaning is usually mindless, calming. Today, I can't stop fretting about my love life. The timing keeps being off, and I haven't found a single good moment to talk to Damien. I need to get it over with. The situation gnaws at me.

I have to admit, he looked ready to throttle Billy this morning. I'm sure the jealousy wasn't about me—Damien just hates losing. But whichever way I look at it, there's no future for us. I've put this off too long already.

Because I can't stop thinking about Billy. I'm surrounded by people I love, people who love me, but with Billy I never feel alone.

I'd thought I was into Damien... until Billy came along. The two men couldn't be more different. Damien is such a *guy* sometimes—a jokester at the pool table, the type who smacks me on the butt as I walk by. Fun, easygoing, everyone's buddy.

Laura teased me about Damien putting a ring on it, but getting to know Billy showed me that Damien isn't the man I'd want to marry someday.

The man I'd want is someone who stands tall, stands for what's right. Stands up for me. Someone like Billy Preston.

My time with Damien has been fun—easy and uncomplicated. And he's a great person who's done so much for my family. I don't doubt he cares about me. But am I in love with him? Do I feel that deep, abiding love people talk about?

No.

The problem is Billy. He said he wasn't competing with Damien—"Good thing I'm not competing with him," to be exact. If he's not even trying, that must mean he's not interested, right?

Not that I expect him to make a move—he's a gentleman. A good guy. And a good guy doesn't move in on another man's girlfriend.

Which means it's on me. Only I have no idea what he feels. I know he likes me, and I definitely feel something. I just don't know if there's room in his heart for anything beyond grief yet.

Billy's older. Maybe he wants someone more experienced, though I'm not as young as I look. Dad's stroke forced me to grow up fast. Running the lodge and tavern has given me plenty of real-life experience.

Either way, it's past time to break things off with Damien. Only then can I figure out whatever this is with Billy. If he's not interested, I need to know now—before I get in too deep.

I finally get Damien alone when he swings by for lunch. One look at his face tells me he knows what's coming, which makes me even more nervous. Damien is smooth, quick. He'll try to talk me out of it.

"It's that sheriff," he says. "You're breaking up with me because you've got a thing for Billy Preston."

"No, that's not—"

"Sorrow Bailey, I've known you my whole life. You can't bullshit a bullshitter. I see what's going on. I get it."

"I... you do?" Relief flares. Maybe this will be easier than I thought.

"Of course. And I don't buy it."

So much for easy. I steel myself. "Well, you have to buy it."

Surprise flashes in his eyes. Good. He's hearing me. But then he changes tactics, stepping closer and tugging the front of my shirt. "Look, babe. You've been swamped. You probably just need a break. Let's take a vacation, maybe head someplace warm. SoCal is nice this time of year."

I picture Billy. I may not know how he feels, but I have to be free to find out. I step back. "I can't. I'm sorry."

"Why not? I'll whisk you away." He leans in, murmuring, "We'll find a nice spa somewhere. Facials. Hot stone massages."

Wow, he's good. It would be so easy to say yes. To float in hot mineral pools and let someone take care of me.

I shake my head. "It wouldn't be right."

"What does that mean?" he asks, baffled.

His easy confidence strengthens my resolve. Damien usually gets what he wants. Not this time. I straighten. "I'd feel like I was taking advantage."

"It's not taking advantage if it's something I want to do. For you. For us."

"I can't, Damien. I'm just not feeling it."

He opens his mouth, and nothing comes out. A pang of guilt hits me. I care about him. I really do. I don't want to hurt him.

"What about me?" he asks. "I've been trying."

This is harder than I thought. "I'm sorry..."

"Let me guess," he cuts in. "'It's not you, it's me'?"

My shoulders slump. I hate that he knows me so well.

He lets out a rueful laugh. "It's okay, Bail. I've given this talk myself a time or two." He taps my chin. "Hey, who knows what the future holds? Stranger things have happened."

After he leaves, I mope around until Laura finds me sitting on our brother's bed. It's the perfect place to think, with hope and melancholy all mixed together. BJ's room is a time capsule from before Dad's stroke, before BJ earned his commission and became a Marine. A Metallica poster. Giants memorabilia. Textbooks. A photo of him with his high school girlfriend.

I stare at the picture. Strange he kept it after all these years.

"Hey," Laura says, startling me.

I set the frame down. "Hi."

"What are you doing in here?" She wanders in, glancing at his books—then freezes, going pale. "There wasn't any news, was there?"

"No," I say quickly. When someone you love is stationed across the world, every ring of the phone feels ominous. "Just came in here to think."

"Jeez, don't scare me like that." She drops beside me on the brown corduroy bedspread. "So what's got you looking like you lost your puppy?"

"Damien and I broke up."

Laura raises a brow. "You mean, *you* broke up with Damien."

I look down, picking at the comforter. "How'd you guess?"

"Who hasn't guessed? You and the sheriff are practically joined at the hip."

I snap my head up. "We are not."

"What's that about, anyway? Some older-man thing?"

"He's like ten years older." When she raises a brow, I amend, "Well, he's hardly ancient."

"Whatever." She flops onto her side. "So spill. How'd it go down?"

"I'm not sure he believed me."

She laughs. "Of course he didn't. The last person to break up with Damien was Paula Richardson in third grade."

I give her a reluctant smile. "Probably true."

"So what'd he say?"

"He wanted to take me away."

"On a vacation?"

I nod. I've dreamed of one, but I'd never use his money like that. "Yeah."

"So what'd you say?"

"That I wasn't feeling it."

Laura waves her hands. "And?"

"And he said he's been trying, and it went on like that..."

"So what now? Are you and Billy a thing?"

I shoot her a look. "Billy doesn't have 'things.' And I don't even know if he's interested."

"Duh. Trust me, he's interested." She sits up, exasperated. "If I didn't know you so well, I'd think you were born yesterday."

"Why do you say that?"

"Why do you *think* he comes around? For Sully's cooking? To chat with Dad?"

A small spark of hope flares. "I guess not."

"She *guesses* not." Laura bumps my shoulder. "Well? Do you want him to be interested?"

My cheeks get hot.

Laura cackles. "Sorrrr-ow likes the sherrr-ifff."

"Shut up." I shove her. "And what about you, Miss Know-It-All?"

"What about me?"

"You're full of advice. Anyone you've got your eye on?"

She looks offended. "In this town? No way."

"Why not? There are lots of great guys here."

"Yeah, great men in the land of low-hanging fruit," she jokes. "But none for me."

"Why?"

She shrugs. "I don't know. They're all so... small-town. I'm just not that into flannel."

Classic Laura. It grates. I cross my arms. "Just because a guy lives in the mountains doesn't make him some backwoods stereotype."

"I didn't say that."

"You implied it. You were born here. What—you live in San Francisco a few years and suddenly you're better than us?"

"That's not it," she says, and she actually means it.

Maybe she is sincere. Maybe I'm the one who's too prickly.

"Whatever." I wave it off. "It's just men. Sorry for snapping."

Laura puffs up dramatically. "An apology. Well, well." Then her eyes gleam. "But the sheriff isn't 'just men.' Little sis, I think you need my help."

"Help," I repeat, deadpan—but suddenly shy. Laura knows men. "Okay, say I *am* interested in Billy. What do I do?"

She laughs. "You tell me. You know him better than I do."

"Be serious."

"What? You're good with guys."

"Yeah—at being the girl next door."

"Jeez," Laura mutters. "How'd you ever land Damien?"

A small laugh escapes me. "I'm pretty sure he was bored."

Her eyes sharpen. "Don't say that. You've really got to quit selling yourself short."

The intensity in her voice catches me off guard, warms something in me. She's right—I can be too hard on myself.

I think about opening up more, but the trust isn't fully there yet. I wave it off. "I didn't ask for a therapy session."

"Fine. Here's a question." She tilts her head. "Is Damien going to need therapy when you're done with him?"

He won't. Honestly, we were good for each other in a way. Our relationship filled a need for both of us. For him, I think it let him imagine a version of himself separate from being the rich kid from the town's most prominent family. I suspect I was good for his ego—I never cared about his net worth, and maybe that encouraged him to see himself as something more.

But I don't explain all that. I look down as I say, "It wasn't true love. We just want different things. He likes fancy restaurants and five-star getaways, and while I'd love to travel someday, honestly, I'd always want to come back here."

Laura softens. "Okay. First, you've got to give Billy a sign."

"What kind of sign?"

"Guys don't need much. Billy watches you all the time. Next time you're alone, just... don't look away. Trust me. He'll take it from there."

"Okay. I can do that. Wait." My heart skitters. "Where should I be? How do I start, exactly?"

"How, exactly?" She studies me. "Well, you could skip the hiking boots every once in a while."

I stretch my legs. "They're all-weather sneakers."

"Whatever. Wear something else once in a while. You've got those cute black boots. And maybe wear something other than your lodge logo T-shirts."

"But they're comfortable."

"I'm not saying you need to be uncomfortable." She grabs my arm. "Come on. We're raiding my closet."

"Really?" I stumble after her. "You'll help me?"

She flings open the closet. "If you mean dress you up and shove you out the door—then yes. Gladly."

I notice the sheer volume of clothes for someone on a "short visit." Then her words hit. "Wait—what do you mean you're shoving me out the door?"

"To his house, dummy." She starts tossing clothes onto the bed.

My stomach swoops. "But he didn't invite me. What would I say when I get there?"

Laura pauses, giving me a long stare. "You really don't know."

I shrug helplessly. "I can talk. I just don't know how to… flirt."

"You do. You just don't know you do." She points at me. "Talk about something you care about. Like food. And spice it up."

"Spice up the food?"

"No, dummy—the banter. Make it sexy." She waggles her eyebrows, making me laugh. "Tell him you're dropping off food to thank him for his help with the freezer. And make something sexy to eat."

"Sexy food. Like… oysters?"

She rolls her eyes. "Something easy and edible. Like drizzly, chocolaty, whipped creamy."

"Got it." Food is my comfort zone; that gives me confidence. "Then what?"

She rolls her eyes. "If you haven't figured *that* out, you're in trouble."

I join her, picking up a purple dress. "How about—"

She snatches it and tosses it aside. "There are better colors for you."

I flop onto the bed. "I can't just swing by unannounced."

"He does it all the time. Make something up. You bought too many groceries and you don't want them to go bad. Whatever." She rifles through her jewelry box and pulls out a silver hoop earring, searching for its mate. "Fastest way to a man's heart is his stomach."

I nod. "I can do that."

"You can." Her eyes light as she pulls out a gauzy black top. "A-ha."

I frown. "That? It's see-through."

"It's *fine*. You own a black bra, right?" She shoves it at me. "Wear it. And don't leave until he kisses you."

Chapter Twenty-Five

Billy

I SHOULD DO SOMETHING, but nothing appeals. It's too early for a movie. I already hit the free weights in my garage, though my heart wasn't in it. I hadn't even bothered with a shirt, just the ancient jeans I pulled on after work. A real triumph in personal grooming.

I can't shake what's been happening at the lodge. Bear Bailey blew off my suspicions—fallen trees, the road closure, appliance failures—calling it mountain living. But the cut freezer lines cast everything in a different light. Somebody's playing a dangerous game.

And one of these days, one of these "accidents" could turn lethal.

I hate the thought of Sorrow caught in the crossfire. I've poked around, but nothing's shaken loose. Bear was right: Sierra Falls is a friendly town. Everybody knows everybody. So who on earth would want to mess with the lodge?

As much as it kills me, I need to let it go. All I want is to storm over there and protect her, but it's not my place.

I yank open the fridge. I'm hungry, but there's nothing worth eating, and I sure don't feel like cooking. I shut the door harder than I need to.

I already had pizza once this week, and that about covers delivery options around here. I consider the tavern, but there's no way I can go there again, never mind that it's the only place I seem to want to go lately.

The early birds are probably rolling in for dinner now. Sully's likely got some meaty special—Prospector's Pie, or maybe those Southwest burgers he hasn't made in a while.

I could get a hot meal and keep an eye on things. If I went, chances are I wouldn't even see Sorrow. She'd probably be busy in the kitchen. I could just swing by, grab a quick bite, make sure nothing's wrong. Not like I'd be paying her a visit. If I saw her, I saw her.

I grab a shirt. Then stop. Wad it up and toss it on the kitchen chair.

I can't go to the tavern. People will talk, if they aren't already. I've lost count of how many times I've been at the Bailey place this week.

Something shifted on that car ride. It's more than wanting to keep Sorrow safe. I want *her*—and for once, it feels okay to want her. Like maybe I even need her.

Except for the damn boyfriend. I can't compete with someone like Damien Simmons—rich, young, powerful, good-looking.

But Sully said she'd be giving the guy his walking papers any day now. Could that really be true? And if it is, would she ever be interested in me?

I could look elsewhere, I guess. If I'm serious about dating again, I could try that bar across town—Chances, such a ridiculous name—instead of haunting the tavern.

But who am I kidding? Sorrow's the only woman I want to see. She's gotten under my skin.

The doorbell jolts me from my thoughts. Six is late for a drop-by. I rake a hand through my hair. Anyone knocking at a man's house after hours gets what they get.

I open the door, and my jaw drops. It's her.

"Sorrow. Hi."

"Hey, Sheriff."

I drink her in—cheeks pink from the cold, a fuzzy bluish green hat that matches her eyes.

She gets prettier every time I see her. Has something changed, or am I just finally seeing her clearly?

"Laura kicked me out of the kitchen," she says, a little breathless. "But I bought too many groceries, and they'll spoil if I don't use them, so I was hoping maybe... I mean, I thought maybe you might be hungry. If you're free. And hungry. I could cook for us."

A minute ago I'd been restless. Now I'm frozen where I stand, every bit of focus locked on her. She's been in my head all day, and now she's here. On my doorstep. Like I summoned her.

Her eyes flick down, taking in that I'm shirtless.

Right. Clothes. Damn.

"I hope I'm not bothering you." she says uncertainly.

"God, yes. I mean—no, you're not bothering me. Yes, I'm hungry." Hungrier than you know. I laugh, step back. "Let's try that again. Hi, Sorrow. Please come in." I take the canvas bag from her, overflowing with groceries. "Let me get this."

I can't figure out what she's doing here. She's like an angel at my door, walking into my house as if she's done it a hundred times.

As we head toward the kitchen, she glances around. I catalog the mess—blanket on the couch, mail on the coffee table, kindling by the hearth. Lived-in, not dirty.

"It's kind of rumpled," I say. "But it's home. And the kitchen's clean." I set the groceries down and pull on my shirt.

"Not rumpled at all," she says, following me in. "It's homey. Comfy. And no mounted heads anywhere." She laughs, thinking of her dad.

"Yeah, I'm not big on dusty antlers." I look at her—so damn beautiful, standing in my kitchen. "So you're really making me dinner?"

She hesitates. "If you want. Is that weird?"

"Are you kidding? Not at all. I was just wondering what I'd feed myself."

"Hungry?"

"Starving."

She looks pleased. "Good."

I start unpacking the bag, anything to keep my hands busy. Melons, prosciutto, lamb, tomatoes, strawberries, champagne. Impressive.

"What did you bring us?"

"Melon and prosciutto skewers to start. Then rack of lamb with *herbes de Provence*, and berries for dessert." Doubt flickers in her eyes. "Is that okay?"

"More than okay." I rein myself in—I can't sound too eager. She's another man's woman. And she's Sorrow. Guileless, not the flirting type. If she's here because of too many groceries, that's the reason.

She still has her jacket on. I step behind her. "Here, stay a while."

I slide it from her shoulders and nearly choke. Her shirt is sheer and black, offering a glimpse of her bra. Sexiest thing I've seen in years.

I cough, glad she can't see my face. "You look incredible."

She turns, waving a hand at her shirt. "Am I too dressed up?"

My gaze snags on the lace of her bra strap, heat shooting through. me. "Hell no." I laugh at how fast that comes out. "Not too dressed up at all. You're gorgeous."

A cold knot hits me. Is she staying? Or is that shirt for

someone else? "Are you... do you have a date with Damien later?"

She looks panicked. "No." Then quieter, "No. We broke up."

"Oh." My pulse kicks. "I'm sorry. You okay?"

"Yes." She fusses with the groceries. "I'm the one who broke it off."

And just like that—Sorrow is single.

"So..." I tread carefully. "Does that mean you didn't love him?"

She goes distant. "I've known him my whole life. I definitely care about him. But not... not in that way." Her eyes lift to mine. "It wasn't love, not like that. I've never been in love."

She starts to say more, and I hold my breath.

God, I'd love to see this woman in love. And the stupid part is, I want it to be with me.

"I see," I say.

She put on that shirt. Filled a bag with food. And came to me. It's not love—not yet—but what if someday it could be?

There's been something between us from the first cup of coffee she poured me. A connection, a spark I was too numb to recognize.

But I feel it now. After years of being half-dead inside, I'm awake. Alive. My gaze drops to her shirt—the low V, the tiny buttons.

She looks around. "We should get started."

Oh, we should. In more ways than one.

"Do you have an apron?" she asks, glancing down at her shirt. A small locket rests just above the neckline.

I force my eyes to stay focused on hers. Someday I'll be the man who sweeps the hair from her neck and hooks her necklace as she's getting ready. I'll stand behind her and rest my hands on her bare shoulders. I'd turn her to face me. I wouldn't give her a chance to finish getting dressed.

"This is Laura's shirt," she says. "I don't want to mess it up."

"Of course," I say, still distracted by my fantasy. I'd be careful with that shirt. I'd take each tiny, shiny button one at a time.

She looks at me expectantly. "So... apron?"

"Apron," I repeat. It'd be a crime to cover up that shirt. Good thing there's no apron. "I'm afraid not."

"No worries." She smiles slightly and starts prepping the lamb. "I hope you're not too starving. I want to marinate this for an hour."

She could marinate it all night—I'm way more interested in the company than the meal. But I just say, "That's fine."

When she finishes, we move into the living room. She stops short and I nearly walk into her. We're close enough that her warmth presses against me.

"I didn't even call," she says. "I'm interrupting your evening."

She sounds nervous, and something fierce rises in me—protective, wanting her to know she belongs here.

"You're making my evening," I tell her.

"Did you already have plans?"

I finally give in and rest my hands on her shoulders. "I did. Grand plans. I was going to spend the next few hours poking at that fire. Care to join me?"

Her smile blooms, bright and open. It takes everything in me not to kiss her. Instead, I turn to stoke the fire. Behind me, I feel her moving slowly through the room.

Then I remember the photos. Keri's photo over my desk. The framed portrait in the hallway.

Sorrow stops in front of that one.

"Your wife was beautiful," she says softly. "Very elegant."

"She was." I brush ash from my hands. For once, thinking of Keri is gentle—a warm ache instead of a stab. I loved her deeply. She'll always be a gift. Her quirks—both the ones I adored and the ones that drove me crazy—come back to me, and I smile. "She was a city girl, born and raised."

"City girls must be appealing."

I hear the subtext. "My wife was something else. But women from the city are like women anywhere... it's the person who matters."

I cross the room to stand behind Sorrow. I study Keri's photo with her—the sleek black bob, sharp eyes, sharp wit. Edgy where Sorrow is soft.

"Do you miss the city?" she asks.

"Honestly? No. Not one bit."

She goes quiet, like she needs more.

It's time. I take a breath. "In some ways, the city took her from me. She was in... an accident." My voice tightens. "I didn't know at first. It took them time to ID her. To track me down. And the worst part was, I'd heard it on the scanner. 11-44, motor vehicle fatality."

"I'm so sorry," she whispers.

My focus shifts from the photo to Sorrow's reflection in the glass—her face soft with sympathy. She's feeling my grief with me. Different from Keri, but no less extraordinary.

I want to give something back. "I always liked the country-side more than Keri did. We used to argue about it. Her idea of camping was staying anywhere that didn't have room service."

"She'd have loved the lodge," Sorrow deadpans.

"Well." I rest my hands on her shoulders and gently turn her to face me. "I love the lodge."

Up close, I see flecks of gold in her eyes. Her lashes thick and brown. Her lips parted, surprised by my touch.

And something clicks into place. I'm alive again. It's time to take my life back.

It begins with steering us from the heavy stuff. "Come sit by the fire," I say, my voice rough.

She nods, but something shadowed flickers in her eyes. Instead of sitting, she steps in front of the fireplace, bathed in flickering amber light.

She turns to me, courage gathering. "Do you think you'll ever marry again?"

She wants to know if I'm still mourning. The answer is complicated, but a little clearer now.

"I think I would like to marry again," I say, steady. I've thought it before, but tonight I finally believe it. "It's been over three years. She'd want me to move on." I feel the truth settle inside me, quiet and sure. "She'd want me to find love."

"But do you... can you..." Sorrow can't find the words.

"Let's find out." I cradle the back of her head, giving her time to stop me if she wants to. Then I lean down.

And I kiss her.

Chapter Twenty-Six

Sorrow

BILLY'S strong arms wrap around me, lifting me onto my toes, sending my heart soaring. After months of wanting him, it feels so good to finally touch him. I clutch him, soaking in the feel of his stubbled jaw, his hair, the strength in his arms and shoulders. I let myself memorize every moment—every warm, steady bit of him.

For months I'd been kissing Damien, and it's startling how different this feels. Even though we've broken up, something about Billy—the newness of him, the intensity—makes me feel a little wild, a little reckless.

Whatever I'd imagined about kissing him, it wasn't *this*. He's gentle and steady in life, and I'd expected the same softness now. But his kiss isn't hesitant—it's sure, intent, sending a rush through me that steals my breath.

He feels so big around me, so warm—his presence wrapping me up in a way that makes the rest of the room fall away. I've always known he was broad and strong in that sheriff's uniform, but touching him like this makes it real. My hands slide over his shoulders, learning the shape of him, the solid reassurance of him. I feel small in his arms, but not diminished—safe. Seen. Wanted.

We kiss like we've been holding our breath for months. All my questions scatter. All that's left is this pull between us, fierce and certain, like stepping toward something I didn't know I'd been waiting for.

A timer goes off in the kitchen.

No. No, no.

I try to ignore it. I don't want to stop. My fingers slip into his hair, holding him close, my breath catching at the feel of him. This moment, this connection, I want to stay right here in it. I want forever to feel like this.

But the timer keeps blaring.

Finally, he pulls back, resting his forehead on mine. "Damn."

I exhale, pained. When our eyes meet, a slow smile forms—wicked and secret at first, then conspiratorial as the timer keeps shrilling, until we're laughing. I step back and slap a hand to my forehead. "Sorry."

"Don't worry. The potatoes might be done, but we're not." He tucks an arm around my shoulders, guiding me toward the kitchen. "You and I are far from done."

He doesn't let me go, and the feel of him—of being wanted so openly—shifts something in me. I want another kiss. I want more of him, more of this closeness, this promise shimmering between us.

Seeing photos of his wife when I'd arrived had scared me. Losing a spouse so young—a person might never recover from a thing like that. My first thought had been, *How could I ever compare to a woman like that?* Pretty, sophisticated, powerful.

But that kiss... he kissed me, and instead of doubt, what I felt was possibility. Something bright. Something real.

As I cook, my skin hums with awareness of him—his gaze, the light brushes of his hand as we move around each other in the kitchen. Every small touch sends a quiet warmth through me. I'm completely attuned to him. Every look, every moment between us feels charged.

If I'm honest, this started months ago. Our bond had been instant, the spark unmistakable. When I started cooking with him, our time in the kitchen felt like a secret courtship... until the morning I realized I was falling in love with him.

We have the intimacy, the connection—and now I want something deeper. Something that moves past the careful boundaries we've both kept.

I slice the shallots slowly, hyperaware of him behind me. Using my shoulder, I nudge my hair out of my eyes and murmur, "You're hovering."

"I'm supervising," he says, a grin in his voice. He steps closer to smooth my hair back for me, and the casual intimacy of it steals my breath. "There's a difference."

"Oh really?" I ask, hoping my voice doesn't wobble.

"Mm-hm." He reaches past me for the tomatoes, his arm grazing mine. "Hovering implies anxiety. I am extremely calm."

I huff out a laugh. "You are *not* calm."

He pauses just long enough to give me a low, knowing look.

"No," he says quietly. "Not around you."

My pulse jumps.

Neither of us is calm.

He shifts closer, his presence warming the space behind me, and the nearness sends a flutter through my chest. I brace a hand on the counter, steadying myself.

He holds up the tomatoes. "How about I chop these for you?"

A dozen thoughts crowd my mind—none of them about tomatoes. But instead I say, "Yes, please."

He works quickly, then leans against the counter, watching me with an intensity that sets my pulse racing. "I still can't believe you're here. What did I do to deserve this?"

"I like cooking for you." I rub my herb mixture into the

lamb, glance up, and catch him looking quickly away. Something warms low in my belly.

"I was about to say I can't think of anything better than your cooking," he says, voice quiet enough to curl around me. "But... I think I could."

His teasing makes me feel lit from the inside. "Food first," I chide, then slide the lamb under the broiler and wash my hands. "Just a few more minutes."

He comes up behind me and runs his hands along my arms, threading my damp fingers with his. "Can't wait," he murmurs.

My breath catches, because I'm pretty sure he's referring to more than just the food.

The aroma of roasting lamb fills the room. He inhales deeply, letting out a satisfied sigh that reverberates through me. "How did they spare you at the tavern? Your father's a fool not to let you cook every night."

I love being seen like this. And I love that no one, except maybe my sister, knows where I went. "They don't even know where I am," I say. Truth be told, *I* barely know where I am. I feel untethered, falling fast.

"Their loss, my gain." He leans a hip against the counter. "Your dad's lucky you don't leave the tavern and become a professional chef."

I shrug. "Nah."

"Nah," he teases, turning me toward him. "What do you mean, nah?"

I think of the lodge, the tavern, my parents—everything that tethers me. "My time has passed."

His expression softens, but his tone is serious. "What do you mean, your time has passed?"

"You know." I give a half smile. "It's too late for me to start something new like that."

"You're young. You can do whatever you set your mind to."

"I'm stuck." I pause, but he waits—truly waits—for me to go on. "Laura and BJ got free. They left me to run everything alone." *Abandoned* feels closer to the truth.

The timer goes off again. He slips on an oven mitt and pulls the pan out himself. "You're cooking one night a week at the tavern— that's a start. We'll convince your dad to up it to two, then three."

I tent the lamb with foil. "That's fine, but then who'll do my job?"

"At the lodge? Get Laura to help."

"Yeah, right." Her 'help' never feels helpful. It always seems like she has something to prove—that she's older, smarter, superior.

"I'm being serious," he says. "You need to ask for help. You need to *make* people help." He pops a prosciutto-wrapped melon ball into his mouth and sighs with pleasure. "Hell, *I'll* help, if it means you'll make more food like this."

I laugh. "It's sweet how you encourage me. Cooking is my dream, but it's just that—a dream. I'll never get help from Laura. Not the kind I want. I don't even know why she's here or how long she's staying."

Something shifts in his gaze. "Something's been nagging at me."

"Uh-oh." I look away. So much for my grand seduction.

He lifts my chin, guiding my gaze back to his. "I need you around me more, Sorrow."

"I... you do?" I'd braced for criticism, not this. The words knock the air from my lungs.

"I do. Why do you think I've been hanging around that lodge? I wanted to see you."

My heart jumps so sharply I feel it in my throat. "Really?"

"Really. But you're always busy. And there was Damon."

I huff a laugh. "Damien."

"Whatever." He shrugs, smiling. "I want to take you on a real date. You deserve the best. But you're running yourself ragged—repairs, budget, food, staff, cleaning? It's too much. We're hiring you a cleaning service."

"A cleaning service?" That's the last thing I expect. "In Sierra Falls?"

"I'll find one. You won't have to think about it."

The idea makes me laugh. But reality sets in. "Not possible. My dad would have a conniption."

"Your dad can deal with it." There's a firmness in his voice that startles me. "If Bear gives you trouble, I'll cite him for child endangerment."

"Okay, okay." I laugh under my breath. "Point taken."

"It's time to demand more help from your family. What do you have to lose?"

"You're right." I've accepted random favors from Damien for months—so why am I afraid to ask the people I love for real help? I plate our dinner, thoughtful. "All right then. What the heck."

It strikes me, why didn't Damien ever help me see this? Billy has managed to upend my life, shifting everything inside me in a matter of weeks.

"You know…" I arch a brow, playful now. "If you help me, I'll have to find some way to thank you." For the first time, I feel fully in control—settled in my own skin. I like the feeling, this sense that what's happening between us is unfolding in complete harmony.

I look up, expecting him to laugh, but Billy's eyes are steady, fixed on me. The intensity there steals my breath. He's kind and thoughtful, yes. But he's also a man who knows exactly what he wants, and that certainty is written in every line of him.

My pulse kicks hard. Something essential inside me wakes up, matching his certainty with my own. Billy Preston may be a lawman, but he kisses like an outlaw. There's a boldness in him, a quiet command, that pulls me closer every time.

And, for the first time, I'm not afraid of where that pull might lead.

Chapter Twenty-Seven

I GATHER my guests in the sitting room. Facing west, it's the brightest, warmest spot in the house—perfect for a February afternoon. It's also my mother's favorite place, and even though the women are here to talk historical-society business, I want Ma with us. I want her to enjoy the chatter, the music, the company. To feel included.

But my mother Emerald is having an off day. She just stares, silent and still. Usually she looks around, tracks voices. Not today.

I've made her favorite French toast, played her old records, and settled her in the corner of the sitting room, where she now sits like a statue. A quiet grief settles in my chest, the kind that never really leaves.

Then Sorrow comes to stand beside me, and I remember I have guests who need attention. "Thanks for having us." She pulls off her hat and fluffs her hair, which crackles with static. "Staying at the lodge all winter makes me stir-crazy."

"I figured a change of scenery would do us all good," I say. Truth is, we have business to tend to, and I wanted to meet on neutral ground. Though considering the tension between Sorrow and Laura, I doubt even Switzerland would be neutral enough.

My gaze drifts back to my mother. Bailey family tension aside, I'm happy not to have to shoehorn three elderly ladies into that Buick.

Sorrow follows my look; the change in my mother is impossible to miss. "I'm glad she's here," she says quietly. "This room is so cozy with all the snow outside."

Sweet girl. I give her a warm smile. A house full of women will be good for Ma—and for me. I've needed this more than I realized.

"Snow?" Laura drops into a wing chair and stretches her legs. "Gray slush, more like it. Grossest winter ever."

"The spring festival will be here before we know it," Edith says.

"Don't remind me." Sorrow heads for the buffet. "There's too much to figure out. I need food first."

I've laid out their favorites—olive-and-cream-cheese sandwiches, pimento spread on sourdough, cucumber with dill and butter. And cookies, of course. Gingersnaps for Ma, iced sugar cookies for everyone else.

"Yum," Sorrow says, taking a plate. "We should meet here more often."

"That town hall is too chilly." Pearl buttons her cardigan as though the thought alone makes her cold. "And Bear's restaurant gets so gusty."

Bear is notoriously cheap with the heat. Not that I've noticed the chill lately—not when Sully's around.

"It's a treat to get away from the tavern," Edith says, ignoring the jab at her husband.

"Totally good to get away." Laura meets her sister's eye. "Did you see Dad this morning?"

Sorrow laughs. "The man was on a rampage."

"Why was your father on a rampage?" Ruby asks, perking right up.

Edith beams. "We got a letter from my boy today."

"That's wonderful, but..." I can't make the connection. "Wouldn't that make him happy?"

"Hearing from him always does it," Sorrow says.

"Thank God he hasn't figured out how to video call BJ," Laura jokes. "That'd really put him over the edge."

"My brother is spending more time in the air," Sorrow explains. "Dad just worries."

Laura grows serious. "He's doing troop transport in that giant helicopter."

All the military talk puts me in mind of Tom Sullivan. He showed Craig some of his medals last weekend. I had no idea he'd been such a hero. He still has his boonie hat—whatever that is—and his dress uniform. My mind drifts. The man keeps himself in remarkable shape; I bet everything still fits.

I refocus. They're talking about BJ, not retired officers.

I pour tea from my great-granny's silver service. "I'd think Bear would be thrilled to hear from the boy."

"He was," Edith says brightly. "Absolutely thrilled."

I give her a look, though what I really want is to demand why Bear gets to be such a sourpuss, and why Edith enables it. Bear acts like... well, a bear, though I suspect she's the one quietly running the show.

She must sense the direction of my thoughts because she adds, "He lives for BJ's letters."

"It's true." Sorrow settles into the window seat with her plate balanced on her knees. "He's practically memorized this one."

"Well, I think it's the strangest thing," Ruby says as she heads to the buffet.

Pearl follows. "If he misses the boy so much, he has a strange way of showing it."

Their judgment hangs thick in the air, but no one calls them on it. Disapproval is practically the Kidd sisters' hobby.

As they load their plates, I find myself wondering how different their lives might've been if they'd married and raised children. They wouldn't have so much time for judgment, that's for sure.

Edith sighs. "Bear is just... frustrated. He hates that we're not in closer contact with our boy."

"Nah," Sorrow says, shaking her head. "Dad just wishes he could put on a uniform and go join him."

Edith gives a fond smile. "My husband is a man of action."

"Action?" Laura stirs Splenda into her tea. "A man of temper, more like."

"Well, he should just say a little prayer when he feels his temper coming on," Ruby declares, mostly focused on dessert.

Laura eyes Ruby's loaded plate. "How do you stay so thin?" She mutters to Sorrow, "Maybe I should start praying more."

"It's genes, dear." Pearl settles into an armchair and raises her voice toward my mother. "Isn't that right, Emerald? The Kidd girls have good genes."

I make Ma a plate. Laura still has only tea. "Aren't you going to eat?"

Laura pulls out an apple. "I'm eating. I'm good."

"An apple's not eating," Sorrow says. "Though it does look good." She picks at her sandwich. "I can't wait till winter's over —produce has been terrible."

"Berries will be in season soon," Ruby says cheerfully.

I drag a little table to my mother's chair and set down a plate of sandwiches and cookies. Patting her shoulder, I say clearly, "Time to eat, Ma. All your favorites."

I study her face, desperate for a flicker of recognition. Nothing. Just that horrible, hollow blankness.

Laura checks the time on her phone. "We should get this show on the road." She pulls a manila folder from her bag. "So, for the festival, I made a marketing plan. Nothing big—just milestones for the next few weeks, a tentative schedule, and a list of tasks and who should handle them."

Everyone stares like she's sprouted a second head.

Laura shrugs. "I couldn't sleep last night."

Sorrow holds up a finger as she finishes chewing, and the whole room goes still. "We need to learn more about Buck Larsen before we finish planning. Like whether he ever returned to Sierra Falls."

Laura crunches her apple. "I still think we need tasks and owners. There's more to do than arranging the bake sale. We should compile a program—some good Sorrow Crabtree quotes, old-timey photos. It's easy to publish books these days; we could sell them at the festival."

Sorrow gapes at her, and I brace. But instead she says, "Laura, that's an awesome idea."

"It is," I agree quickly. Hoping to keep things civil, I steer us back to safer territory. "But Edith tells me you haven't finished reading the letters."

"That's the thing." Sorrow flips through them. "I've tried, but some passages make no sense."

"That old-timey handwriting is a real pain in the—" Laura pauses at Sorrow's cleared throat. "A real pain in the... rump."

"That's where you ladies come in," Edith says to the older women.

Ruby pulls a lap blanket over her legs. "We're not that old-timey, dear."

Pearl waves her off. "You know what they mean." She nods to Sorrow. "Read them aloud, dear. We'll help when you get stuck."

For the next hour, Sorrow reads, and the room is spellbound. It's impossible not to feel the truth in her thrice-great-grandmother's words—a woman dreaming of more, trapped with no escape.

Then Sorrow suddenly stops.

"What is it?" Edith asks.

"Just a second." Sorrow flips back and forth. "These are out of order."

Laura frowns. "What do you mean, out of order?"

Sorrow drops to her knees, spreading pages across the floor. "Okay, remember this one? *My Mama told me to live life for me... Just me and our boy. With or without you.* That was dated 1851." She sets it aside.

"Now look at this." She holds up another letter. "We read this one first—the one about the dance hall, making a life for herself, and *a babe in my belly.* We assumed it was the same time period. But it's not." She matches page numbers. "This one's dated 1853."

The women gasp.

"She had another baby," Edith murmurs.

Pearl clucks. "Poor luck from the day she was born."

I give her a look. "Some see a baby as a blessing, Aunt Pearl."

Laura drops to the floor beside her sister and reaches for the pages. "Let me see." For once, Sorrow hands them over without hesitation. "Wow. You're right. Listen—*He moves in my belly. A boy, like your beautiful son. I'll raise them both up to be good men.*"

Edith tilts her head, peering. "Was Buck the father?"

"No," Sorrow says. "Buck Larsen never returned. There must've been another man."

"She was a fast woman," Ruby says.

Pearl grunts. "Two fathers, no husband."

"A life of toil and fatherless babies," Ruby adds. "That's what being a fast woman gets you."

"That's enough," I say, tired of the implication. What it suggests about my own mother.

But Pearl isn't finished. She purses her lips. "I wonder if it runs in the blood?"

Laura rolls her eyes. "That's us. Baileys of the spoiled blood."

Sorrow shoots Pearl a look. "Who says she was fast? Maybe it means things got better for her."

"Shush," Laura says, trying to read. "How did you get through this, Sorrow?"

"What does it say?" Edith presses.

"Give me a second." Laura squints. "Handsome... first sight... blah blah... okay, here. *My Silas is an angel. As dependable as God's love, he comes to town once each month, letters in his bag and love in his heart.*"

Sorrow shrieks. "She was in love with the mailman!"

"Those guys were actually pretty badass," Laura says. "Snowshoeing all over the wilderness."

Edith's eyes widen. "*First sight... angel...* When we read it before, I thought it was about the baby."

"We all did," Sorrow says.

I lean forward. "And the date is definitely 1853?"

"Read more, read more," Sorrow urges.

Laura finds her place. "*All's I need is a simple man. I once thought I needed a man like you, but your promises are as empty as that fine suit you wear.*"

She keeps reading, but I stop listening. Those words hit too close.

Have I been chasing the wrong things? Men in suits. Nice houses. Boats and convertibles. Things that look like security but aren't. I had a husband who was successful—a fancy home, shopping trips to Reno, a new coat every fall. And what did it get me?

My four boys—good, loving men. For them, I'd do it all again.

But my ex-husband? After he left, I doubted myself. I felt angry, abandoned. But did I ever actually miss him?

I glance at the Kidd sisters—and my mother. Ma still hasn't eaten. She hasn't moved. She sits there, blank-eyed, not even looking out the window. Life keeps marching on. One day these women will be gone and then I'll... what?

Suddenly everyone is talking at once, jolting me back.

"You have to finish," Sorrow insists.

"*The only things... the things...*" Laura squints harder. "Nope. I can't. This handwriting is killing me."

"Let me see it, dear," Pearl says, holding out a trembling hand. She slips on her glasses, studies the page, and brightens. "Ah! It says, *The only things you regret in this life are the risks you don't take.*"

I go pale. It feels like Sorrow Crabtree herself has reached across generations to speak to me.

My life has been all about the roads not taken. Caring for my husband, then my sons, now my aunts and my mother. Always the responsible choices. The choices with no choice at all. No room for risk.

Sorrow puts a warm hand on my chilled shoulder. "You okay, Marlene?"

"I'm fine." I paste on a smile. "Let's keep reading. We've been looking forward to it." I glance at my mother. Maybe she's still in there somewhere, able to enjoy it, too.

My mother lived a life of risk—leaving home, falling for a man, returning pregnant. Why haven't I ever asked her about it? Asked the hard questions? And now, the one woman I wish could give me wisdom sits across the room, empty as the prettiest seashell.

People think that if someone's still alive, there's no reason to grieve. But I know better.

I grieve my living mother every day.

Chapter Twenty-Eight

Sorrow

MY PHONE BUZZES, and I juggle a lid, a ladle, and an oven mitt to reach it. Worth it when I see who's calling.

Memories of last night flicker through me—Billy's kiss, the warmth of his hands at my waist, the way we both pulled back before things went too far, breathless and a little unsure. He'd walked me to my car afterward, quiet and steady, and the thought of it has been humming under my skin ever since.

"Billy, hey." I don't even try to hide the relief in my voice. "You coming by soon? It's Ladies' Night," I add, teasing. Tuesday's my night to cook at the tavern, and Dad dubbed it with the silliest name imaginable. But I'm following Billy's advice—take opportunities where I can get them.

"That's why I'm calling."

His somber tone snaps me to attention. "What is it?"

"I've got to work a double shift. Marshall's got the flu—poor guy looks awful."

"How much crime can there be in Sierra Falls? Can't you just let people speed for one night?"

His laugh is gentle. "You know I can't. But I'll be thinking of you. Wish I were there to help."

"I wish you were, too. I'm using a Dutch oven that weighs about a thousand pounds."

"What'd you end up making? The chicken or the pork loin?"

"Chicken. Coq au Vin, technically." My sauce needs thickening, and I'm stirring madly. "If I can get my roux to cooperate. It's broken twice already."

"Damned roux," he says, perfectly deadpan.

I laugh. "I miss you." The words slip out, and I instantly regret it. We've kissed, sure, but I don't know where he stands. I know he's carrying a lot of emotional baggage, and I need to play it cool.

But he surprises me. "I miss you, too." There's real affection in his voice, and it settles something inside me. "Save me some. I'll stop by later. I promise."

I'm sliding the meat into the oven to braise when a hubbub ripples through the tavern. I pull off my bandanna, wipe my brow, and push through the swinging door.

"I swear, Helen," I say, stepping out. "I don't know how Sully does it. I'm roasting in there. Could you please get me—" I spot Damien and his parents settling into a window booth. "—some ice water," I finish, lamely.

Dabney and Phoebe Simmons—what are they doing here? If Damien is the prince of Sierra Falls, these two are the royal elders. Moneyed, sophisticated, and impossible to hate because they're also genuinely kind.

Dabney's always been especially sweet, joking that I need to make his boy an honest man. Like he's actively lobbying for a proposal. I've never understood it—maybe Damien was a hellraiser as a kid and I mellowed him out.

They must know about the breakup by now. Did Damien send them to convince me to reconsider? I dread the idea of disappointing not just him, but them.

Helen hands me a big tumbler of water and sings under her

breath, "Oh yes, it's ladies night, and you're feeling right." The little snort she adds doesn't feel entirely nice.

I glare over the rim as I chug, then set the glass down with a thunk. "If you're quoting the song, I think it's 'and the feeling's right.' And thanks—the only thing I needed more than seeing Damien's family was Kool & The Gang stuck in my head."

Phoebe and Dabney are debating the menu. The chicken is in the oven—now's the moment to go say hello.

"Need something stronger?" Helen whispers.

I have a joke ready, but one look in her eyes stops me. She's serious. Drinking might be how she'd handle this, but that's not how I roll.

Still, she means well. "No thanks, Helen. No drinks. I've got too long a night ahead."

I'm gathering my courage to approach when Damien beats me to it.

"Heya, Bailey." He saunters to the bar with a confident smile. Apparently not even a breakup can dim Damien Simmons. I don't believe he's accepted it. Showing up with his parents feels like part of a plan.

He looks good, as always, and I give myself a quiet second to check my own reaction. No regret. No desire. Nothing.

"You're looking good," he says, echoing my thoughts. "Cooking agrees with you."

I take the compliment and smile. "Nothing like a hot, stuffy kitchen to put color in the cheeks." We'll never be best friends, but he's a good guy. Maybe someday we'll get back to where we started—just casual friends.

He gestures toward the door. "Hey, your bear box is open." Up here, everyone keeps their trash locked up unless they want a several-hundred-pound visitor. "I tried to shut it, but it looks like the latch is broken. If you've got some tools, I could look."

"Nah, I got it." No way I'm asking for his help—I don't want him thinking we've slipped back into old patterns. And I'm perfectly capable of managing my own bear box.

Outside, sure enough, the door swings on its hinges. Not many bears this time of year, but the last thing I want is to wake a hungry brute. I lean into it, try the latch. Broken.

I'm not wearing gloves, I don't have tools, and I've got two Dutch ovens of Coq au Vin going. This is tomorrow's problem.

Back inside, annoyance needles me. Everyone's in the kitchen now—Dad dragged them back to show off our new freezer.

I have a ton left to do and no time for tours. I catch Mom's eye, plead silently, but she just shrugs. *What can you do?*

Dad's unstoppable once he gets rolling. He's droning on with talk of gaskets and cam-lifts and electro-polished shelves. Dabney and Phoebe don't show a flicker of judgment.

I slip behind Phoebe and give her shoulder a grateful squeeze. "It's a freezer all right," I whisper, rolling my eyes. "Not like it's going to feed starving orphans."

Dad stops midsentence, the light in his eyes dimming. Mom shoots me a disappointed look, and shame hits hard. Bad daughter.

"Very impressive," Dabney says, saving me. A rich landowner with a timber business employing half the town, he's Sierra Falls' resident benefactor. "Damien tells me you got quite a deal."

"I hear you have the sheriff to thank for that." Phoebe catches my eye and gives me a sad smile. She leans in. "He'd best be as good as he sounds, Sorrow. You were supposed to marry my Damien, you know."

But Dabney overhears. He wraps an arm around me. "If

that man doesn't treat you right, I'll go over there with a shotgun and see that he does."

I laugh, relieved it's all out in the open. "It's not like that. I mean… we had one date, that wasn't really a date, and—"

A thin trickle of black smoke slips out as warning. A fireball erupts with a boom followed by a raging blaze.

Screams echo through the kitchen. A body slams into me—Damien, shielding me.

"Get out of the kitchen!" he yells. To his father: "Get them out!"

Mom yanks the faucet hose, and Damien lunges to grab her hand. "No! No water!"

"What the hell, boy?" Bear barrels across the room, reaching for the faucet.

"It's grease." Flames climb the back wall, no longer contained. Damien covers his nose and mouth, squinting through the smoke. "Call 911. Sorrow—fire extinguisher."

Everyone flees. I'm across the room and back in seconds with the extinguisher. Damien snatches it and sprays. Black smoke fills the kitchen as the alarm screams.

Coughs tear through me, and Damien shoots me a look. "Get out!"

I shake my head, struggling for breath, and grab our restaurant-sized bag of baking soda. But by the time I get back, the fire's out. I dump the soda on the stovetop anyway, adrenaline shaking me.

Damien scoops me up and half carries me to the dining area. Outside, everyone's huddled together, shivering and chattering. Dad's expression is as dark as the smoke.

"Guess who's getting blamed for this," I mutter.

Damien tips my chin up. "I'll talk to him." He smudges soot from my cheek. "See? I'm good to have around, right?"

My guard snaps up—I need to tread carefully. "I never said you weren't."

His voice goes low and husky as he leans in. "So can I get you to come to your senses?"

Apparently, he didn't get the memo. I set a gentle hand on his chest and step back. "Damien, I'm sorry. It's really over."

"C'mon, Bailey. You know we're good together." He chucks my chin, light and teasing, wearing his trademark grin, only now I see it masks something. Damien Simmons isn't as confident as he pretends.

"I need you," I say. "As my friend."

His eyes shutter. "You've already hooked up with Billy, haven't you?"

"Hooked up?" I pray my voice doesn't squeak.

As if on cue, Billy barrels through the door. Red-and-blue lights from his SUV strobe across the tavern walls. His gaze goes from me to Damien to Damien's hands on my shoulders.

And just like that, the sheriff looks ready to answer Damien's question—with his fists.

Chapter Twenty-Nine

Billy

THE RADIO CRACKLES—FIRE at the Thirsty Bear Tavern—
and a bolt of fear goes through me. For one terrible moment,
all I can think is: Sorrow.

I've known my feelings were serious, but this kind of panic
leaves no room for doubt. I care about her more deeply than
I've let myself admit.

I speed toward the tavern, passing the volunteer engine.
They only called for the truck, not the ambulance, but I need
to see with my own eyes that she's safe.

It's obvious now—someone's targeting the Baileys. She's in
danger. They all are. And if this doesn't convince Bear, nothing
will.

But when I burst inside and see Sorrow's ex holding her,
my fear flips into fury.

I want to rip his hands off her. Take her someplace safe and
check every inch of her for injury.

Urgency surges through me—the need to show her what
she means to me. She's breathed life back into me without even
knowing it. I want to tell her... everything.

But I'm in uniform. I force myself to keep control.

I flex my hands. I will not physically remove this man
from her—

But then Sorrow pushes from Damien and launches into my arms.

I wrap myself around her, sweeping my hands over her hair, her back, her sides. Let people think what they want. I need to know she's whole. My heart hammers so hard she must feel it. "Are you okay?"

At her faint nod, I pull her closer. Damien shoots me a look, but I barely register it. All I care about is her warmth against me and the fact she's unharmed.

"What happened?"

The door bangs open, and Bear storms in behind me. "What in the hell happened in there?"

"Grease fire," Damien says, his expression stiff, like he needs to save face.

Bear glowers at his daughter. "I knew your cooking was a bad idea."

Sorrow tries to pull away, and though I loosen my hold, I keep a hand on her. She won't stand alone.

"It wasn't my fault," she says, a barely-there tremor in her voice. It guts me. "Grease fires happen all the time."

"Not in my restaurant."

"That wasn't an accident," I cut in. It's one coincidence too many for the Bailey family.

The SFFD fire chief, Mike Haskell, strides in.

"It's okay, Mike," Damien says. "Sorrow and I put it out."

I give Damien a grudging nod.

Mike sniffs the air. "Trying to burn down the place, Bear?"

The joke doesn't soften Bear's scowl. "No, but my daughter is."

"It wasn't my fault," Sorrow insists. She turns to me, eyes pleading. "This wasn't my fault."

I run through the facts. I know Sorrow. I know Sully.

They're careful. And this fits the pattern—cut freezer lines, the blocked road, the downed tree. Now fire.

"Sorrow's right," I say. "This wasn't her doing." Through the window I see Scott Jessup pull up in the old Parks Department Bronco. Good. She needs more friendly faces tonight. "Something else is going on here."

"Not your theories again," Bear mutters, then swings to Sorrow. "I told you I didn't want you cooking. First the freezers, now this."

"I didn't break the freezers."

Scott steps inside, takes one look at the tension, and winces. "Smells like you're serving barbequed kitchen tonight."

Bear looks close to exploding, and Mike jumps in. "Scott, about time you showed up. Let's take a look at that oven." He claps Bear's shoulder on his way past. "We'll leave you folks to it."

Laura rushes in. "Did Sorrow burn down the kitchen?"

I shoot her a look that stops her. To my surprise, she wilts a little and squeezes Sorrow's shoulder. "Seriously—are you okay?"

Before Sorrow can answer, Bear cuts in. "Yeah, but my kitchen's not."

"I didn't do anything to your kitchen," she says, steady but strained. I'm impressed with how she's holding up.

"Sully's been cooking twenty years and never had a fire."

Mike calls from the kitchen, "Grease fire all right. Looks like drippings on the bottom of the oven."

Bear's eyes narrow, but Sorrow jumps in. "No way. Not from me. I keep a spotless kitchen."

Damien's parents appear. "Sweetheart," Phoebe murmurs, hugging her, "I'm so sorry your big night was ruined."

Dabney gives her a warm nod. "You'll get another shot, kid."

"She spilled grease in the oven," Bear insists.

"There's no grease in my Coq au Vin," Sorrow says, dangerously calm.

I tighten my arm around her. "Nobody keeps a cleaner kitchen."

"Well something was in that cocoa van of hers," Bear mutters. "I told you that kitchen's too big for you."

That does it. Sorrow steps forward, arms crossed tight. "Too big? *Too big?*"

Phoebe steps in before things can escalate and hugs her goodbye. "One of these days this town will eat something besides Tom's chicken poppers, and my money's on you."

Dabney jerks his chin at Damien. "Come on, son. We're your ride."

Damien hesitates. "You sure you're okay?"

Sorrow nods. The Simmons family leaves, followed by the last of the lingering crowd.

Chief Haskell calls as he heads out, "It's just a grease fire. Oven's still good."

"Thanks, Mike," Sorrow says.

"Anything for a pretty lady." He winks.

I clap his shoulder. "All right, Chief. Don't you have a wife waiting on you?"

He laughs. "Understood. Can't wait for the festival, Sorrow. Should be a good one with all the Buck Larsen stuff."

She musters a tired smile. "Let's hope."

The sight twists in my chest. I turn to Bear. "First the freezers, now this. These aren't accidents."

"That's enough for one night, city boy." Bear jerks his chin toward the door. "Time for you two to get out of here. I'm airing out the tavern. With the stink and the cold, business is dead anyway."

Sorrow stiffens. "It wasn't my fault."

"It was somebody's fault."

I step in. "We'll lock up, Mr. Bailey. Go join Edith."

Laura loops her arm through his. "Come on, Dad. TV time." She winks at Sorrow.

With a grunt, Bear lets her lead him out.

Sorrow gives me a wan smile. "He needs his recliner and some alone time."

"Do you need to head back too?"

"Are you kidding? Not until he's out cold."

I take her in my arms. "I know it wasn't your fault."

She sags into me with a deep breath. "Thank you. I just don't get it." She meets my eye. "There's no grease dripping from a Dutch oven. Sully keeps things spotless. So what happened? Usually the most exciting thing in town is old man Ziegler getting drunk and driving his snowplow into a ditch."

"Which sounds dangerous," I say.

"It was. Christmas about fifteen years ago. Probably why Marshall finally became a deputy."

I chuckle. "That explains a lot."

We fall silent, thinking. This isn't random. But I don't want to scare her.

"Your dad thinks it's just bad luck…"

"A lot of bad luck."

"All at once."

"To a crazy degree."

Our eyes lock. She swallows. "These aren't accidents, are they?"

"No way." I exhale. "I just don't know who'd want to hurt you."

"Hurt me?" She gives a weak laugh. "Maybe it's Laura—everything started when she showed up."

I can't help laughing. "You're awfully calm about this."

"If by calm you mean making jokes so I don't cry, then yeah." She drops her forehead to my chest.

"You're a remarkable woman, Sorrow Bailey."

"So what do we do?"

"Without a suspect, not much. The best thing is to keep you close." My hands slide down her back. "There *are* better ways to handle the stress."

She lifts her head. Her expression is grave, but her eyes twinkle. "And the uncertainty. There's lots of uncertainty."

I grab her coat and guide her toward my SUV. "Let's go."

"Whoa, cowboy." She locks up. "Aren't you on duty?"

"This is my duty." But I stop myself—tonight rattled her. "Unless you'd rather stay home..."

"Billy." She steps closer. "You're all I want right now."

Her certainty hits me hard. I see it in her eyes—not fear or hesitation, but something like relief. Like she's been wanting this as long as I have.

"Then we're a pair," I say quietly. "Because I want you, too."

She nudges me with a smile. "What about speeders and lawbreakers?"

"Calls route to Silver City after ten. Marshall's listening."

"I thought he was sick."

"I offered him a raise."

She gives me a look. "So this is how a sheriff finds trouble?"

"No." I open her door for her. "This is how a sheriff makes trouble."

As I get behind the wheel, a flash hits me—what could've happened tonight—and the relief is so strong it borders on desperation. I've wanted her a long time, but after tonight... I just want to hold her. To keep her close. To feel her there beside me, alive and safe. I crave her light, her quiet strength. The way something in me settles whenever she's near.

When we get to my house, I pause at the door. There will be no going back from this. She looks up at me, and whatever she sees in my face makes her reach for my hand. "Take me inside, Billy." Not a question, not a doubt.

Once inside, everything hits the floor—keys, coats, her bag —the moment the door shuts. I take a second to put up my belt and sidearm, then I'm reaching for her, pulling her close, my mouth finding hers. The kiss isn't tentative. It's driven by the echo of how close I came to losing her tonight. She answers with the same urgency, her fingers gripping my shirt like she's afraid I'll disappear.

When I finally pull back, we're both breathing hard. I rest my forehead against hers. "If we do this, there's no going back. I don't do casual."

She cups my face, her palms warm on my skin. Her eyes hold mine, clear and unwavering. "Good. Because I'm already in this, Billy. I've been in it for a while. I don't want casual— not with you. I want this. Us."

Her words hit me square in the chest, knocking the air out of me. The honesty in her eyes damn near levels me. This thing between us is real. I didn't know how much I needed to hear it until now.

I pull Sorrow closer, and she comes willingly, her arms sliding around my neck. I never expected to get a moment like this again, not in this lifetime. Something fierce and certain surges up in me—want, yes, but more than that. It's *her*.

"You gonna frisk me, officer?" The naughty gleam in her eye breaks the tension just enough.

My laugh is low. "More than that." I guide her toward the hallway, and she goes, fingers laced through mine.

What follows is everything I didn't let myself imagine. Her warmth, her softness, the way she says my name like it means something. The way she looks at me after—like I'm exactly where I'm supposed to be.

And for the first time I can remember, something in me settles. Locks into place. When I was young, I thought I'd understood what forever meant. I didn't. Not until now.

With all the pain and years behind me, I truly recognize what this is. How rare. How precious.

For the first time, I feel like the man I'm supposed to be. Like Sorrow pulled me back to myself.

I've gotten a second chance at life.

And it's because of her.

Chapter Thirty

I SNEAK another glance at Tom Sullivan out of the corner of my eye. The theater is dark, but the movie's glow flickers over his features. In the shifting light and shadow, he looks carved from granite.

He catches me looking, and I snap my gaze back to the screen, heat flooding my cheeks. When was the last time I acted like such a schoolgirl? Probably the last time I'd gone on a real date, and I can't even remember when that was.

I felt like a girl again when Sully picked me up tonight, drove us to Silver City, took me to a nice Italian place—not a chain—and bought tickets to the movie I'd chosen. The last time my ex-husband took me out like that, we must've been in high school. We'd gone straight from the Homecoming Dance to diapers and bills.

Somewhere along the way, I lost him. And I lost myself, too.

I try to focus on the film, but a low buzzing breaks through the soundtrack. It takes me a moment to realize it's coming from my purse. My cell phone. I barely use the thing, and whenever someone calls, the sound always throws me.

I slowly unzip my bag—every inch of the zipper loud in the quiet theater—and close my fingers around the phone. It vibrates like an angry beetle. It's either a wrong number or an emergency. I pray for the former.

I glance at Sully, unsure. They announced that phones had to be off.

Guessing my dilemma, he leans in and whispers, "It's okay."

But all I register is the warmth of his breath on my cheek, the faint scent of his aftershave.

I nod and check the screen. The number is familiar, but it takes me a second to place it. Ruby. My heart kicks up. Oh dear Lord. She wouldn't be calling unless something was wrong—especially not on a night she and the others made such a fuss about.

Sully senses my panic. With a steady hand, he guides me up and out of the row. It was supposed to be a simple, friendly date. Just a Tuesday night he'd had to talk me into.

Yet here he is, his arm around me, keeping me upright.

"Go ahead," he murmurs once we reach the lobby.

The overhead lights feel harsh as I fumble to answer. Too late. I missed it. My hands shake as I redial. Part of my mind is always braced for bad news. The hazard of caring for three elderly women.

"Ruby," I gasp when she picks up. "What is it?"

The blood drains from my head. I end the call and meet Sully's eyes. "It's Ma. She fell. They think it's her hip. An ambulance—"

My voice breaks.

Sully has me in my coat and out the door before I've fully processed what's happening. "They'll be taking her to Silver City Memorial," he says.

I'm grateful I don't have to think. Tom Sullivan just knows... how to navigate town, where to park, who to talk to.

By the time we reach the right curtained room in the ER, the ambulance has only just arrived.

And then we wait. Time collapses until I feel like I've either just walked in or been sitting here forever.

Ruby and Pearl show up soon after. I watch them from a distance—asking questions, fetching coffee, organizing everything—and I'm struck by their calm, their independence.

Suddenly I'm a child again, and they're the adults. Memories I'd forgotten rise like dust motes in sunlight: dinners they made me when Mama wasn't home, how they'd insist I wash up and finish my homework. I realize how much of my childhood has drifted from memory, the tiny daily moments that make up a life.

Sully had slipped out, but he returns to sit beside me. He takes my hand, giving it a gentle squeeze.

His touch is warm and steady. It's so unexpected, offering such comfort. I see in his eyes that he has news, and I want to hold onto this quiet moment before the next blow lands. "My husband never held my hand like this," I say, stopping him.

"Your husband was a fool," he replies without hesitation.

I squeeze his hand, thinking of Frank. How would he be acting right now? He never held my hand. Never courted me. Never took me to nice restaurants, and he'd never sit through a romantic comedy just because I wanted to.

I meet Sully's eyes. "I'm glad you're here, Tom." And I am. I'm an independent woman—I raised a houseful of boys, ran a household, cared for my mother—but right now, having a man beside me is reassuring in a way I hesitate to acknowledge. "What did the doctor say?"

"Your mother broke her hip. She's not responding, but that's the Alzheimer's. Other than the hip, she's in good physical shape."

I swallow hard. "Ma was always fit as a fiddle. Mountain living."

"Something like that." He wraps both hands around mine, cocooning my fingers in warmth. "They've hooked up an IV for feeding, Marlene. But you're going to have some decisions to make."

I blink back tears. "Can I see her?"

"Of course." He helps me stand. "They're moving her now."

As we walk to the room, all I can think is that Mama wouldn't want to be here, not in this bright, sterile place. Even if her mind is mostly gone, the woman who raised me would want her cookies, her TV shows, sunlight through her own windows. Years ago, the younger Mama would've been begging to take the car out with the top down, angling for a picnic even in bad weather.

"Hi, Ma," I say quietly. My throat tightens.

Sully pulls a chair closer. "You sit with your mother. I'll get you some coffee, find your aunts."

He's nearly out the door when Mama's eyes sharpen, fixing on him. "Wait," she snaps.

"Mama?" Her voice should reassure me, but it's more alarming than her silence. I touch her arm, and it feels like crepe paper over bone. When did she get so thin? Should I have put her in a home? She hasn't been eating well. Guilt shears through me.

I gesture Tom closer, forcing brightness into my tone. "You remember Tom Sullivan? Sully? He helped me. He drove me to see you."

But I don't need to introduce him. Mama's eyes are locked on him. Her voice is suddenly strong, startlingly clear. "I don't regret you for a minute."

Sully shoots me a wary look but comes to sit beside her. "I

beg your pardon?" He takes her hand without thinking, and I love him a little for that.

When Ma speaks again, her gaze sharpens with unnerving intensity, her hand gripping tight around his. "I don't regret our running off. What I regret is that we didn't keep running."

"She thinks you're someone else," I whisper.

"Gus?" she cries, suddenly frantic.

I go still. Gus. I've never heard her say the name. My father.

Tom stays calm, his voice low and sure. "Yes, Emerald? What is it?"

His tone soothes her—and me—and one wild thought shoots through me: how on earth is this man single?

Mama's chin trembles, but her voice rings clear. "If I had it to do again, I'd stay. I loved you, Gus. And I love you still. Daddy said I was reckless and I believed him, but my mistake wasn't going off with you. It was listening to anything besides my own heart."

I watch as she drifts into sleep, wearing the most peaceful expression I've ever seen. Sully quietly slips his hand from hers and tucks it beneath the blanket. Then he takes my hand again.

I look into his dark blue eyes, so steady on mine that something in me settles. It's time to learn from my mother. Time to let my heart run free.

And as I hold Sully's gaze, I know: my heart is safe with him.

Chapter Thirty-One

Sorrow

MY EYES SNAP OPEN, heart pounding. Something woke me. For a disorienting beat, the room feels unfamiliar. Then relief washes over me. Billy is warm at my back.

Billy. Wondrous, amazing, hot-as-hell Billy.

The ringing finally registers. A phone. My heart kicks harder.

He sits up, instantly alert, and answers. His voice goes all business, but his warm hand settles on my suddenly chilled shoulder.

BJ. My mind leaps straight to him—late-hour calls are terrifying when you've got someone in the service. But they don't call, I remind myself. They come. Early.

Dawn light filters through the blinds. What time is it? Would my parents have tried to reach me here?

The clock reads 7:17 AM. Early, yes. But too early for a Marine Corps chaplain at my parents' door?

"What's up?" Billy asks, then mouths, *Marshall.*

I jolt upright, sheet clutched to my chest. Why is the deputy calling? Was there another incident at the lodge? Billy believes the culprit is after me, but if they think I'm home in bed...

Billy's voice stays calm as they go back and forth. Then he glances at me and hesitates. "Yeah, she's here."

I lean into the headboard. "What is it?" I whisper.

He holds my gaze but doesn't answer. Instead he says into the phone, "I'm sorry to hear that. We'll be there in no time."

The second he hangs up, I pounce. "What is it? What happened? It's not BJ, is it?"

"BJ?" He looks confused, then gets it. "Oh! God, no, Sorrow. BJ and your folks are fine. It's Emerald. I'm sorry—she passed last night."

"Oh." I slump, letting it sink in. "Poor Marlene." Emerald had been fading for a while, but that doesn't soften the blow. I frown. "But why ask about me?"

"Your folks were looking for you. The lodge was up at dawn. Your mom apparently has a bee in her bonnet to hold a reception this afternoon. Marlene's mother was well loved."

"We all loved Emerald." In a small town, when grief hits, you feed people—or get fed. The kitchen's probably humming already. "But how did they know to call here?"

"When they realized you weren't in your bed, Bear called dispatch."

I groan and press both hands to my forehead.

Billy laughs. "Our secret's out."

"I'm sorry." His job keeps him in the public eye—does he really want the extra attention? The speculation? I'm ready to dive in with both feet, but what about him?

"Sorry?" He gently takes my wrists, easing my hands away from my face, and then draws me against his chest. "What kind of nonsense is that? I'm not sorry. You were here with me. I'm walking on air, Sorrow. I'm thrilled people know."

Walking on air. No one has ever said something like that about me. "You are?"

"Absolutely. And honestly? Do you think anyone's surprised?"

I give him a shy smile. "No, probably not." Damien

and whatever reaction he'd have is a problem for another day. I start to slide out of bed, Emerald's passing nudging in at the edges of my thoughts. It makes Billy's warmth feel all the more precious. "I guess we've been summoned."

"Oh no you don't." He tugs the sheet up over both of us and shifts, gathering me in, rolling me gently back on top of him. "They won't miss you for another half hour."

A pang moves through me—Emerald, of all people, had known the value of seizing life. The only sister who'd once left Sierra Falls for love.

Billy brushes a hand down my arm, steady and warm. "You need time to shower, and get ready, and eat something... all kinds of things that take a while." His hands settle at my waist —not urging, just holding me close.

My hair slips forward around his face, and he looks up at me the way a man looks at discovered treasure. The intimacy of it makes my breath catch.

"You sure we have time?" I murmur.

He lifts a hand to tuck my hair behind my ear, his expression soft but certain.

"Life's short, Sorrow," he says quietly. "We'll make time."

LAURA LOOKS from me to Billy. "Well, look what the cat dragged in."

"Morning to you, too," Billy says, unbothered.

Heat rises in my cheeks, but I'm not playing. Today isn't about us. "What happened?" I ask.

Laura's teasing drops instantly. "Emerald fell yesterday. She was on the porch, trying to go down the front stairs in her slippers and robe. Ruby and Pearl were in the kitchen when it happened."

"Those poor women. They must feel awful." It's not the first time something like this has happened, but you can't watch someone every second. Even the best care can't prevent every accident. "Where was Marlene?"

Laura lifts her brows. "On a date. With Sully."

A smile slips out despite everything. "Really?"

"Yes, really." Laura exhales. "And she feels terrible. Thank God she made it to the hospital in time. Emerald passed peacefully during the night."

"What do you need us to do?" Billy asks.

She gives him a look. "So you're sticking around, are you?"

"Marshall's on duty. You're stuck with my ugly mug." He slides my coat off my shoulders. "Go help your mom. I'll keep Bear out of your hair."

When he's gone, Laura grins. "You go, girl."

What I have with Billy feels too special to gossip about, so I cut her off. "Let's get to work."

Laura's shoulders deflate. "Fine. But you have no idea."

"What do you mean?"

"Just follow me."

We walk into the dining room, and I stop short. It looks like the breakfront exploded. Every piece of blue Wedgwood is stacked on the buffet, the good silver is spread across the table, cut-glass vases wait to be dusted, and blackened polish rags lie everywhere. "What's the story?"

"The story?" Laura shrugs. "Mom's losing it."

As if on cue, our mother bustles in clutching two tablecloths. "Which one?" she demands, eyes wild. "The gingham or Meemaw's runner?"

"Meemaw's," we say in unison.

Mom still looks unsure.

"Meemaw was close with the Kidd sisters. It's a nice touch." I take the cloth, and Laura helps me move the silver so we can spread it out. Before Mom rushes off again, I grab her hands. "What's the plan?"

"It's a luncheon," she says.

"Okay." I glance past her at the growing mountain of food on the counters. "But if people are coming soon, we need to clean up and get everything on the table."

"I loved Emerald," Mom says. "I want it to be perfect."

"I loved her too. And it will be perfect enough." I start returning the silver to its felted tray. "Nobody cares if it's the good silver."

"Amen," Laura mutters.

I shoot her a look, then focus on Mom. She looks like she's aged a decade overnight. "Have you eaten? Sit down." I steer her into the kitchen. Her shoulders feel fragile beneath my hands. "Have a cup of coffee and make a list. Lists help." I set a pad and pen in front of her. "Tell us what you need, and we'll do it."

Back in the dining room, I let out a heavy sigh and meet Laura's eyes. What next?

Billy reappears. "Your dad's settled in his recliner. We're lucky college basketball's on. You'll have to unplug the TV to get him up."

He stands beside me, resting a steady hand on the small of my back. I give him a quiet smile. He manages to be loving and solid without making a show of it. It's exactly what I need.

We hear banging from the other room. A scrape of a chair on the floor, the clatter of plates.

Laura gives me a look. "Mom is freaking out." The anxiety in her voice is so rare it makes me feel like the big sister for once.

"It helps her feel in control," Billy says. "Keeping busy is probably what's holding her together."

I look to him—he's suddenly my compass through this. If anyone has wisdom about how to navigate mourning, it's Billy. Emerald's passing wasn't a shock, but it still hits hard. The whole town—especially Mom—will want to stay busy, rally around each other, *do* something.

"You're right," I tell him. "Mom grew up with the Kidd sisters. Putting together a big spread is the most therapeutic thing she could do. For all of us."

"She's been different since Dad's stroke," Laura says quietly. "I think she's clinging to life harder than ever."

It's a surprising insight, especially from her. Dad's stroke reminded all of us how fast things can change. Neither of our parents has been the same since.

"Yeah," I agree. The silence holds for a moment—the kind that doesn't need filling.

Then she exhales, brushing her hands on her jeans, and leads me into the kitchen. "All right. I made a few plates this morning—now that we're not polishing silver, we can actually put everything out."

I'd braced to handle all the food myself, but the spread she's assembled stops me in my tracks. "Wow. This is great. How'd you manage all this?"

Mom joins us. "She did a nice job, didn't she, Sorrow?"

I look at my sister and see her differently. I've spent so long thinking I lived in her shadow that I forgot who she really is— capable and bright. "Yeah, big sis. Nice work."

Laura shrugs, a little shy. "I went shopping yesterday, and there were enough veggies, dips, and deli meats to throw together some trays. And I found random frozen stuff this morning—mini quiches, pot stickers. Figured we could heat those too."

"That's a great idea." I give her a sad smile. "Nothing like putting on a Costco memorial."

Chapter Thirty-Two

Marlene

IT'S BEEN a week since Ma's funeral, and I keep picturing the photo we displayed at the wake—a black-and-white studio portrait from her younger years. She wore a white polka-dot dress, her lipstick a perfect dark bow. It captured the mother I remember best: vibrant, mischievous, quick with a cheeky joke.

"Marlene."

The sheriff stands over my table, warm concern softening his features. "How are you doing?"

He's the kind of man who'd see through a pat answer, so I think before I speak. "I'm... I think I'm okay." And I am. I'm meeting the festival committee for an early dinner, and it feels good to be out. Good to be surrounded by friends, even if Bailey family sparks are a possibility. It's been a tear-soaked week, but I'm grateful to feel steadier tonight. I gesture to the empty spot beside me. "Want to join us?"

"On duty, I'm afraid."

His eyes track Sorrow across the room, and I smile. Exactly the kind of little intrigue Mama would've loved. Life goes on, and it's good.

"You let us know if there's anything we can do," Billy adds. "Sometimes it hits hardest once the vases are packed away and the well-wishers have gone."

He'd know. I give him a grateful smile. "I've got my family

around me." And Tom now, too. I spot him through the pass-through window, his white T-shirt clinging to his back in the kitchen heat.

The words my mother spoke on her deathbed reverberate through me. *My mistake wasn't going off with you. It was listening to anything besides my own heart.* She'd wanted to live by her own compass.

Isn't it time I learn to do the same?

A crash outside shatters the room, followed by the screech of metal. My hand flies to my chest. "What happened?"

Tom bursts out of the kitchen and comes straight to me just as there's another crash, followed by shouts. He rests a reassuring hand on my shoulder, playing it calm, but his eyes meet the sheriff's, sharp and alert. "Sounds like a couple of fender benders. We'll check it out. Don't you worry."

He's back moments later with the sheriff and Sorrow. Eddie Jessup and Helen follow, with Dabney Simmons close behind, holding tight to his shaken wife.

Laura drops into a chair beside me. "What's going on?"

"Black ice," Sully says. "A sheet of it on the driveway. Smooth as glass."

"That's weird." Laura's gaze flicks to Eddie. "Nobody was hurt, right?"

"No, thank God," Sorrow says, joining us.

"Just some bruised fenders and egos," the sheriff adds. "Eddie's new pickup took the worst of it."

"I salted yesterday. It's been dry." Sorrow twists the edge of her apron. "I don't know how this happened."

An uneasy look passes between her and Billy. I reach out to reassure her. "Don't worry, honey. These things happen."

Sully still looks doubtful. "It is strange."

"It's more than strange," Sorrow says. "It's a nightmare.

Mister Simmons's Mercedes has a huge dent. And poor Helen —her old Dodge slid right into it."

"Poor Helen is right." I glance toward the bar, where she's tying on her apron with trembling hands. It'll take months of tips to cover damage like that. "I hope she has insurance."

"We wouldn't dream of making Helen pay," Phoebe Simmons says from behind me, knuckles white on her Chanel handbag.

There was a time her affluence would've stung. No longer. I once thought I wanted the BMW and a lake house. But after Ma I know... those aren't the things I'll mourn at the end.

"Come sit with us," I tell Phoebe. "Have something for your nerves."

"I am a tad rattled." Still, she glides into a chair with effortless grace radiating off her. "A glass of water should set me right."

"On it," Tom says. He returns with two glasses—one for me, too. I offer him a shy smile.

Phoebe sips, already calmer. "Laura, it's so nice to have you back in Sierra Falls. Edith says you might stay awhile."

"I think I just might."

Sorrow sits stiff as a plank. I try to catch her eye. I heard about her breakup with Damien, and I can't tell whether she's shaken by the accident, by Laura, or simply by sitting across from her ex-boyfriend's mother.

Phoebe tries to smooth things over. "You deserve a rest, and Sorrow sure could use the help." The simple kindness raises my opinion of her another notch.

Laura straightens, energized. "I'd love to transform this place from a dusty old hunting lodge into a cozy destination resort."

"Oh, charming," Phoebe says, surveying the room. Her gaze lands on a set of antlers above the dining table.

Laura laughs. "First order of business: lose the animal heads."

Sorrow says nothing, practically vibrating with tension. I try for a gentler tone and say, "Some of us like local flavor."

"I'd keep some flavor," Laura says quickly. "I'm talking to an old friend about designing a website that really showcases that gold-rush-town vibe."

Sorrow's mouth tightens. "Have you talked to Dad about this? Because you sure haven't talked to me."

"Not yet." Laura waves that off. "I'm building the marketing plan. It'll be comprehensive—new interior design, stronger online presence—and it'll all connect with my festival ideas. I thought we could even have a gold rush menu. Sully's Prospector's Pie, and maybe a special dish Sorrow could make. What do you say, sis? You could debut it at the festival."

Standing at the bar, Eddie and Helen exchange a look, then Helen slips away to finish her shift. Dabney clears his throat, collects his wife, and the Simmonses make a quiet exit. The second the door shuts, Sorrow rounds on Laura.

"This dusty old tavern is open for business, in case you forgot. Now is *not* the time to announce your grand takeover plans."

"Please don't—" I start, but Laura cuts me off.

"It's never the right time for you," she snaps. "And I'm not trying to take over."

I take a long sip of my water.

"You go around second-guessing everything I do," Sorrow says. "Don't you have enough to do in your fancy job? Do you need mine, too? As I recall, you couldn't get out of here fast enough."

"How could I forget when you remind me every time I'm home? I'm just trying to help."

"Scheming about redecorating is *not* helpful."

Laura pouts. "I thought you'd like the gold rush dinner idea."

"It's cute. And that's not the point."

"Then what *is* the point? You barely have a handle on things here." Laura gestures around the room. "Why are you so resistant to my help? Like with the festival." She turns to me. "Tell her, Marlene. I've contributed a lot."

I swallow. "Oh dear, I..."

Edith swoops in, a mother's sixth sense razor-sharp. "Dinner's up, and I'm sure Marlene's hungry." She takes Laura's arm. "Honey, help me bring out our plates? Helen's still too shaken."

They disappear into the kitchen, leaving Sorrow slumped at the table.

"I'm sorry," she murmurs. "I shouldn't have done that in front of you. I just... I haven't slept much. It's been some week. I really am so sorry."

"Oh, hush." I take her hand. "What are you apologizing for?"

"For me. For my stupid sister." She sits up, shoulders still low. "Nothing is going right today."

"Do you think this is the first sisterly fight I've witnessed? Don't forget who I live with." I can't help but smile. "Don't give it a second thought. You're young. You'll figure it out."

I watch Laura at the pass-through window balancing plates. "Try forgiving her. Life's too short not to. And open your mind to her ideas—I think a little change around here would be lovely. And if Laura stays awhile? Good for her, following her heart."

And it's time I do the same.

Chapter Thirty-Three

Billy

A COUPLE of weeks have passed since Sorrow and I got our wake-up call and the whole town found out about us. Now I'm back at the Bailey house, sitting stiffly, wondering if it's expected—or frowned on—for me to grab a beer from the fridge.

I've already screwed up once, taking Edith's preferred spot on the couch. Not that Sorrow's mom is about to sit and watch basketball with Bear and me.

When her dad mentioned the Colorado/Brigham Young game, I jumped at the chance to join him. I have a thing or two I want to say to the man, but so far, the bulk of our conversation has gone like this: Bear grunts, "Colorado, huh?" and I answer, "Yes, sir. Econ major."

But I can't complain. I'm still shocked Sorrow's dad even remembered my alma mater. It tells me there's more going on in his head than the old grump lets on. Progress.

Sorrow pops her head in, eyes bright and mischievous. "You boys need anything in here?"

I catch the look she gives me—quick, teasing—and it's all I can do not to grin. "Oh, I think I've got all I need," I say.

She checks that Bear's attention is glued to the TV, then flashes me a saucy little smile.

I make myself wait a full minute before springing off the

couch. "If you'll excuse me, I think I should see if your daughter needs anything."

Truth is, I'm genuinely here to help. Being around the house like this feels right. I want to ease things where I can, take a little weight off her shoulders.

I come up behind her as she wipes down the counter. "Reporting for duty."

She snorts. "Are you kidding? You've already gone above and beyond watching a game with my dad."

"That's nothing." I reach past her and take the rag. "Give me something more to do."

But when I see the tension in her shoulders, I set the rag in the sink and rest a gentle hand between her shoulder blades. "Starting with this. You're wound tight."

She exhales, leaning back a little. Her shoulders loosen under my touch, and the shift in her melts something in me.

"I like this kind of help," she murmurs.

"That's good," I say softly. "Because I like giving it."

I wrap an arm around her waist, drawing her just a little closer. Just enough that she feels me there, steady behind her.

"Well hello, Sheriff," she teases. She tilts her head, giving me a look that lands like a spark. "You seem... enthusiastic about helping."

I bite back a laugh. "Morale matters."

"I thought you were here for lunch prep."

"This is prep," I say, brushing my palms lightly along her arms. "You can't chop onions when you're tense. Safety hazard."

She nudges me, trying not to smile. "If you're trying to distract me—"

"Distract you?" I ask, all innocence. "Never crossed my mind."

Her laugh is low and warm. I could kiss her right now. Forget the whole house, the whole town, everything.

But I was serious about lending a hand, so I force myself to step back. "All right. Give me a job."

She looks around. "We need to get this place in order. We have two parties of two coming in this afternoon. A Big Bear Lodge record."

The lights give a quick flicker, and for half a second I think I imagined it—just me losing track of everything but her. Then they flicker again, sharper this time, and the room drops into darkness as the power cuts out.

Sorrow's hands fist in my shirt, her eyes going wide in the dim light. "What was that?"

I keep my voice calm as I smooth my hands down her arms. "It's okay. Probably just a simple power outage."

But the fact is, I'm not so sure. And I'm not about to take chances.

She gives a nervous laugh and presses a hand to her chest, still rattled. "Sorry. Just a little jumpy these days."

"We all are." I keep a hand on her, but send part of my attention outward, listening. "Where's the fuse box?"

"Garage."

I need her safe inside. "I got this. You wait here."

Bear yells from the living room, "What the hell was that?"

Sorrow groans under her breath. "That man." Then she huffs a laugh, sounding a little more like herself. "Well, isn't this great? We've got guests on their way, and now no electricity."

I press a kiss to her forehead and step back. I have a hard time believing this is just a simple outage—nothing about the Bailey lodge ever feels simple. "I'll go see if a fuse blew."

She grabs my shirt, stopping me. "Hey, rain check on the whole morale thing."

"You got it, darlin'." I swoop in and steal one last hard, quick kiss. "I will cash that rain check."

"Best get going, then." She gives me a playful shove, then digs a flashlight out of a kitchen drawer and hands it over. "Just in case."

The living room is dim, and Bear is hauling himself to the edge of his lounger, trying to get up. "Wait," he grunts. "I got this."

I move to his side and lean down to offer an arm. "Let's go take a look."

He flinches away, angry. "I'm not an invalid. It's my house, and I'll take care of it."

"Of course. So how about I come with, in case you need me to hold the flashlight?" Someone could be waiting out there, and I'm not about to let Bear get jumped in the dark.

He shoots me a suspicious glare, and as I watch him struggle up from the chair, a puzzle piece clicks into place. Sorrow's father was raised to be a man's man—hunting for fun, logging for pay. Having a body that no longer cooperates has to be a blow to his ego, to his sense of who he is.

He might be moving slower, but the man isn't dead yet. Someone needs to remind him of that.

I plant myself in front of the chair, blocking his path. "Permission to speak frankly, sir?"

"Stop sirring me." He wobbles for a moment, getting his balance.

I bite back a smile. "Permission to speak frankly, you old hard-ass?"

Bear laughs. "I been waiting for you to speak frankly. Because I can't figure you out."

Not the response I expect. "There's nothing to figure. What you see is what you get. I care about your daughter, and

I'm not going away anytime soon. At least, not if I have anything to say about it."

"I don't know how I feel about her breaking it off with that Simmons boy," Bear says, and I'm pretty sure he's testing me. "The kid practically prints money at that job of his."

He clearly wants to be contrary. Fine. That's his right. Doesn't mean I'll take the bait. "Damien has money, that's easy to see. Doesn't mean he's the right man for Sorrow."

"Sometimes I wonder if the girl would know the right thing if it came up and bit her on the backside." Bear shrugs, his face screwed into mild distaste. "So, this is you speaking frankly?"

"No. This is me speaking frankly: you need to stop being such a stubborn old bastard. Hollering at the women in your life doesn't make you a better man, it just gives us all a headache. I know your body isn't what it was, and I'm sorry for that. But Bear, last I checked, getting old sure as hell beats the alternative."

He scowls hard at the word old, but I keep going. "You want to be powerful again? Put that daughter of yours up on your shoulders. Support her. Make sure she's set up to fly higher than you ever did. That's a weight only a real man can handle."

Bear's features go utterly still. Whether it's anger or he's actually listening, I can't say. "What are you saying?"

"I'm saying you need to let your girl spread her wings."

He frowns. "Last time she spread her wings, she almost set the tavern on fire."

My response is instant. "I don't believe that was her fault."

"You would say that. New sheriff and all. We pay you to be suspicious."

"Look, Bear. Think what you like. But if you shared more of the decision making, things would get better around here. If

Sorrow wants more say in the tavern, give her a shot—what the hell, right? I'd bet good money Sully would welcome the help. Maybe it'd even prevent incidents like that fire."

"Girl's got no time for all that," he grumbles.

"That brings up my next point."

"How many points you got, Sheriff?"

I ignore the jab. "Sorrow could use some help around the place. An assistant maybe." His eyes go wide at that, but I push on before he can cut me off. "She runs around like a one-armed paperhanger. She's in her twenties, and as far as I can see, her closest friends are a bunch of retirees."

"Laura's back in town," Bear protests. "She's been helping." His tone is firm, but it sounds like he's losing steam.

"You need to hire someone. Right now, in addition to handling repairs, the budget, and the reservations, you've got Sorrow cleaning rooms. For God's sake, Bear. If you hired someone, if you had more help, you could handle more business. You'd bring in more tourists. Think on it."

"You done?" He doesn't look happy, but at least he doesn't look like he's swallowed a box of nails.

I let out a breath. "All done." I have a feeling I've gotten through to him, at least a little. I'll take it. With Bear, even half an inch feels like a mile.

Bear's the one person around here who really needs standing up to, but not many people do it. His kids know how to rebel, sure. But rebelling against a man and challenging him are two different things.

"Then if you're finished flapping your jaw, let's go see what happened to my power." He's proud; he'll never admit anything. But hopefully an attitude adjustment is in his future.

I clap him on the back. "Lead the way."

We huddle in the dim garage while Bear flips fuses on and

off. I angle the flashlight, illuminating a tangle of frayed wires under the breaker panel. "It's all chewed up."

"Raccoon maybe," he grunts.

"Maybe." I lean closer, certain this isn't any animal's handiwork. Raccoons don't go after fuse boxes. "Either way, you'll need to call an electrician."

Bear creaks upright. "That'll cost a pretty penny." His lip twitches as he takes that in, clearly not pleased. "Nothing for it, though. I'll get Eddie on the phone."

A couple of hours later, it's all patched up. Eddie Jessup came straight over—one half of Jessup Brothers Construction, with a schedule that was, conveniently, wide open.

"You're all set," Eddie says as he joins everyone in the living room.

"It's done?" Doubt creases Bear's face. "All fixed?"

"Bear Bailey. When I say 'all set,' I mean all set."

Bear harrumphs and mutters, "I guess we didn't need Damien after all."

Over his shoulder, I catch Sorrow's eye. We share a smile. "I guess we didn't," I say, laying it on a little.

Biting back a smile, Sorrow stands and hands Eddie a foil-wrapped bundle of fresh-baked cookies. "I made these before the power went out. Spiced molasses."

Eddie takes them eagerly. "I'd have worked for free if I'd known I was going to get some of your cookies. I swear they get better every time."

"It's to thank you for getting here so fast. We have some guests arriving tonight, and the last thing we need is a power outage."

"No trouble fitting you in," Eddie says. "I had a hole in my schedule."

I grin. "I'll bet." It's not hard to guess why his schedule had a hole in it. "I saw those skis tossed in the back of your pickup."

Eddie laughs, easy and rolling. The guy lives and breathes outdoor sports, with the snow-tan and prematurely earned smile-and-squint lines to prove it. He treats every hill like an invitation and would veer off the road in a heartbeat if he thought he could ski it.

"You caught me," Eddie says. "What can I say? It snowed last night. Not much, but just enough for some fresh tracks out east of the falls."

Bear is staring at the cookies in Eddie's hands, apparently stuck on the idea that he could've gotten the work for free. "That mean you're not going to charge extra for coming early?"

"Bear. I'm offended. But"—Eddie sets down his toolbox and shrugs into his jacket—"I will accept partial payment in the form of something tall and cold." His smile stalls as Laura walks into the room. His eyes track her, and I hear him murmur, "Speaking of tall and cold..."

He's slack-jawed, and no surprise. Wearing only short shorts and a see-through mesh top over her jog bra, Laura is dressed—barely—for a workout.

"You can shut your mouth now," she says, not meeting Eddie's eyes.

That snaps him out of it. A huge grin splits his face. "Well, well, well. The Big Bad Bailey Sister is still here. Whatcha running from on that treadmill, little girl?"

Laura tosses a towel over the monitor and climbs onto the machine. I'd swear she's blushing. "It's an elliptical trainer," she says primly.

Sorrow makes a coughing sound that's suspiciously like a swallowed laugh.

I start backing out of the room. "Well then. You all look like you've got it under control here."

"Yeah," Sorrow agrees quickly. "I told Billy I'd help him

with... a thing." She catches my eye and jerks her head toward the door.

Bear harrumphs. "What about our guests?"

I watch Sorrow's shoulders tense, and apparently Laura catches it too, because she hops from her machine and says, "Oh, please. Like she's the only one who can do anything. I can work out later. Sorrow, go. Take the rest of the day. You two clearly need to... handle whatever you're handling. I've got it from here."

Eddie looks up at that, eyebrows shooting high. Laura pointedly avoids his gaze, which only makes him grin wider. He steps back like he's giving her the floor, giving her the space she clearly wants.

Sorrow blinks, the need for a break warring with her old habit of taking on everything. I give her an encouraging nod.

"You sure?" she asks finally.

Laura wanders closer and says in a low but firm voice, "Yes. You've been working all day. The rooms are ready. Sully's got dinner. Everything is prepped." She narrows her eyes, insisting, "Go. Before Dad asks Billy to help him chop wood or something."

Our eyes meet and she gives me a *what-the-hell* shrug.

A flicker of satisfaction runs through me. She's finally letting someone else shoulder a little of the load. It's new... and damn good to see.

The moment we're safe in my SUV, she says, "That was..."

"...something else," I finish.

We laugh, but even so, I can feel a thread of tension humming under her skin. When our laughter fades, I say, "At least I seem to have risen in your dad's estimation. I've gone from accused to merely a person of interest."

"I'm afraid Dad's a 'guilty until proven innocent' kinda guy."

I fall quiet for a moment, then ask, "Was he that much of a grump before the stroke?"

"He was always a tough guy. But no, he's gotten worse. Isn't that what they say happens with age? Can't teach an old dog new tricks, and all that?"

"Maybe so." But I'm not entirely convinced. "Might be he's just frustrated he can't get around like he did before."

She nods slowly, letting that sink in. "Yeah, I've been thinking about what you said before. It's got to sting, letting go of so many responsibilities." Then she laughs. "Either way, I thought his head was going to explode when the TV went out."

"Hey, speaking of electricity, there sure were sparks flying between Laura and Eddie."

"Laura? No way. You thought my dad was proud? My sister will sprout wings and fly before she hooks up with a Sierra Falls man."

"Hey, what's wrong with Sierra Falls men?" I reach across the car to give that irresistible hip a playful tweak.

She squirms away with a squeak. "You know there's nothing wrong with Sierra Falls men. We attract only the finest." She reaches across and rests her hand on my thigh, growing thoughtful. "Laura hightailed it out of here after high school and wants nothing to do with the place. I'm sure she pictures herself in some urban loft somewhere, shacked up with a tech bazillionaire."

I cut my eyes from the road long enough to give her a puzzled look. "Then why is she still hanging around?"

"Now that's the question." Sorrow leans back, propping her feet on the dash. "Maybe she's hoping her dream bazillionaire will drop from the sky and check into the lodge."

"Or maybe there's something else going on with her. Have you thought about just asking her?"

"I tried," she says, brushing it off.

"I don't mean in the middle of an argument. I mean have a real sisterly heart-to-heart."

"Uhh, no thanks. I've grown fond of my head and would prefer to keep it attached to my body."

I laugh. "It's obvious she's wound pretty tight, but… I don't know. She was a pretty big help at Emerald's memorial. And she's stepping up today. Maybe you underestimate her."

Sorrow stills, and for a moment I wonder if I've gone too far. Then she admits, "I guess she has done a lot for the festival. She asked if I'd cook a special gold rush dinner."

"That's great."

"Yeah, I guess it kind of is." She shrugs. "She's constantly online, doing whatever she does. Some historical journal is even coming out next week to do a write-up on Buck Larsen and his days in Sierra Falls."

"That's cool. That's something. It'll bring in more tourists. It does seem like you have more guests than usual."

"All this buzz is great, sure. But the place is falling apart at the seams. Every time I fix one thing, something else breaks. And now, apparently, somebody may or may not be out to get us. Having more visitors is all well and good, but it means more mouths to feed, more rooms to keep perfect, and more things to stay on top of."

"You don't have to do every single part of this job alone. Let her pick up some of the pieces you don't love, and you can focus more on what you *do* love—the food."

"Pick up some of the pieces…" Sorrow's feet slide off the dash and thump to the floor. "Who's going to pick up *my* pieces when Laura decides she's done and takes off again?"

Alarms go off in my head. There's tricky history between the sisters—Sorrow's more hurt than I realized, carrying it deeper than I guessed.

I make a snap decision to broach a topic that might not be quite ready. "Well, if she decides to take off again, I think we might have some other help for you."

"What do you mean?" Sorrow lets out a rueful laugh. "First the Laura hard sell. You're not going to foist Ruby and Pearl on me, are you?"

"Better than that. Bear's hiring you an assistant. At least I think he will." I wait, watching it land.

She just stares at me, like I've started speaking Greek. "Assistant? What kind of assistant?"

"The helpful kind. Someone to make the beds, answer the phones, do the grocery runs."

"An assistant." She says it in a dreamy voice. "How fancy. I'll believe it when I see it."

"Well, you'll need one. Because next week I'm taking you to Silver City."

"Cool." She pauses. "Why?"

"Remember my restaurant buddy?"

It takes her a second. "You mean the freezer guy?"

"That's the one. He pulled a few strings at work and managed to snag you a night in the kitchen. A real kitchen, under a real chef."

"Get out! I'll get to act like a sous-chef?"

"Something like that, yeah." I steal a glance. One look at her, cheeks flushed with excitement, and I'm a goner all over again.

"Wow," she breathes. "Working with a real chef. How can I ever thank you?"

I practically skid into my driveway. "I've got some ideas."

Chapter Thirty-Four

Sorrow

"CAN'T SLEEP?" Billy's voice is low in the dark. He pulls me closer, tucking me against his chest, steady and warm. "Want me to distract you?"

I let out a soft laugh and turn to face him. "You've already done a pretty good job of that tonight."

"Then stay," he murmurs, tracing a slow line along my arm. "My bed. I can protect and serve, and all that."

But when he catches the tension in my expression, his whole demeanor shifts. "Hey." His hand settles gently at my back. "I've got you. You're safe."

"I know." I breathe out, but relaxing still feels impossible, even with Billy being—well, Billy. My thoughts won't slow down. Dad insists a raccoon caused the electrical damage, but I don't buy it for a second. Someone was in our garage. Probably while we were home. The idea crawls under my skin. "It just... it feels creepy. Personal."

"It *is* personal," he says quietly. "But we've got this. We'll figure out who's behind everything."

Moonlight slices through the blinds, catching the edge of his face. Strength radiates from him, even in shadow. I draw on it—on him—because I trust him completely.

But my mind wanders back home. It feels like just yesterday my father was swinging me onto his shoulders, and now I'm worrying whether he can manage the stairs. He's so stubborn. What if someone breaks in again? What if next time it's worse than cut wires? "I'm worried about them."

"Your folks?" Of course he knows exactly who I mean. At my nod, he says firmly, "They'll be fine. Eddie's crashing in one of your spare rooms. Those Jessup boys are tough—he can handle whatever comes up." A low laugh. "The question is, will Eddie survive your sister? Do they have history or something?"

A smile tugs at me. "Laura totally denies it."

"What's the line... the lady protests too much?"

"Something like that."

We go quiet, and when he speaks again, his tone turns grave. "I hate to say it, but without you there, I don't think anything else will happen tonight."

A shiver runs through me, because I'd been suspecting the same thing. "Who's doing this?"

"Whoever it is, I'll find them and throw their ass in jail so fast their head'll spin. If I don't wring their neck first."

I laugh at the fierceness in his voice. "Thanks. You know, I believe you will."

We lie in the dark a little longer while he strokes slowly up and down my back. I let out a deep sigh. I feel safe with Billy. Safe in his house. Safe in his arms.

But I still can't sleep.

"That's it." He slips out of bed and pulls on his boxers. Handing me his robe, he says, "You're coming with me." He grabs a pair of wool socks. "This time of night, you'll want these."

I swim in the green-and-navy flannel, but there's nothing more intimate than wearing my man's clothes. We walk downstairs hand in hand, and curiosity edges into my voice. "Where are we going? It's got to be past two."

"I'm making you a cup of tea. And—" he snags my purse from the dining table—"we'll need this."

"We'll need my purse?"

"We need what's in your purse."

"What's in my—?" My eyes light as he pulls out the thick packet. "Ohh. The letters." Ever since the fire, I've kept Sorrow Crabtree's letters close, wrapped in plastic and tucked safely in my bag.

It's not just their historical value. As the trouble around the lodge has escalated, I've felt an even deeper connection with my great-great-great-grandmother. She faced hardships I can hardly imagine. Pioneer women must have been made of steel. Plus, I figure if she could weather the old days as a single mother, then I can buck up and handle a little lodge drama.

"Don't think I haven't noticed how you read these every chance you get." Billy helps me into a kitchen chair, squeezing my shoulders. "Have you finished them yet?"

"No, I'm going slowly." I ease the pages from their layers of plastic, the paper crisp and yellowed with age. "Her story takes my mind off my troubles. I want to make it last."

I want to savor every moment. And since Emerald's death, the need to understand what the older Sorrow went through is sharper than ever. Why hadn't I asked Marlene's mother more questions? About Sierra Falls back in the day? About Marlene's childhood? All those pieces now lost forever.

I half listen as Billy putters around the kitchen, pulling out tea bags and filling the kettle. "Would you read one to me?" he asks.

I look up, checking if he's serious. My breath catches—he looks so handsome in the dim light, scruffy, wearing just his T-shirt and boxers. I still can't believe this guy is mine. "Really?"

He freezes mid-motion, teakettle suspended over the stove.

"I told you, I'm in this for keeps. What makes you happy—I want to know it. I want to be part of it."

"Oh." It slips out, small and startled. I drop my gaze, overwhelmed by the simple kindness. I can't remember the last time someone cared about my happiness just because. "Okay."

"And hey, it's not exactly a stretch." He's still busy at the sink, missing my sudden embarrassment. "Those letters are amazing. To think Buck Larsen was prospecting for gold before he got elected as one of the first California representatives."

"I guess he must've bought his post with gold rush money." The man was infamous for appearing out of nowhere, firing his advisors, then resigning midterm when politics bored him. Bribe rumors trailed him for years. He went on to build a railway empire, but no one really knew where he came from.

"Guess all his money didn't come from bribes after all. Maybe some of it came from gold." The kettle whistles. Billy pours the tea and joins me at the table. He nods at the letters. "Where'd you leave off?"

I shuffle through. "Let's see... she didn't date half of these, so they're not in any real order yet. Last thing I read, Sorrow Crabtree was writing about the town's judgmental biddies."

He gives a thoughtful shrug. "Couldn't have been easy, pregnant and alone. Life was hard and cheap back then, especially for women."

"Well, aren't you the strong, sensitive type?" I tease, squeezing his hand. He was right to bring out the letters. The more we talk, the further away my worries feel. "But it wasn't just the men making money. Some of those gold rush dancers made a fortune."

Billy leans in to study the writing. "Maybe I've seen too many Westerns, but I bet there were other types of women than just dancers. You know, *those* kinds of women."

"My ancestor, a lady of the night? She couldn't have been... could she?"

"Read it and see."

I trace my finger down the page. "Here's where I left off. She wrote, *Thank the Lord for Madame Lizzie. I know what you'd say—you'd be like to call her a harlot or worse. But to me, she's my angel. She invited me to live with the Parlour Ladies, but she don't make me dance no more, nor worry about any of that other business on account of my swole belly. Swole with your child, Buck. Maybe I can see how you'd walk away from me, but I don't understand how you could walk away from your son.*"

Amused, Billy raises a brow. "Doesn't make her do that other business?"

I set the letter down, meeting his eyes. "Wow. She moved into a..."

"A house of ill repute?"

"Yeah, that." I take a sip of tea. "Seems the Madame was a *Madam* Madam."

Billy playfully guides my mug back to the table and gives me the letter. "You can't stop reading now."

I grin and dive back in. "*Some folk carry a Bible in their hand and judgment in their heart. But not the Madame. She has only kindness. Says we women must look out for each other. I think maybe she once had a man who left her, same as you did me. But I'm done being angry. It burned through me, and I've vowed to let it go. Each day brings more love instead, feeling the strong kicks of my baby. My baby, Buck.*"

I put the letter down. "Jeez, he sounds like such a jerk."

"I can't believe the infamous Buck Larsen knocked up a dance-hall girl and left her alone in a pioneer town. He's even more of a bastard than everyone thought."

"Pregnant, alone, and living in a... a house like that," I

murmur. "At least it sounds like she didn't have to do the, uh, extra duties."

"She must've done something to earn her keep."

I read on. "Wait—listen. *Trouble came round this morning. I was in the parlour when some men came. They looked at me funny, all demanding-like, wanting to buy my time. They said some nasty, un-Christian things, and I had to say a quiet prayer not to curse you, Buck. But then just when it seemed I was a goner, the Sheriff stepped in. I suppose Madame Lizzie told him about my babe, and he sent those men packing.*"

Billy grins. "See? Us sheriff types come in handy."

I beam at him. "Too bad Sorrow Crabtree ended up with the mailman instead of the sheriff. That would've been too perfect." I flip ahead. "Should I stop? It's getting late."

"No way. You can't stop now."

My smile widens. I love these old letters—love getting to know my ancestor this way—and I'm tickled that Billy seems to love them too.

"Okay." I turn to a page filled with cramped script. The beginning is mundane—food, weather—then it gets juicier. "Buckle up for this next part:

"*Madame L says from now on I'm just to work at the cooking and laundry. It's hard and my hands bleed from it, but it's better than lying under a man. Some of them come round with their suits and pocket watches, and they remind me of you. And I'd rather my hands bleed, Buck. How do you like that?*

"*One fellow came by yesterday with a newspaper from Sacramenno. And whose name would you figure was on the front page? Mister Buck Larsen, all right. News is you were voted to Congress man. My compliments. I guess the folk of California believed your promises just like I did. Fools, all of 'em.*

"*But I tell you, Buck, maybe it stung extra bad because today is an angry day. None of my dresses fit no more. I let them out all I could, and now I had to sew an extra panel just to cover my belly, but all I had was an old bit of calico from my apron. And I tell you, Buck, that bit of calico makes me spitting mad. At you. Angry how you had your pretty words for me. You told me I was so lovely. Like a winter bloom on the mountainside, you said. But you plucked that bloom and left me, no good for no man now."*

I look up at Billy, making a face. "Yikes. Pregnancy hormones, you think?"

He lifts his hands. "I'm not touching that with a ten-foot pole."

I laugh and continue. *"I should've known watching you glad-hand folk. You wanted me on your arm, so pretty you said. Like a picture. You'd've shown a picture more care though. The moment the Rassmussens came to town with their fancy Foreignn money, you jumped fast enough for their girl. 'Tis unkind of me to say, but I get comfort thinking of those teeth of hers like a Truckee River beaver, and trying to picture you kissing on her. I swear, I hope you have a flock of beaver-faced children. Not this babe in my belly though. He's a fine boy. I can feel it.*

"And he's getting big too. I move slow now, but it don't matter. Madame L lets me hide in the kitchen with my cooking, and it's fine by me. I work and I think about the places I'll take my boy someday."

A warm, startling connection flares in me, across decades, across bloodlines. "She liked to cook. It was an escape for her."

"Just like you," Billy says quietly.

I look at him. Stubble shadows his jaw, his hair a little wild. Being here with him, in the middle-of-the-night calm of his kitchen, hits me with a fierce rush of emotion. I feel seen. Whole. Maybe even loved.

"You get it, don't you? Get me."

"Of course I do." He scoots his chair closer and brushes my hair back, tucking it gently behind my ear. "And I'm the luckiest man alive that you let me in."

Chapter Thirty-Five

Sully

WHEN I WAKE, I know instantly—spring is here. It's in the warm shift in the air, in the way I kicked off the covers overnight.

My bare feet hit the timber planks as I raise the shades. The snow has melted to a thin, crusty layer. Water drips from the eaves, catching the dawn light like crystal. Clear sky, and the birds are already at it.

I've been waiting for a day exactly like this.

I call Sorrow, surprised when she answers groggily. She's usually first up. I smile to myself—none of my business, but I hope the sheriff is the reason she's dragging. That girl deserves some happiness.

"No problem," she says when I request a personal day. She even sounds excited. I figured she would be—any excuse to dive into that kitchen and cook up some exotic breakfast guaranteed to irritate her father.

I move fast, wanting to surprise Marlene before she heads out. I pack a simple picnic with what I've got on hand—fruit salad, deviled eggs, bread, cheeses, juice, a thermos of coffee.

On my way out, I give my Harley a longing look. Feels like spring, sure, but Marlene's not ready for the bike. Not yet.

She answers her door, and the sight of her hits me. She's always elegant, always put together, but today she's in jeans and a plain red sweater that makes her cheeks glow. She looks so fresh, so beautiful, I forget what I meant to say.

"Tom," she says, startled. "What are you doing here? Is something the matter?"

"Yes, something's the matter." Grief is a routine that doesn't quit. Even with her aunts around, she'll still be moving through the motions she had with her mom, reaching for tasks that no longer exist. The days ahead will feel long and empty, and if I can help her avoid some of that, I will. I hold out my hand. "You need to come with me."

She touches her cheek. "I need to finish putting on my face."

"Your face looks just right to me. Prettier than this spring morning." I don't even try to hide my staring. If she doesn't already hear the truth in my voice, I don't know how to make it any plainer. "Come with me, Marlene."

"I'll get my coat." She nods, grabs her jacket and purse, and joins me on the porch.

She moves quickly, and I have to keep a straight face—she's actually coming.

Her keys slip in her hands, so I gently take them and lock the door for her. "Where are Ruby and Pearl?"

Her eyes widen. "Shopping. They took the old Buick all the way to Silver City. There aren't even any sales on now."

"Good for them." I get the car door for her.

"What's the emergency?" she asks once we're in. "It's not the lodge, is it?"

"Nope." I pull out of her driveway toward Route 88.

"Where are you taking me?"

"The falls."

"There's an emergency at the falls?"

"No, ma'am." I savor the confusion on her face. "There's a picnic at the falls."

"A picnic?"

"Our picnic." I point toward the pack in the backseat. "Supposed to hit the mid-fifties today. I figured we'd walk to the falls. The rocks warm up nice in the sun."

"We're hiking to the falls?" Her bafflement is adorable. "I don't have the right shoes."

"I've got snowshoes in the back," I say, keeping a straight face, "but I doubt we'll need them."

"Snowshoes?"

I laugh. "Marlene. I saw your shoes. They'll do fine. I was out here last week. The fire road's clear, and the trail's chewed up and dry. No trouble at all. It's a short walk."

The fire road is a couple miles, but the day is too glorious to care. Snow still blankets the pine boughs, wrapping everything in heavy silence. Farther in, the trail glitters—ice catching the light and spears of sunlight making the place look like a postcard come to life.

When the falls come into view, her breath catches. "It's magnificent."

Her whisper—the awe in it—swells something in my chest. *I* brought her here.

She slows, taking her time. The water is flowing again after the long winter, but ice still clings along the edges, glowing white-blue in the shadows. "It's like a fairy tale."

I take her hand. "Then come on, princess. Time for your feast."

The fresh air sharpens our appetites, and she devours the food as hungrily as the landscape. "I've never been here in the winter," she says.

I set down my fork, more interested in her than anything else. Sunlight dapples her cheek, and the wonder in her eyes makes her look twenty years younger. "It's my favorite time," I say.

She takes a bite of fruit salad, studies me, and shakes her head.

I raise a brow. "What?"

"Another surprise from you, Tom Sullivan."

"What do you mean?"

"You're not usually the biggest talker."

"I'm more a man of action," I say with a wink, and she makes a small, startled sound that hits me right where I live. My voice goes low, and her answering flush just about undoes me. "Is it the action part that surprises you?"

"No," she says slowly. "It's that... just when I think I know you, you open your mouth and say the darndest thing."

"How's this, then?" I take her hand. "Marlene Kidd Jessup, when the weather warms up, I'm bringing you here on my bike."

She coughs. "Oh goodness. I could never ride a motorcycle."

"Why not?"

"Why not," she echoes, thinking it over. She starts to speak, hesitates, and closes her mouth. "Well, I don't know why not, precisely."

"You can be your own woman, Marlene. Heed your own heart." I'm thinking of her mother's last words, and I know she is too.

"I don't even know how I'd start," she admits quietly.

"I can help. We'll figure it out together."

"Could we?" She sighs. "Sometimes I wonder if it's already over for me. I don't know when it happened, but I woke up one day and I was old. And now all I do is mind my aunts, nag my grown children, and wait for the years to pass."

"Seems to me your aunts do a damned fine job minding themselves."

"Seems that way, doesn't it?" A reluctant smile tugs at her

mouth. "So here it is: my kids don't need me, my mother is gone, and my aunts don't need me either. Not really."

"Then you'd best start living for yourself." I want to touch her again, to comfort her with more than words, but there's time. She needs to grieve a little longer, to find her own footing. Then—soon—I'll take her hand, and we'll take off together.

"You're right." Her eyes brighten, clear and fierce. "And you're on, Tom Sullivan. When the weather clears, we're getting on that bike of yours."

Chapter Thirty-Six

Sorrow

"I'm so sorry." I shepherd the couple out the door, hauling their suitcases with numb fingers. Waking up to screaming will do that—flood your body with adrenaline, leaving your limbs chilled and useless. "We'll refund your stay, of course."

"You bet you will," the woman snaps, her collar buttoned as tight as her expression.

Her husband yanks their roller bags from my hands and shoves them into the trunk. "One doesn't expect to encounter wildlife on a historical research trip."

I start to reply, but the car doors slam, cutting me off.

I stomp into the kitchen, muttering, "Newsflash, Professor. One generally does encounter wildlife in the mountains."

Mom stands at the sink, watching through the window. "Good heavens, that woman's scream could wake the dead."

I lean against the counter and blow out a breath. "I guess all their copious reading didn't cover how to handle a simple black bear encounter."

"Sit down, honey." Mom guides me to the table. "Your hands are trembling."

I shake them out. "I'm fine. I need to call Scott." Marlene's second-oldest is our local park ranger. If there's a bear foraging through Sierra Falls trash cans, Scott Jessup needs to know.

I pace as it rings, staring out the window. I thought I'd fixed the stupid bear box, but this morning it was hanging wide open again, trash exploded everywhere in a veritable bear buffet. Someone must've tampered with it. There's no other explanation. Someone messed with the box, practically summoning every bear within sniffing distance. We're lucky a whole crowd of them didn't surprise our guests.

"Scott's on his way," I tell Mom, setting down the phone. "What do you call a group of bears? Like, there's a gaggle of geese, a murder of crows, and a what of bears?"

"Oh, honey. Relax." She presses a cup of tea into my hands. "Drink this."

I smell it. Chamomile.

"Drink it, Sorrow."

"Dad's gonna flip." I take a sip and glance outside again. "That couple couldn't get out of here fast enough. We could've used that money. And the mess..."

Mom points to the chair. "Sit down. The trash will wait. And your father will survive."

I think about what Billy said about Dad. My father's from a generation that didn't turn to therapy to talk through their problems. No support groups for men like Bear Bailey. There are so many ways he could still help around the lodge—he just doesn't see them.

"You know," I say, sitting, "Dad can't stand for long, but if I dug out his old fishing stool and set him up with his tools, I bet he could fix that bear box."

Mom's face lights. "That's a lovely idea."

Wow. Based on her immediate, grateful reaction, Billy was definitely onto something. "Yeah, no problem. I can think of other things, too." Possibilities spin through my mind.

"Sometimes," Mom says gently, "I think your father has given up a little. Be patient with him. His bark is worse than his bite."

"I'll set him up as soon as I deal with that disaster out there." I shudder. Chicken carcasses, wilted greens—it's disgusting. "Did you see it? Do we really have that many leftovers at the tavern? What a waste. I need to talk to Sully."

Mom stirs honey into her tea. "Where's your sister? Maybe she can help."

"Laura? It's an emergency, Mom. Duh. In an emergency, Laura is nowhere in sight." A tiny pang of guilt hits, but I shove it down.

She touches my hand. "Breathe, Sorrow. We're all in this together."

I warm my hands on my mug, remembering how Billy said almost the same thing. Everyone's right—it's time for me to unclench a little. Ask for help. Even if it doesn't come naturally. "You're right." I let out a breath. "I know I've been wound a little too tight. I'll talk to Laura when she gets home."

But two hours crawl by, and I can't wait anymore. I call her cell. "Where are you?"

"Running errands," she says—and then I hear her whisper, "Thank you," to someone.

"Where are you? I asked you to pick up milk and toilet paper. How long does that take?"

"I drove out to Silver City."

I freeze. "For groceries? That's my car you took. If I'd known you were emptying the tank, I wouldn't have let you borrow it."

"My trunk's too small. I needed some other stuff, too."

"What stuff?"

"Looks like I'm staying in Sierra Falls for a while," she says. "But I totally don't have the clothes for it."

My patience snaps. "You went clothes shopping?"

"Yeah. Jeez, Sorrow. Chill out. You have things like hiking boots—why can't I?"

"Let me guess. You've decided to stay… because you saw an opportunity to accessorize?"

Her tone goes frosty. "What's that supposed to mean?"

"It means you talk big about wanting to be a part of things, but I'll believe it when I see it."

"That is so unfair," she fires back. "I've come up with a million ideas, and you shut down every one without even listening."

I don't let her continue. I've been holding in this diatribe for years, and it bursts out, fast and hot. I know I'm going too far, but the words are already pouring out. "You took off the moment you graduated, but it looks like you failed in the city —or at least I'm guessing you did, because you haven't told us anything. Saying you're taking a sabbatical tells me nothing, except apparently it involves buying hiking boots. You can't just drop in like nothing's happened, like it's no big deal you disappeared for years, like you're still the big sister in charge. It takes more than dressing like you live here to be an active, contributing member of this household."

"I am totally an active member," she shouts. "I'm practically pulling this festival together solo. But do I ever bug you about it? No. Did I make you help with online publicity, or ask for money for the ads I placed? No. Did I—"

"I didn't ask you to do any of that," I cut in, my voice hard and measured. "Weird stuff is happening, the lodge is falling apart, and it shocks me that you haven't noticed. So yeah, stupid Buck Larsen is the last thing on my mind."

"Ha!" She barks a harsh laugh. "Don't get all holier-than-thou. The lodge is also the last thing on *your* mind."

I grip the phone tighter. "Meaning?"

"Meaning, lately you spend more time with that sheriff than in your own house."

I want to scream. "Are you so bored with your life you came home to meddle in mine? Why are you even here?"

"To help the family."

"Oh, yeah, right." I roll my eyes. "Because you're sooo committed to Mom and Dad. How am I supposed to believe you?"

"You want honesty?" she asks flatly.

I mutter, "This should be good."

"I lost my job, Sorrow. My boyfriend broke up with me. And I feel like a failure. I wake up every morning and my life is empty. I've dated all the wrong guys, chased all the wrong things. I've got my stupid condo and my stupid car, but nobody who cares about me."

"Laura... come on." I rub my forehead, already regretting half of what I've said. But seriously, how can we come from the same family and still feel like we're from different planets?

"Look, I just need to figure some stuff out, and I need to be home to do it."

The silence hangs as I stare out the window, a stab of guilt hitting me. Have I been spending too much time with Billy? Neglecting things?

"Okay," I breathe. "Please don't bring my car back empty." I hang up.

I know my sister is trying—I know she genuinely wants to help—but right now it all feels like talk. And this place is a full-time job; someone has to keep it running. I yank on rubber gloves, grab heavy-duty trash bags, and get to work.

Some time later, the door slams and Mom steps out. "I thought you were waiting for Laura."

"Nope. Dealing with it myself." Under my breath: "Again."

Her eyes flick to the trash bags, then to my face, reading more than I'd like. She hugs her cardigan tight. "Where is she?"

"I let her take my car for a couple errands," I say, wiping my forehead with my sleeve. "But apparently she decided some shoe shopping was in order."

To disappear for a while—what a thought. To go shopping. I'd buy sexy lingerie. I'd shower off the stink of tavern scraps, slide into lacy silk under my jeans and sweater, and go to Billy's.

His place has become my haven. *He's* my haven.

I've been spending a lot of time there. I worried it was too soon, but he wants me there as much as I want to be there. Instead of fading, our connection only grows deeper. He eats lunch at the tavern almost every day, and every time I see him, my heart skips. The way he shows up—solid, capable, all-in—it gets me every time. And that smile, the way his eyes soften just for me... I never stood a chance. Pretty sure I'm in love with him, and I'm pretty sure he feels the same.

"Can Billy help?" Mom asks, hope in her voice. I've clearly been staring into space.

I shake my head. "On duty."

"Can you call him?"

"Nah." Though I know I could. Billy would make time for me. But I try not to bug him while he's working.

The house phone rings, and Mom darts inside. A minute later, she peeks out, hand over the receiver. "It's Eddie Jessup," she says, puzzled. "He says it's urgent."

"Urgent?" An uneasy sensation prickles up my arms. Eddie never calls the lodge phone. I jog inside, peeling off my gloves.

The call is quick. "Oh God."

Mom barely waits for me to hang up. "What is it?"

I meet her eyes. "There's been an accident."

Chapter Thirty-Seven

Billy

I HOLD Sorrow in the antiseptic waiting room, her head tucked under my chin. She leans into me, and I try to will strength into her. She'll need it.

"Thanks for coming to get me," she says.

I came right away, rushing her to Silver City Memorial with her parents following in Bear's truck.

I squeeze her closer. "What good is a police vehicle if I can't get you to the hospital fast?" I kiss the top of her head. "We're lucky Eddie drove by when he did. He's got a work site near the Simmons place—found Laura way out on Old Mine Road."

She nods against my chest. "It's our shortcut. Old Mine hits a couple back roads that dump you onto 88 to Silver City."

"I know the route." A chill moves through me. The car rolled into a deep ravine. "It was a miracle Eddie even saw it. That road's narrow and winding—rock face on one side, a steep drop into pines on the other. It's the foothills. People could've driven by and never noticed her."

Keri's accident flashes in my mind. Oakland. The middle of the city. Hundreds probably drove past, rubbernecking.

I pull Sorrow tighter, thinking I might never let go. I know firsthand just how lucky Laura is. How lucky we all are that she survived.

The waiting-room door swings open. Sorrow lifts her head,

hopeful, but the nurse calls in someone else. Her shoulders fall. "I hate hospitals."

"Who doesn't?" I smooth a hand over her hair. "You'll see her the second she's out of radiology."

"Do you think she broke her collarbone?" she asks again. She asked the same thing five minutes ago. It's guesswork, but if speculation keeps her steady, I'll indulge it.

And it buys me a little more time before the news I need to tell her.

"Whatever happens," I say for what feels like the hundredth time, "she's going to be okay. You two will be back at each other's throats in no time."

She bursts into tears. Panic spikes through me. I replay my words, trying to hear what I got wrong. "What is it?"

"I said such horrible things the last time we talked. What if those were the last things I ever said to her?" She scrubs at her face. It's almost a relief to see her finally cry—she'd ridden all the way here stiff and silent, and I'd worried it was shock.

"It's okay." I hush her gently, rubbing her back, brushing tears from her cheeks. "I promise, Laura knows you love her. And she will pull through. She was lucky. It could've been so much worse. I talked to the guys on scene—your old Chevy is completely totaled."

Fear grips me again. I lost one woman before; I won't lose this one. I take her chin, lifting her eyes to mine. My voice comes out grave. "I want you in a better truck. With air bags everywhere. Steel beams. One of those giant SUVs. Or hell, a tank. I need you safe, Sorrow."

She laughs, grateful for the moment of humor. Emotion slams into me—she's so strong, so steady. The words *I love you* flash through my head. I can't say it, not yet, so I crush her close instead, my voice cracking. "I'm so relieved it wasn't you behind the wheel." An accident took someone I loved once. I can't face that again.

Something shifts. The sheriff in me takes over. "We're lucky," I say firmly. "And I'm going to do everything in my power to keep it that way. There's something we need to talk about. Silver City PD told me a few things."

"What? Was it her fault?" She pulls back, sensing I'm bracing her for something.

I take her hand, guide her to a corner seat, away from everyone else. I walk slowly, choosing the right words. "That's the thing, Sorrow. It wasn't an accident. Your sister said a blacked-out SUV was on her tail. She slowed to let it pass, but as it pulled alongside, it slowed too. It matched her speed."

"That sounds like something out of a movie." She frowns. "You mean, he was driving side by side?"

I nod. "He—or she. Laura didn't get a look."

"So what did the driver do?"

"A car came from the other direction. Your sister saw it and panicked. The SUV edged her off the road. That's why she lost control and flipped."

"Oh my God." She drops her head into her hand. "Poor Laura. That should've been me doing the errands."

"That's exactly my point." My tone comes out fierce enough to make us both pause. "Any other day it would've been you behind that wheel," I say, softer now. Do you hear me? Someone did this on purpose. Someone who thought *you* were driving."

Rage coils in my gut. I want to take my truck and hunt every road until I find the bastard.

Her face has gone pale. "This has something to do with all the accidents at the lodge, doesn't it?"

She looks so vulnerable I want to shelter her, hide her until this is over. I pull her close, kiss her temple. "I believe it does.

And as sheriff, this is my only priority now." Technically, it's Silver City jurisdiction, but SCPD's being cooperative. And even if they weren't, nobody's stopping me.

She wipes at her eyes, pulling herself together. She's strong, my Sorrow.

She takes a sharp breath. "Okay. Tell me what I need to do."

"I need you strong. Lay low. Stay off the roads when you can. And Sorrow..." I hesitate. She won't like this next part. "I want you to stay away from Damien."

Her eyes fly wide. "What?"

Everyone in town loves Sorrow. Everyone wishes her well. Everyone—except maybe Damien.

"The accident happened near Simmons Timber land," I say, letting it hang. "Who might have a grudge against you?"

"Nobody. Especially not Damien or his family." She's immediately sure. "They love me over there."

"Well, somebody doesn't. And they've ramped this up. First small incidents, then a fire, now a hit-and-run." I lift my brows. "Have you thought about whether you hurt your ex more than you realized?"

"Are you saying you think Damien tried to run me off the road?"

I shrug. "Think about it."

"That's ridiculous," she says flatly.

I can't tell if she's confused or angry. I'll take either. She can be mad at me—I just want her safe. "You can think it's ridiculous. But right now, for me, everyone's a suspect."

The intake nurse pokes her head in. "Miss Bailey?"

Sorrow jumps to her feet. "Thank God."

I stand up, searching her face. "So... you're not mad at me?"

"Mad?" She gapes at me, looking rattled. "Of course not. It

doesn't mean I believe Damien had anything to do with this. But I trust you."

"I'll find the truth."

"I know you will." She gives me a tired smile that twists at something in my chest.

I cup her cheek. "Don't think about any of this right now. I'm on it. And I swear to you, I'll find who did it. I won't stop until they're behind bars."

She hesitates, reluctant to leave.

"You go to your sister," I tell her.

"Do you want to come with me?" she asks quietly. "I can ask if it's allowed."

I kiss her forehead. "Family only." Someday I'll be family, if I have anything to say about it.

For now, I have work to do. My mind is already two steps ahead, tracing the path back to Simmons Timber.

But I don't want to load her with more worry, so I soften it. "I need to get back anyway." I rest my hands on her shoulders, fighting the urge to pull her into one more embrace. "You going to be okay here?"

She manages a weak smile. "I'll get a ride with Mom and Dad."

I slide my hands down to twine my fingers with hers. "I hate to leave you."

She breathes in deep, and I see the raw affection in her eyes. "You just go find the bad guy."

Chapter Thirty-Eight

Sorrow

I STAND IN THE DOORWAY, watching my beautiful, vital, energetic, pain-in-the-butt sister lying broken and asleep in a hospital bed. The sight dredges up a tidal wave of feelings.

Laura's left arm is in a sling, her shoulder wrapped tight, an IV in her other arm. Her face is bruised, and the sight sends a sharp spear of anguish through me. For all her bluster, she's fragile. What if she hadn't survived? What if I'd never gotten the chance to take back the awful things I said the last time we talked?

Her eyes flutter open, and we just stare at each other.

"Hey, sleepyhead," I say finally.

"Sorry about your car." Her voice is small and cracked. She coughs, trying to clear her dry throat.

I'm beside her in an instant, easing onto the bed and pouring water from the bedside pitcher. "Forget the car." I smooth her hair back. "Honestly, you did me a favor. It's a miracle that thing still ran."

"Remember when Dad got it?" she asks, and we both laugh.

"Totally. He used to wax it every weekend, right before Sunday night football."

Laura leans back, a wistful smile ghosting over her face.

"There were times," I say, "when I wondered who he loved

more—us or that car. I was shocked he handed it down to me. I thought for sure he'd save it for BJ."

"Nah. Of course it went to you." She looks away, eyes glimmering, her breath shuddering. She's trying not to cry. "I always screw things up."

"Are you kidding?" I take her good hand and give it a light squeeze. She's the golden girl—the one who never screws up. "That's the painkillers talking. You know you're the family princess."

She pulls her hand back. "What are you talking about? You're Dad's favorite. You always have been."

I stare, stunned into silence.

"Don't give me that look," she says. "Dad would never have let me take over the lodge."

I find my voice. "As if you'd ever want to."

"Oh, please." She scoots higher in the bed. "I'd have loved to work more around the place. But Dad always second-guesses me. Why do you think I took off? It's not easy being the oldest."

The room hums with the low whirr of machines. I've spent years feeling abandoned by her. But what if she hadn't run from us? What if she'd felt pushed out—like leaving was the only way to prove herself?

"You really want to stay?" I ask. "Like... live in Sierra Falls again?" I still can't quite believe it.

"It's what I just said." She sighs, then winces at the pain it causes.

I pour her a cup of water, thinking as she sips from the straw. "Seriously, Laura. *Permanently* permanently?"

"Permanently," she says. "I swear it. I pinky-swear it."

I look at her in a new light. "You're serious."

Laura, staying for real. The idea hits me sideways—not as a

burden, not as competition, but as... family. Now, after almost losing her, it feels like the only thing that makes sense.

A laugh slips out of me, raw and relieved. "You know shared duties means shared blame when things go wrong."

Laura gives a shaky laugh. "Oh, I know."

"We need you. Please stay." I grip her hand. "You'd be amazing—you've got more business experience than the whole town put together."

She looks away, fiddling with her IV line. "Dad would never have it."

"Shut up." I nudge her good arm gently. "Mom and Dad would be thrilled to have you back."

"Okay," she admits, laughing a little at my intensity. "Maybe I'm being unfair. But sometimes I think Dad respects me more in theory. Like... he likes the idea of his oldest daughter driving around in a fancy car, being Urban Business Barbie, but he doesn't want to deal with the actual person. All the... chaos." Tears shimmer again. "And believe me, there's a lot of chaos."

"Forget that," I say. "You'll be Sierra Falls Rural Business Barbie. And we'll embrace the chaos together." I beam at her. "Oh my God, Laura. You don't get it. I'd give anything to spend less time with ledgers and plumbers and snow shovels."

"I didn't say anything about snow shovels. Kidding!" she says, seeing my expression. "I'd be happy to share it with you." She gives me a pointed look. "I've been trying to tell you that since I got here."

"You want responsibilities? I've got them coming out of my ears."

Her laugh breaks into a cough, and I'm quick to bring her the cup again.

"First, we need to get you better." I watch her trembling hand steady the cup, her throat working slowly as she swallows.

"I'm so grateful Eddie came along when he did. I'm giving the guy a big kiss next time I see him."

Laura lifts a brow. "Won't the sheriff be jealous?"

"You know what I mean. Actually…" I narrow my eyes playfully. Now that she's staying, it feels like a whole new game. "I think *you* should give him the big kiss."

"What does that mean?"

"You should go for Eddie. I've seen the looks you give each other."

"Eddie?" She scowls. "If you ever saw me give Eddie Jessup any look, it was either scorn or distaste."

"But he's cute."

"I've learned my lesson—I'm steering clear of cute. If I date anyone, it'll be some nice businessman."

"What's that supposed to mean?" A spark of annoyance flares. "Just because he's outside all day, doesn't mean he's not a businessman. Eddie and his brother built an incredibly successful business. Plus he works with his hands. And his body. That's pretty hot, if you think about it."

"I'm not interested in a man who's obsessed with his… equipment."

Biting back a smile, I raise an eyebrow.

She rolls her eyes. "Okay, Miss Dirty Mind, if we're being specific, I'd never be interested in a guy who spends all day covered in sawdust."

"So then why are you blushing?"

"I am not blushing," she snaps. "I haven't blushed since seventh grade."

"Maybe that's part of the problem." And it hits me exactly how Laura's attitude could get adjusted. "Maybe a mountain man who makes you blush is exactly what you need. Ditch the tech bros in khakis whose idea of foreplay is talking about mutual funds."

Laura guffaws. "Wow, someone's fired up today. Jeez, the girl gets lucky with the sheriff and suddenly she's an advice columnist." She jokes, but she's considering it—and then she shudders. "He drives a vehicle best suited for monster truck competitions. That giant red pickup. Can't go there."

"What's wrong with Eddie's pickup?"

"It's... a lot. Like he's overcompensating."

"You know what they say about the size of a man's truck," a deep voice says from the doorway.

Laura's cheeks flame pink.

I grin at the sight of the Jessup brothers. "Eddie, Mark, hi!" Under my breath, I sing, "Blushh-innng."

"We found the doctor," Eddie says, shoving his brother forward. "But I don't know if you can trust him. I hear he sucks."

Mark, still in his white coat, elbows him back. "You're only jealous I got all the brains."

"Whatever, dude. Mom likes me better." Eddie gets a wicked look and steps up to Laura's bedside, tipping her chin with a finger. "Plus, I have the biggest truck. Isn't that right, sugar?" He winks.

I snicker as Laura's cheeks go crimson.

"Jessups," she croaks. "They're everywhere."

"Can't get away from us." Eddie perches on the edge of the bed, and she inches away.

Mark grabs her chart from the foot of the bed. "Haven't seen you in a while, Laura."

"Not since you graduated high school," she says. "I was in eighth grade. So, yeah. Long time."

"Wish the circumstances were better than a fractured clavicle."

I read over his shoulder. "You and me both, Dr. Mark."

"We need to figure out who did this," Eddie says, his tone turning steely.

I nod. "Billy's investigating."

Mark raises a brow. "*Billy*, huh?"

Now it's my turn to blush. "The sheriff and I have become friendly." I shift into business-as-usual. "He thinks too much has happened around the lodge. And now, with the accident... it's just too suspicious."

Eddie pins Laura with a look. "Good thing Miss Fancy-pants here will be running off again soon. Staying safe. Right on schedule."

Laura looks like a deer in headlights, so I answer for her. "Laura's sticking around this time."

"Oh, is she now?" Eddie's eyes glint. "Sounds like something *I* need to investigate."

Chapter Thirty-Nine

Billy

I NEED TO QUESTION DAMIEN, and if I can't get him into an interrogation room, I'll do one better: a bar. The Thirsty Bear Tavern, to be exact. I considered a neutral spot like Chances across town, but if I want to take a man's measure, it's best to hit the sensitive spots, get under his skin. Which means meeting him here, ground zero for Damien's history with the Bailey family.

"Thanks for meeting me," I say when he comes in, wearing an easy smile I don't feel. Sierra Falls seems to adore the guy, but from the start he's struck me as arrogant, slick, and too young to know better.

"Yeah. You bet." He shrugs out of his fleece jacket, movements stiff. "Though why do I get the sense this isn't a friendly visit?"

Because we're not friends. Instead, I laugh, light and casual. "Shall we get some drinks?"

His posture loosens. He nods toward an open stool at the bar.

I cut him off, wanting some privacy. "How about a booth instead? Easier to kick back."

His gaze flicks to the booth and back. "Whatever you say, Sheriff. How about I snag the first round of beers?" A nervous laugh. "I hope by drinks you didn't mean diet sodas."

The Simmons boy has always struck me a little entitled, and nothing gets a guy like him talking like his pal Johnny Walker. I give him a wide smile. "Why mess around? I'm off duty. How about a couple shots with a beer back? My treat." I catch the bartender's eye. "My tab, Helen."

By the time Damien returns, his features have hardened, nerves tucked away. The guy knows the best defense is a good offense. He settles into the booth, leans forward, and slides my drinks across.

"Cut the shit, Sheriff. Why am I here? Don't tell me you need a new drinking buddy."

I raise my glass. "Points for the brass balls, Simmons." I down the shot. "You're right. I'm not looking for a friend."

His lip twitches, bracing.

"I just want to make sure it's all cool—with me and Sorrow."

His eyes narrow. He tosses back his own shot. "Yeah, sure. It's cool."

"Good." I keep my face neutral. "Sorrow has enough on her mind without worrying about bad blood. You heard about the accident, I guess."

His expression doesn't shift, not even a blink. "Tough break."

Tougher nut to crack than I thought. Time for the big guns. I gesture to Helen for the bottle.

Damien's brows flick up, wary.

"Don't sweat it," I say. "My buddy Scott's coming later. He'll drive us home."

"You're the sheriff," he says flatly. He peels at the label on his beer. "So, she okay? Laura, I mean?"

Helen drops off the Scotch, lingering on Damien. "I hear you're single."

He doesn't miss a beat. "And I hear you're still married."

When she walks off, he drags the bottle closer and pours a shot. "Women," he mutters.

Watching the amber pour, I say, "That's the way." *That's right—loosen up.* I slide my glass over for a pour. "I don't know how you and Sorrow left things. She's no gossip, and what happened between you two isn't my business. But far as I can tell, there's no reason two men can't have a friendly drink."

He meets my eyes and holds them as he throws the shot back. "Or five."

I laugh. "Whoa, cowboy." Either he's more torn up about the breakup than Sorrow realized, or he's got something heavy on his mind. Guilt, maybe?

If I want any credibility, I've got to match him drink for drink. I knock mine back and exhale hard. "Don't think you can drink an old man under the table."

He gives me a half smile. "I bet I can." A beat. "Speaking of age, don't you think you're maybe a little too old for our Bailey?"

I bark a laugh. "I'm not dead yet."

He waves it off with a brittle chuckle. "Okay, you're right. Foul ball." He sighs, sounding suddenly tired. "Hell, I don't know anymore."

He pours another and raises it. "I hate to admit it, Sheriff. But for her sake..." He pauses, sobering. "I've known Sorrow my whole life. She's good people, and any friend of hers is a friend of mine."

That surprises me. I sift his words for any hidden edge, but they ring true. In my mind, he drops from villain to just plain jerk. I clink my glass against his and toss mine back. We'll never be best buds, but I remind myself to stay open. First rule of law enforcement—nothing is ever quite what it seems.

Still, trusting too easily never ends well. Time to steer things back. I keep my tone casual, eyes on the table. "So, I hear the accident happened close to Simmons land. Hope that doesn't bring bad publicity."

"Dad once told me, no publicity is bad publicity."

"Your father must know what he's talking about. He's successful enough."

"Truer words."

"You're lucky," I add. "Hell of a mentor to have."

"Who, Dad?"

"Do you work closely with him? I imagine he treats you like his protégé. You'll inherit Simmons Timber someday."

He drains the rest of his beer in one long pull. "I'm pretty sure my father just wants me to be a suit."

I pour us each a smaller shot and keep the bottle. The kid's drinking too fast. "A suit?" I echo, nudging him to talk.

"Yeah. You know, a good ole boy in a suit. Says it's the lynchpin of a business like ours—hunting trips with the guys, that sort of thing." He snatches the bottle and tops himself off. "I have ideas, though. I try to be a good guy. A responsible guy."

"Responsible how?" Like by running Laura Bailey off the road?

He holds my gaze. "Newsflash, Sheriff: logging isn't exactly politically correct these days. I drive into the city and say I'm in timber? Women can't run away fast enough." He tosses back the shot. The kid can hold his liquor—good for the questioning, bad for my liver. But the booze is loosening his tongue. "These days all women wanna talk about is composting. Vegan stuff. Things like that. You'd think I was out there clubbing baby seals. Like cutting down trees is the devil's work."

I see him differently now—vulnerable, maybe even lonely. Sorrow probably hurt him more than she knew. It's easy enough to imagine. If Sorrow left me, I'd be wrecked.

I tread carefully. "Seems to me the ladies would love—let's be honest—that car you drive."

"Yeah," he says flatly. He spins his empty glass. "Some girls go for the money."

He sounds more jaded than a young, wealthy heir should. Clearly he doesn't want gold diggers. So what's his story? Maybe there's more to him than I thought. And why should that surprise me? Sorrow wouldn't date a complete idiot.

When I speak again, it's more guy-to-guy than sheriff-to-citizen. "Have you tried talking to your dad? I don't know much about running a big company, but change happens from within. Environmental initiatives can actually be lucrative—good press, too."

"I tried, man. I went to the Simmons board once—just said the word sustainability—and they laughed me out of the room. Like I was a moron. I know people need paper. Paper's not going anywhere... yet. I get that. I'm not stupid. But Dad? All he wants is build, build, build." Damien laughs, dark and low, leaning back to stare out the window. "It drives him nuts that Bear's sitting on so much prime land. I love it."

I freeze. The Baileys are struggling. I've always assumed all they had was the tavern and a roof over their heads. "Bear owns land? And it borders Simmons Timber?"

He laughs again, softer this time, worn out. "Yessir, Sheriff. Old Dabney Simmons calls it green gold."

Chapter Forty

Sorrow

THE LUNCH CROWD THINS, the tavern door whooshing open and shut as I stand at the bar refilling salt shakers. I glance over my shoulder and hold my breath.

Damien. Making a beeline straight for me.

He leans against the bar. "I have a proposition for you."

"Hello to you, too." My heart jumps to my throat. Billy and my ex met for drinks last night, and even though he didn't come away Damien's biggest fan, he didn't think him capable of hurting Laura. According to him, things were "all cool"—at least for now. He said we'd talk more at dinner tonight.

So why is Damien here?

"Don't give me that look."

"I'm not doing a look."

"Sure you are. It's your oh-crap face." He laughs, clearly seeing how flustered I am. "Relax, Bailey. I know you're off the market. I had a sit-down with your new boyfriend. Didn't he tell you?"

I nod warily. "He told me."

"So you know it's all good." He chucks my chin. "Your sheriff's not that bad. For a relic." His pointed look pulls a reluctant smile from me. "Yeah, that's the Bailey I know. Here." He hands me a box. "I even brought you a peace offering."

I take it—one of those decorative tins—and heft it suspiciously. "What's in it?"

"Cookies. Fancy ones. Look for yourself. And before you thank me, don't. My folks got them for you."

I pop the lid. Chocolate-dipped madeleines.

"Because of Laura's accident," he says.

"Oh, wow…" The gesture hits me hard. It means more than wishing my family well. It means forgiveness. I broke up with their only son, but they don't take it personally.

"I think they're from France," he adds. "Your fancy sister should like that."

I laugh. "Cookies? It's obvious they don't know Laura."

"No, goof. It's obvious you deserve a treat." When my eyes narrow, he adds quickly, "As a friend. You're as pretty as ever, but like I said, Billy and I cleared the air. We're cool."

"What is it with you men? Everything is 'It's all good. It's cool.'"

He gives me a broad smile. "That's because it is, Bailey."

I close the tin. "So this is your peace offering? Cookies your mom picked out?"

"No." He sounds defensive. "Well, okay, partly. The cookies are gravy. I'm really here because I need to show you something."

"What?" I ask, instantly on guard.

"You have to come with me to see it."

Billy and I have agreed Damien wasn't capable of something as calculated as a hit-and-run. Still, something niggles. "Can't you just tell me? Why the mystery?"

His eyes go cold. "Don't look at me like that, Sorrow. God, you make me feel like a criminal. I found something you'll think is cool. I wanted to surprise you. Sort of a last hurrah for the two of us." At my skeptical glare, he adds, "A platonic hurrah. Come on. I'll have you back in an hour."

My misgivings soften. I feel ridiculous for being suspicious —I've known Damien my whole life. Still, I have an honest excuse. "I'm busy."

"The dinner crowd won't be here for hours. And Sully's back there, right? He can hold down the fort."

I check the clock—a shellacked wood slab that's hung there forever. "I haven't even eaten lunch yet."

"We'll pack sandwiches." He grabs the tin. "We can bring these too. C'mon." He pleads again, making me smile. "I've got no meetings till three. Just sixty minutes, for an old friend. Closure—don't you women always want that?"

A laugh bursts out of me. There he is—the mischievous Damien. The one I've always known. That decides it. Closure *would* be nice. I'd love to stay friends with him, and an impromptu picnic feels like the right first step.

I throw together a couple of simple sandwiches, grab apples, refill my water bottle, and we're off. Fresh air will do me good. I haven't been out since Laura's accident, and spring is in full force. I'm dying for blue sky. And with him driving, I'll be safe. Whoever this mysterious bad guy is will assume I'm at the lodge.

But as we get farther from civilization, doubts creep back in. He takes us down an old fire road, deep into Simmons Timber land, well off Irish Camp Road. "Where are you taking me?"

"I told you. I have something to show you."

I trust he won't hurt me. I do. Still, I can't help joking, uneasy. "You're kind of freaking me out here."

He sighs and pulls onto a dirt road, stopping almost immediately—his sports car won't go farther. Hurt flickers in his eyes. "You used to trust me, remember? What happened between us, Sorrow?"

I sit stiffly, not unbuckling. "Is that why you brought me here? To talk about our relationship? Take me home. Now."

He leans back, looking tired. "Give me fifteen minutes. Then I'll take you back."

"First, you have to answer something." When Billy mentioned his initial reservations about Damien, I'd scoffed. But now, in the middle of nowhere, everything rushes back—every crisis at the lodge, every moment Damien happened to be right there to swoop in and help. Too many coincidences. "Have you been sabotaging us?"

His face hardens in stunned disbelief. "What?"

I almost take it back, but the words are out, hanging there. No going back now. Might as well keep going.

"There've been so many freak accidents at the lodge," I say carefully. "And you always seem to be right there."

He stares at me, stunned. I expect guilt, maybe revelation. What I see instead is confusion, comprehension... and something like despair.

Finally he speaks, his voice low and raw. "Jesus, Sorrow. I know I can be an ass, but I would never sabotage you. Never."

I watch him, searching his eyes. "How can I be sure?"

"How could you even think that? I've been trying to help. You've been so in over your head." He grips the steering wheel, jaw tight. "Why would I ever hurt you? I care about you."

I rack my brain for reasons. "Maybe you're jealous."

"Of Billy? Yeah, sure, I admit, at first I got pissed every time I saw his damned cruiser in your lot. I mean, what's the appeal? He's older, he doesn't try worth a damn, yet every woman in town swoons for the guy."

"Seems to me you're the one they're swooning for."

"I don't know. Whatever. It doesn't matter." He stares out the window, voice soft. "You always talk about feeling stuck,

Sorrow. Abandoned in Sierra Falls by your siblings. But think how I feel." He meets my eyes, and his are dark with anguish. "I'd give my left nut for a sibling. You think you're stuck, but I'm the one trapped being everyone's golden boy, handed an empire I never asked for. What good am I when my own girlfriend doesn't want me—when I'm the guy who's supposed to have it all?"

My eyes go wide. "Are you kidding? Damien, you're like... the prince of Sierra Falls. You were the star quarterback. You're going to inherit half the town."

"You still broke up with me."

"It wasn't because of you. You're amazing. I just connected with Billy."

He gives a bitter laugh. "The old 'it's not you, it's me' talk. But the thing is, Sorrow, it was me." He shakes his head. "You don't get it. Billy Preston is the kind of man I could never be. Simple, loved."

"You're loved."

"Sure thing, Sorrow." His expression shutters. "Forget it. This isn't why I brought you here, whatever you're thinking. Look, I'm glad you found Billy. If you're happy, I'm happy."

"Then what do you want?" I ask quietly.

"All I want—all I ever wanted—was to look out for you."

Chapter Forty-One

"Look out for me?" Ice rushes through my veins. "From what?" I glance out the window—towering pines and not another soul for miles. "Damien, you're scaring me."

He practically yanks off his seat belt, pinning me with a look. "I keep getting misunderstood, and I need to make it right."

Damien gets out and opens my door for me. He holds out his hand, his arm rigid. "Please come with me. I swear I'll keep you safe." Something in his expression cracks when I don't take his hand right away. His arm drops with a sad, tired sigh. "I wanted this to be fun. Hell, Sorrow, before that sheriff started showing up, it felt like I was the only one who cared whether you kept your head above water."

I stare up at him and see emotions I've never seen on Damien's face—earnestness, anxiety, even pain. Such a contrast to the easy confidence I'm used to. This is the Damien I'd always suspected was there.

I make my decision. I take his hand, letting him haul me up. "Fifteen minutes."

We hike in silence. The trail is overgrown, and even though we only go about half a mile, it's slow going.

I pause to catch my breath. "So this is Simmons land?"

He leans against a tree, pulling out a water bottle and offering it to me first. "You don't know where we are, do you?"

I chug, suddenly thirsty, and look around—nothing but pine trees. "How could I?"

He points to the right. "See that?"

"See what?"

"That's your land."

"My land?"

"Bear's land, at least. There's a strip extending south of the lodge. Not enough to do anything with except sit on. Which is exactly what the Baileys have been doing since, probably, the days of your Sorrow Crabtree." He drinks and tucks the bottle away.

I huff a laugh, because honestly, what else can I do? "Then why aren't we rich? Looks like a lot of land to me."

"You ever heard the phrase land rich and cash poor?" At my nod, he says, "Welcome to my world."

He walks on, and I follow. "What do you mean, your world?"

"Timber's not exactly the road to fortune in the twenty-first century. My family's been land rich and cash poor for years."

He ducks through a thick patch of greenery, holding branches aside for me. He starts heading straight uphill.

I stare, horrified. "Are you sure?"

"I got you." He holds out a hand. "I promise you'll love it."

I practically crawl, clutching his hand and grabbing roots to haul myself up. At the top, he steadies me.

"Careful." He leads me along a narrow ledge. "I need you in one piece so you can see—" He sets his hands on my shoulders, turning me. "This."

I gasp. The path leads to a black hole in the hillside. Rotted timber posts at the entrance tell me it's more than a natural cave. "What's that?"

"An old gold mine," he says, giddy as a kid. "Come on, I'll show you."

I grab his shirt to stop him. "Is it safe?"

"Sure." He tugs me forward. "I've been here a bunch of times."

Closer now, I see the deep hallway and timber scaffolding. "Wow. It really is a mine." These foothills are gold country—tourist spots everywhere—but I've never been inside an actual mine. "And this is on our land?"

"Yup," he calls from inside. "All yours. Too bad it's not worth a dime."

"I'll say." I follow him, stopping to let my eyes adjust. Dark, but not pitch-black. A sharp, pungent smell hits me—like urine. "What is that? An army of homeless prospectors still living down here?"

He laughs. "It's okay. Just bats. They won't hurt you."

I scowl, not convinced. "If you say so."

He comes back, guiding my shoulders. "Promise. It's safe. I've been exploring here since I found it."

Curiosity wins out. The place is surprisingly intact—wooden support posts, old rail-cart tracks, exactly like in the movies. "How come nobody knows about this?"

"I did some research at Town Hall. The mine was a bust."

"You did research?"

"Yes, Bail. I did research." He walks ahead, leaning on a railing. "The Comstock Lode hit, and folks forgot this place."

I step up beside him, then jerk back with a yelp. He's standing at the edge of a narrow shaft. A rusted pulley hangs overhead, ropes dangling like cobwebs. A ladder leads down into darkness so complete the floor could be an illusion. "Creepy."

"I thought you'd like it." He picks up a rock and tosses it down. It lands only one level below, but the echo goes on and on.

"You're such a guy. Don't do anything crazy."

"It's pretty safe."

"Pretty safe?" I shiver and back up. "I'll take your word for it. It is cool, though. How'd you even find it?"

"I didn't. Coop did."

"Your dog found it?"

"We were hunting. He scented a fox and wouldn't let it go. He followed her to a den outside. Whole litter of kits—must've been a dozen of them."

"Please tell me Cooper didn't eat them."

"Never fear. Coop wouldn't hurt a fly." Damien laughs. "It's why he's such a terrible hunting dog."

A faint hissing comes from outside. I step to the entrance and see a drizzle starting—a soft Sierra mist. I settle between the rails and slide to the ground, leaning against the tunnel wall.

He drops his pack and joins me. "Hungry?"

"Starving." A cool breeze carries the scent of damp pine needles, the setting both serene and a little eerie. I dig into a turkey and Havarti sandwich. Between bites, I ask, "So you really just wanted to show me this place?"

Damien eyes his sandwich, then chooses an apple instead. He takes a huge bite, grinning as he chews. "Maybe I wanted one more shot with you."

"Damien!" I nudge his foot.

He gives an exaggeratedly innocent shrug. "So. You sure it's over?"

"Yes, I'm sure." I narrow my eyes. "Hey, you said your intentions were innocent. You lied."

"I didn't lie," he says, matching my glare with a smile. "Not really."

I glare harder.

"Okay, fine. Maybe a little white lie. Can't blame a guy for trying."

I try to be mad, but it's too classic Damien. Oddly, I feel a stab of affection for him because of it—affection mixed with firm resolve. He's still the smooth-talking lady-killer he was in high school. But I'm not in high school anymore, and sitting here with him, I know more than ever how I found my perfect man in Billy. The realization makes me strangely at ease with Damien. "You just want to keep dating me now that you know I'm a gold-mine heiress."

"Dream on," he shoots back, but then his expression shifts. "You really like that sheriff, huh?"

I finish the first half of my sandwich, brush off my hands, and reach for the second. "Yup. I really like that sheriff."

"He's a lucky man." He works the apple down to the core, looking genuinely hungry.

The compliment makes me shy, so I focus on his lunch choice. "I swear, between you and my sister…" I nod at the untouched sandwich. "A carb and some mayo won't kill you."

"A guy's gotta stay ripped." He flashes the familiar confident smile, cocking an eyebrow. "Especially now that I'm single."

"Hey, this was supposed to be a hurrah. You'd think, just this once, you could eat something besides beef, berries, and protein shakes."

He laughs, pulling the cookie tin close. "Then forget the sandwich. If I'm eating processed, it's gonna be sugar."

"Alert the media," I say gleefully as he shoves an entire cookie in his mouth. "Damien Simmons eating carbs. Apocalypse is nigh."

He laughs and downs a second cookie. "You should try one," he says, mouth full.

"Very appetizing. Don't worry, I will—if you manage to save me some."

He grabs a third cookie, bites off the chocolate end, and pops it in. "That sheriff better take care of you. I worry about you in that lodge."

I freeze mid-bite, studying him. "Why?"

"The place is a..." He hesitates.

"A dump? Is that what you were about to say?"

"No, of course not. Though it is halfway there. Why do you think I keep coming by?"

The realization hits with a sharp pang. I hadn't loved Damien, but for a while I'd enjoyed his company. "I hoped it was because you were my boyfriend."

"I was, Sorrow." He meets my eyes, earnest. "I care about you. A lot. Say the word and I'm back on board, baby. Your sheriff is lucky. Any man would be. But when it comes to the lodge, you're flying solo. You can't run that place alone. It's like a demolition zone. Someone needs to look out for you."

The unexpected tenderness makes my eyes burn. Little does he know how much protection I actually need. And even though Billy would disagree, I find myself confiding. "Billy thinks everything that's been happening... he doesn't think those were accidents."

Damien goes still, his mouth slack. "What do you mean, not accidents?"

"Think about it." I lean my head back, rattling it off. "The tree branch, the bear box, the black ice—sure, stuff happens. But the kitchen fire? That wasn't my fault. Sully and I keep a spotless oven. And then Laura's hit-and-run. She was driving my car." I look up. He's wearing a strange expression. "What?"

"Just..." His brow is creased in a frown. "Who would want to hurt you?"

"I don't know." I stand abruptly, a hand on my stomach. Nausea churns—not just at the thought of someone out there wanting to hurt me, but at the sudden, wrong feeling in the air.

"Are you sick?" he asks, eyes focused hard on me.

"No, I just..." I trail off. Something's wrong. At first I think Damien's reacting to me, but then I notice his breathing—open-mouthed and shallow. "Damien. Are *you* sick?"

He rakes a hand through his hair, frowning. "I feel weird. Thought maybe you did, too." His laugh is thin, forced. His skin looks gray, his face drawn. "What'd you put in that water bottle?"

"Nothing," I say, alarm flaring.

"Oh shit." He turns his back to me, scrambling toward the railing. "I think I'm gonna be sick."

I rush to him, rubbing his back. "Can you make it outside?" I try to joke. "Pretty sure the bats won't appreciate you puking in their territory."

He laughs weakly. "Gross, Bail." He tries to smile, but his face goes slack. "I need some fresh air," he mumbles, the words slurred.

He tries to stand and stumbles into me. I brace against the railing. He smells like chocolate.

An alarm bell goes off in my head. "Are you allergic to anything? Maybe something weird in the cookies?" I grab his arms, trying to pull him away from the edge. He needs air, and I need to call an ambulance.

"Shhii—" He blinks heavily, slurring harder.

"Can you breathe?" My mind races. I check my phone—no bars. I want to try his, but it's in his pocket, and I can't reach it with his weight on me. "We need to call an ambulance."

He shakes his head. "Ressep... resss..."

No reception. "Got it. Let's get you outside. Can you walk?"

He nods, swallowing hard. Maybe he won't vomit after all. The thought spurs me into action.

"Ready? On three. One, two—" I brace against the railing, trying to heave him off me so we can shuffle side by side.

He stumbles and lands hard. There's a sharp crack—and suddenly I'm falling. Nothing beneath me but open air.

Time suspends, an eternity in half a second—then I crash down and pain explodes. I hear a horrific snap, then feel it a beat after. My arm. That sound was so awful, I know it'll haunt me. I cradle it close, breathing through my teeth.

Then, strangely, calm clarity settles over me. I assess. Everything hurts, but nothing else feels broken. Damien is shouting.

"I'm okay!" I call up. I pray there aren't any bats down here. The floor is wider than I expected, metal tracks disappearing into darkness. It's the eeriest thing I've ever seen. I force my voice steady. "I'm on some kind of platform."

"Don't move," he says, still slurred, but sharper with panic now.

"The ladder." I inch toward it with my good hand, but the wood crumbles in my fingers. Tears sting my eyes. "Rotted."

"Told you... don't move." His words come slowly, but at least they're clearer. "I'll... get help."

"No! You can't drive like this. I'll be okay." I hear him moving around above and shout, "Don't you dare leave, Damien Simmons!"

"It's... no good, Sorrow. I'm... been... coward... enough."

His footsteps scuffle away, and then nothing. Just the echo of my breath in a cavern twenty feet underground.

Chapter Forty-Two

Billy

I STORM INTO THE TAVERN. Dispatch relayed a thirdhand message from the EMT—an accident.

Keri flashes through my mind.

Not Keri, I remind myself. Sorrow wasn't on scene. But she's in danger, and I have to find her.

The tavern door slams against the wall as I shove it open. Heads turn.

Bear spins on his stool. "What the hell's gotten into you? Coming in here like a bat outta—"

I cut him off. "There's been an accident. Damien went off the road. He's injured and getting medevacked to Silver City." According to the EMT, he was slurring, barely conscious, doubled over with abdominal pain—just ranting that they needed the sheriff. That Sorrow was hurt and he'd tried to get her help. That they had to go to the mine. Whatever the hell that meant.

"Sorrow was with him, and now she's not. She's out there somewhere, and I think she's hurt. He said something about an Irish mine. I need you to tell me what that means."

Mines mean shafts, unstable beams, blind drops. Dark places where no one can find you.

It's unthinkable.

At first, I thought Damien was behind Sorrow's troubles. Then he innocently said two words: green gold.

And it clicked. Not Damien. Dabney. His father. If Dabney thought Bear's property was worth something, he'd make his move the moment anything happened to the owner.

I had a motive but no proof, so I kept digging first thing this morning. Damien had been at Town Hall, combing through old mining records. The clerk, thinking it was Simmons Timber business, mentioned it to Dabney. Hearing there was an old gold mine on Bear's land must've shocked him as much as it had shocked me.

It was coming together fast. Mines mean gold. And yellow gold is worth a hell of a lot more than the green kind. Worth enough to kill for. Unfortunately, the pieces didn't land fast enough for me to warn Sorrow. I tried calling right away, but it went straight to voicemail. My texts are undelivered. Wherever she is, there's no reception.

Dabney caused the trouble—but he wasn't behind the wheel of the SUV that pushed Laura off the road. He'd have known which sister he was looking at. Which means he didn't do this himself.

En route here, I checked with the El Dorado County parole officer. The Simmons family gardener popped up—time served for breaking and entering. Men like Dabney run background checks. They always do. He knew exactly who he was hiring.

The gardener drove the SUV. Dabney pulled the strings.

And now the driver's sitting in the county lockup with a fresh set of charges. The minute I find Sorrow, I'll make damn sure Dabney Simmons joins him there.

Now the question is, what really happened to Damien—and where the hell is Sorrow.

Edith's voice quavers. "What do you mean, Sorrow's hurt?"

"I don't know." My voice sounds hollow to my own ears. Is this going to be like Keri? Not being there when she needed me? Not knowing until it was already too late?

I can't let that happen again. I won't.

I came to Sierra Falls planning to bide my years quietly. I didn't expect to live much of a life. And I sure as hell didn't expect to fall this hard for someone again—not like this.

Somewhere along the line, she didn't just get under my skin—she changed the shape of my days. Made me look forward instead of back. Made me careless with my own safety, because hers matters more.

I love her. It's that simple.

"I need to find her. Which means I need to find this mine."

The Baileys can help. They know this town better than I do, and right now I'm only panicking them. I force myself to breathe, to speak slowly. Act like the sheriff, not a man coming apart.

"The EMT said Damien was agitated. Kept repeating Sorrow's name, and something about a mine. He was fading in and out, so it was hard to follow, but he might've said an Irish mine? Does that mean anything? Maybe he meant Irish Camp Road?"

Silence. Too much of it. I want to bolt out the door, tear down every road until I find her. But I keep my voice steady and look at Bear.

"The mine, Bear. I need to find this mine."

He nods, grave. "I know the place."

"You do?" Edith breathes.

Helen blinks. "There's a mine in Sierra Falls?" She's not the only surprised one.

"You follow Irish Camp past 88," Bear says. "There's an old fire road. I played there as a kid. Lots of digging and panning back in the day. This one shut down when my granddaddy was just a boy."

I shove my hat back on. "Then that's where I'm going. Edith, Bear—rally the troops. We'll need everyone to help track her down. Helen, call the hospital. No—call Dr. Mark. Maybe he can get inside info, see if Damien's coherent yet. Hell, call everyone. And I mean everyone."

"Should we call 911?" someone asks.

"I *am* 911." I grit my teeth—didn't I just say to call everyone? "But sure, get the deputy on his cell. Scott can help, too. Maybe the Ranger Department knows this mine. They might have old survey maps."

Edith jumps up and follows me to the door. She's barely holding it together. "Please bring my girl home."

I pause long enough to meet her eyes. "I'll find her."

Bear's right behind us. "We'd be lost without her." His voice edges with panic.

I level a hard look at him. Fear strips away my filters. "That's something you could show her once in a while."

Emotion twists his face, aging him in an instant. "Then bring me with you."

"You won't move fast enough for me."

Bear snatches his coat from the hook. "And you'll never find the mine without me."

"Then make tracks, old man."

I push through the door, Bear on my heels, moving faster than I've ever seen him.

Chapter Forty-Three

Billy

WE SPEED TO THE TRAILHEAD, Bear glowering in the seat beside me. "There's one thing I don't get," he says. "Damien drunk? This time of day?" He shakes his head. "He'd never get behind the wheel like that."

I have to agree, but for different reasons. It takes a hell of a lot to get Damien drunk. Something else is going on.

"Let's just hope he had his wits about him enough to send us to the right place." The dirt road disintegrates until the wheels spin, spitting rocks against the undercarriage. I throw it in Park. "This is as far as she goes."

Bear peers out the window. "We're not close enough. You using your four-wheel drive?"

"I know how to drive in the mountains." There's no time for this. I unbuckle, jump out, then lean back in. "You gonna show me the mine, or do I need to find it myself?"

"Damned if I let you get all the glory." Bear hops out, looking surprisingly spry. He struggles with a limp, sure, but he's keeping up remarkably well for someone who's given up on good health.

The trail is slow going, and I'm crawling out of my skin with frustration. But Bear was right—the mine would've been impossible to find without help.

I slow to let Sorrow's father catch up. The pace is maddening, my fear for her consuming, and the words just spill out. "You want to know what I think?"

"Nope," Bear says between heavy breaths.

"I think you're not as feeble as you worry you are."

He doesn't look up from the trail. "I'm not feeble."

"I didn't say that. I said you *think* you're feeble. I think that stroke scared the hell out of you," I press. "I think you're afraid of testing your limits. But you were lucky. A lot of people don't survive it. You're lucky you've got a kid like Sorrow who knew the signs and got you to the hospital early. You need to think on that—on how much you have—instead of what you've lost."

"Son, here's what I think: I think I'm done hearing your claptrap theories." He looks like he's swallowed a lemon, but his brow furrows, and I have to hope my words land. Bear mutters, "I'm not afraid of you or anything, Sheriff."

A hill rises beside us, and instead of continuing on the trail, Bear faces the steep incline with a heavy sigh. "This is it."

I study the rise, picking out roots, rocks, and footholds. "Up it is, then. I'll go first." What I don't say is that I'll haul Bear up as I go.

He's trembling by the time he reaches the top. "That way." He points along the ledge, trying to catch his breath. "You'll see it. On the right."

He needs a minute to recover, but I can't wait. "You'll be fine here?"

"Right behind you," Bear says. "I told you. Not feeble."

If I weren't looking for the mine, I'd hike right past it. Just a small black hole in the rock face—no wonder folks forgot it over the years.

I shout for her and strain to hear a reply. Sorrow answers quickly, but her voice sounds strained and far away. Relief hits me. She's alive.

I break into a run—a stupid, precarious thing to do on this ledge, but I can't stop. I need to get to her.

I duck into the mine and stop short, waiting for my eyes to adjust. The air is close, the cool pine breeze at my back mixing with the still scents of dirt and abandoned nests.

"Sorrow!" I shout again, and bats explode from the darkness, a shrieking, flapping cloud.

Sorrow screams.

I run toward the sound, scanning the ground. I've been careless, but it'll be unforgivable if I fall to my death now. "It's okay. Just bats. They won't hurt you."

"Easy for you to say." Her voice wavers, but that little attempt at humor gives me hope.

I spot the broken railing in the shadows, a timber skeleton guarding a narrow black hole in the ground. I edge closer, not trusting the floor beneath me. Below is a mineshaft, as narrow as a well.

I drop to my belly and inch forward. "I'm here, babe." A ladder snakes up to the surface. She's halfway up it, startlingly close.

"Help me," she says, and my relief flips to alarm.

Her pain bleeds through every word. My eyes adjust fully now, and I take it all in. At least half the rungs have crumbled to dust, and she holds one arm tucked tight to her side.

"Stop," I order. "Good God, Sorrow. What are you doing? You're going to kill yourself."

I lean over the edge as far as I dare, stretching my arm toward her, but it's no good. She's just out of reach.

I run my hand down the ladder rails. Between us there are only a couple of nubs where rungs should be. "Looks like you can't go any higher. Can you ease yourself back down?"

She gives a tight shake of her head. "A bunch of rungs snapped when I stepped on them."

She's too high to climb down. Her arm's broken, and God knows what else. I can't risk her falling. The only direction she can go is up.

I scan the shaft. The remains of an old pulley system hang overhead, ropes rotted decades ago. Why don't I keep rope in the car? When we get out of here, I'm reassessing every piece of safety gear in my SUV.

Bear's scuffling footsteps echo behind me. "You sure ran off half-cocked," the old man says.

"Dad?" Sorrow's voice breaks on the word.

"I'm here, girl. We're getting you out." Bear steps to the edge, sucking on his teeth, thinking hard. "We'll need something for this."

"It's too tight for me to ease down beside her." I look up at Bear. "Any ideas?"

"Be right back," is all he says.

Sorrow makes a tiny whimper, and as much as I want to soothe her, I know what she needs is distraction. "Hold on," I say firmly. "I'm right here. Talk to me, Sorrow."

She makes a sound that's half laugh, half sniffle. "Talk to you?"

"Yeah, babe. You can start by telling me how you managed to get halfway up a mineshaft with a broken arm, using nothing but a rotting ladder."

Silence for a moment, her breath echoing in the narrow shaft. "A lot of shimmying," she says finally, her voice shaking.

She's trying, so I try, too. I keep my tone light. "I'd like to see that sometime."

But she doesn't take the bait. When she speaks again, her voice is fragile, cracking like a kid's. "My dad really came?" She forces a weak laugh. "I bet he's just worried I won't get the roast in the oven in time to feed the early birds."

Her doubt in her own lovability guts me. "Aw, hell, Sorrow. Of course he came. He loves you. We all do."

The words roll out before I can stop them, and I feel Sorrow hold her breath. She looks up at me, her face pale and dirt-smudged, glowing in the shadows. "You do?"

"You know it." My voice is steady. "I do, Sorrow. I love you. And the moment we get you out of here, I'm going to show you just how much."

"Cool your jets," Bear grumbles behind me. "Son of a gun, Sheriff, can't you control yourself for two minutes?"

I feel like slugging the guy—until I see the giant branch he's dragged in behind him. My eyes widen. "Where the hell'd you get that?"

"From a tree." Bear mutters, "Fool city boys."

I roll my eyes. "A tree, he says. I figured that much for myself, old man. I mean, how?"

"Just used my belt to pull it down." Bear tries to look casual, but pride shines in his eyes. "Back in my timber days, we called it tree fishing. Best way to clear the deadwood. We used rope, but a belt works just fine."

I give him an admiring look. "Apparently."

Bear steps to the ledge and calls down to his daughter, "Got to get you back for the early birds. They think you're making pot roast."

"Told you," Sorrow exclaims, but there's humor in her eyes now. It's exactly what she needed.

I lower the branch down the hole. The thing must be a good twenty feet long, scraping along the ceiling as I feed it in. Dust and bits of rope shower onto Sorrow. She turns her face away, eyes squeezed shut. Debris pelts me, but I don't move—I can't take my eyes off her.

I worry the branch might snap, but it's dead, not rotten, and still has enough give to bend. Too spindly at the top to hold her weight, though. Leaning against one side of the ladder, it gives just enough traction for her to shimmy up. I don't need her to go far—just high enough for me to grab her. She scrambles, and I hold my breath. Finally she's within reach.

"Grab my hand, Sorrow. I got you."

"Reach, girl," her dad echoes. "You're there."

She hooks the elbow of her broken arm around a jagged rung, wincing. Her good hand stretches until her fingers brush my arm. I grab her forearm and scoot backward, hauling her up and over.

Still on the ground, I pull her into my arms, careful of her injury. I drink her in—filthy face, cobwebbed hair, a goose egg rising on her head the size of a baseball. I don't really see any of it. All I know is I'm holding my future wife. "You're one helluva woman, you know that, Sorrow Bailey?"

"I know it." She gives me a wide smile. "Oh, and Sheriff? I love you, too."

Bear turns away, giving us a moment. "If you kids are done, let's get the hell out of here. I've got a neck to wring. I plan on killing Damien Simmons with my bare hands."

"It wasn't Damien's fault," she says as I help her stand. She sways, and I pull her close.

"Like hell it wasn't Damien." Bear snarls. "He brought you here, didn't he?"

"No, Dad. My falling was an accident." Sorrow clings to me for balance as we leave the mine, and I think I might never let her go again. "I think he ate something that made him sick."

I nod and say, "Something from his parents, I'll bet."

"Wait"—she stops—"What? Dabney and Phoebe sent us cookies. How'd you know?"

I keep us moving, talking as we walk. "All the problems at the lodge, Laura's hit-and-run... it was Damien's dad. He's been sabotaging you all along." She stumbles, and I hitch her higher, taking more of her weight. "We need to get you to the hospital."

"You need to tell me what happened," she insists. She's striding along the path, looking nothing like a woman who spent the afternoon trapped in a mineshaft.

There's no stopping her. I shake my head. "Dabney wanted your land. At first he wanted the timber. Then he found out about the gold."

"But that mine isn't on our land," Bear says.

"And Damien told me it was a failure anyway," Sorrow adds.

"It's true," I say. "The lode was played out, and that mine *was* a failure. Thing is, that wasn't the mother lode. The mother lode is on Bailey acreage."

"Get out," Sorrow says. "Are you saying there's gold on our land?"

"That's exactly what I'm saying."

"How do you know?"

"Once I learned that Dabney knew about the mine, it was a no-brainer. There aren't many surveyors around. It took me fifteen minutes to track down the one he hired out of Sacramento. Modern tech's turned prospecting into a whole different ball game. The guy was happy to tell me all about it. They found gold—a high-grade vein."

"I still don't get how Dabney could've done all this," Sorrow says. "He was with us in the kitchen when the oven exploded. It was his car that got hit when Helen spun out on the black ice."

"Dabney didn't do it alone. He had help from his family gardener. The man has a record as long as your arm."

"Crazy," Sorrow says. "But you know what's crazier... we're rich."

"Easy," Bear says. "That ain't how it works. My granddad

was panning for gold before Dabney Simmons was a light in his mama's eye. We're all sitting on gold out here. It's the mining of it that's hard. Dabney's too much the fool to know that." He looks at me, getting back on point. "So if it's my land, why did he pick on my daughter?"

I pause to help them both down into a ravine. "It makes sense. For all my doubts, Damien turns out to be a decent guy." I slide my arm around Sorrow's waist, adjusting her so I take most of her weight. "Every accident at the lodge nudged the two of you closer. When you had trouble, Damien came running. If you'd eventually married him, the mine would've become just another part of the Simmons empire. Or at least your share would've been."

"Then why try to run me over? I can't marry Damien if I'm dead."

"The game got deadly when you had the good sense to break up with Prince Charming. That's when it was time to sabotage the lodge and take it by force." I glance at Bear. "I'm guessing Dabney's long-term plan was to drive your business into the ground and then make you an offer you couldn't refuse."

Sorrow staggers as we reach the bottom of the gully, and I scoop her fully into my arms.

"Put me down," she protests instantly. "I'm too big to carry."

I give her a little bounce, careful of her arm. "You feel just right."

She wraps her good arm around my neck, and the feel of her is like a puzzle piece snapping into place. She whispers in my ear, "Thanks for finding me."

I nod toward Bear. "Couldn't have done it without that man."

"Your mom and I would be lost without you, girl." Bear's

cheek twitches, and I chuckle, seeing how hard it is for him to open up. "Thought I'd have to come drag you out of that mine myself. Your sheriff was moving slower than molasses in January."

"Wow… rich or not, we're sitting on a gold mine," she repeats. "You know what that means? I'm definitely getting an assistant."

Her comment draws a laugh from her grumpy father. She joins in, and it's a wonderful sound. She tucks her head into my neck and I hold her close as I carry her back to the car.

She's wrong—she's a feather in my arms. I could carry her forever if she lets me. I hope she will.

I'll never forget Keri—she was my first love, and there's no greater gift than that. But I've aged a lifetime in these past years, and my heart and soul have found peace here with Sorrow.

I let Bear walk ahead on the trail. Sorrow nestles closer. "Thanks for carrying me."

"I was just thinking there's nothing better than holding you." I hug her tighter, overwhelmed by the need to keep her close.

She nips my ear, whispering, "I could think of maybe one thing that's better."

We head to Silver City Memorial, where she gets bandaged up. Then I drive her back to my place, eager to test that theory.

"You sure you don't want to lie in bed?" I'm torn. I want to be gentle with Sorrow. But I also want her—to love her, take care of her. To show her I'll do all of that for the rest of her life if she'll let me.

Sorrow uses her good hand to grab a pillow from my couch and toss it in front of the fireplace. "I'm very sure I want to lie right here, with you, in front of the fire that you're about to make for me."

I add a couple more pillows, building a cozy nest. "I'm about to make you a fire, am I?"

She nods, settling under the afghan. "Mm-hm. A nice big hot one."

"I best get to it, then." I crouch at the hearth, stacking kindling and logs. I glance back as I twist newspaper into tight rolls for tinder. The sight of her arm in a cast knots my gut. It could've been worse—she could've needed surgery. Or I might not have found her at all.

I shove that thought away. I'll stay here with her, in this moment, looking toward the future, finally at peace with the pain of the past.

"Hey, Sheriff." Sorrow's eyes shine with a saucy light I'm getting to know well. "You almost done over there?"

I chuckle. God, I love this woman. "Oh, I'm done... with the fire, that is." I stand, wiping my hands on a rag. The kindling catches, crackling warm at my back as I turn to her. "I was thinking maybe you wanted me to do something else."

"How'd you know?" She lifts the afghan for me. "You're going to join me."

"Join you?" I kneel beside her.

"Definitely. A girl gets cold on the floor. And lonely."

"Cold and lonely. We can't have that." I slide in next to her, and she turns to face me, wrapping her good arm around my neck. "You okay?" I ask, helping her adjust her injured arm.

We prop her broken wrist on a pillow above her head. "I'm good now," she says.

I let out a satisfied sigh. "You are. You have no idea how good." I stroke my hand up her side, feeling her relax beneath my touch. At the hospital, she couldn't get her sweater back over her cast and was shivering in just her tank, so I put my flannel on her. Just like I imagined, she's sexy as hell in the oversized red and black plaid. "You warming up?"

She shifts closer under the blanket, her smile telling me everything. "It's getting downright hot in here."

"I'll say." I slip my hand beneath the flannel, pulling her closer until there's no space left between us.

She catches her breath, clinging to me as the fire crackles behind us. "Now I'm burning up," she whispers.

I brush her hair from her face. "You're so beautiful." My gaze drops to her mouth, soft and glistening. "I could kiss you forever."

Her lips curve in a wicked smile. "I was hoping you had other things in mind."

We kiss until we're breathless. "Maybe we should slow down."

She meets my gaze, steady and sure. "I don't want to slow down."

I freeze. "Are you sure?" My body is on fire, aching after the fear of almost losing her, but I won't push her one inch past what she wants. "I can wait."

"Well, I can't." She holds my gaze, firelight painting gold along her cheek. "Billy, I've never been more sure of anything in my life."

I smile, and it's the first easy breath I've taken all night. "Then I know what we need to do." I roll onto my back, and she gives a surprised little chirp as I lift her over me. "How about this?"

She gives me a naughty smile as I pull her into my lap. "Mm. This." She leans down to kiss me. "This is good," she whispers against my mouth.

I draw her close, the firelight flickering around us, and rest my forehead against hers. "I'll keep you close forever, Sorrow. If you'll have me."

And she does.

Chapter Forty-Four

Sorrow

IT's a perfect day for a festival, under a cloudless, robin's-egg blue sky. The spring snowmelt sends the falls rushing in bright, frothy flashes between the pines.

Someone steps up beside me. I don't even need to look to know it's Laura. I tuck my hands into my pockets and lean gently into her shoulder.

For all our bickering and rivalry, when things finally shifted between us, it happened quietly. I see clearly now how the lodge is Laura's place. It's my turn to spread my wings.

Handing over my management duties was a giddy day. Laura's first order of business? Putting me in charge of revamping the tavern menu. Dad grumbled, but there's no arguing with a united front. And Sully was thrilled—claimed if he never baked another Prospector's Pie, it'd be too soon.

We've been a team ever since, and today's festival is the latest thing to benefit. It's still early, but the place is already hopping. For a moment, we just stand there in a shared, satisfied silence. With Laura's marketing savvy and my way with people and food, this might be the most successful event our town has ever seen.

Laura wraps an arm around me and squeezes. "You done good, little sis."

"Me?" I step back to meet her eye. "You did all the behind-the-scenes work. This festival wouldn't have happened without you." I lift a hand to stop her argument. "Seriously. This town wasn't the same without you. I should've seen it sooner."

Screams and laughter rise in the distance. Laura tilts her head. "Pie toss."

We spot Ruby and Pearl Kidd headed our way. Marlene and Sully are a few paces behind them—holding hands.

"How awesome is that?" Laura whispers.

"The absolute awesomest."

"Wonder what the old aunties think?"

I snort. "They probably think Marlene's become a fast woman."

"Well, good on her." Laura grins. "We fast girls need to stick together."

As the entourage approaches, I murmur, "I'll regret to my dying day that I didn't see them the day I fell down that mine."

"You missed it." Laura stifles a giggle. "Those two showed up like a SWAT team. They were quite the sight, bouncing along in Marlene's old pickup, Ruby clutching a fistful of survey maps."

Tears of laughter sting my eyes. "If Billy and Dad hadn't found me, Pearl and Ruby would've tracked down that mine and rescued me themselves."

"Don't you know it. You should've seen Mom's face. 'Lord help us, it's the Kidd ladies.'" Laura mimics Mom's high-pitched alarm, making me laugh even harder. "When they peeled into the driveway, I thought they'd take out the porch."

"Shhh." I try to tamp down my giggles. "They'll hear you."

"Congratulations to us!" Pearl calls as they near. "It's a smash!"

Ruby beams. "It's an attendance record! Tourists, historians, even folks from the Bay Area. I just wish Emerald were here."

"Oh, Emmie." Pearl sighs. "She'd think this was a hoot."

Marlene kisses us on the cheeks. "Ma would've loved it."

Pearl tugs impatiently on Laura's arm. "Did you know there's a reporter from the Sacramento Bee here?"

"A reporter," Marlene says with awe, facing Laura. "That has you written all over it."

"Could be." Laura shrugs, though she can't hide the smile. "I might've known someone who knew someone."

I add, "The biggest news seems to be how our 'Buck Larsen Festival' turned into the first annual Sierra Falls Gold Rush Women's Festival."

Laura meets my eye. "Can't hold a festival for someone who was a jerk."

I grin at her. "Thanks for shifting course. I love the new theme."

She nudges my shoulder. "What man in his right mind leaves a woman named Sorrow anyway?"

The comment makes me shy, but in a good way. Only now do I realize how loved I am in Sierra Falls, and Billy helped open my eyes to it. Seeing the town through his outsider's view, I recognize how precious it is. Snowcapped peaks, sparkling lakes, the roar of the falls, the thick scent of pine—I'm suddenly seeing my home anew.

The mountains are in my blood. I'm not trapped here—I carry this place in my heart. I feel woven into Sierra Falls, just as I feel tied to my thrice-great-grandmother, Sorrow Crabtree, a woman like me, trying to find love and her own path.

I meet Laura's gaze. "Dedicating this to pioneer women was genius."

"Except"—Sully nods toward a booth—"your father's over there complaining he didn't win the cakewalk."

Everyone laughs. Laura claps me on the shoulder. "Dad's her biggest fan."

I shrug, my smile easy. "Go figure."

"So Bear finally saw the light." Marlene smiles.

"And more power to her," Sully adds, looking proud. "New head chef of the Thirsty Bear—been a long time coming."

Our regular diners all know by now. Hard to miss, since Dad struts around bragging about how people better make reservations because they're booked solid with his youngest daughter as head *chef*—always stressing the word like it's French.

"Will you miss it?" Laura asks Sully.

"I'm happy to say good-bye to burgers for a while." Sully tucks Marlene closer. "My Harley's in the shop getting tuned. Me and Marlene are taking a trip in June. Maybe up to Oregon."

"We'll miss you," I say.

"You'll be too busy to miss us," Marlene teases, her wink implying more than my kitchen duties.

I'll never forget the day my parents told me their plan. "You're going to cook," Dad said. "Every day of the week, if you want."

It was such a sudden shift that I didn't fully believe it. "I thought you were upset... about the oven, I mean. That it got ruined on my watch."

"The oven?" He'd scoffed. "Hell, girl. Everyone knows that damned Dabney caused the fire. Screw the oven." His voice had gone gruff and ragged. "I could've lost you."

His emotion humbled me, and it shocked me, too. Something changed that day at the mine, and part of the credit belongs to Billy, who'd seen right through my father's gruff exterior.

"You're our baby," Mom said.

Dad nodded, practically an outburst for him. "We rely on

you. We already have one kid too far away." His face pinched in that way that looks angry on anyone else but on him it means he's feeling too much.

Mom stepped in, gentler. "What your father is trying to say is we rely on you. How would we—how would I—have managed without you?" She shot him a look. "He's held on to the past too tightly. Maybe he thought a firm grip would keep you from running off like the others."

"I'm not running anywhere. I just want credit. Responsibility."

Dad gave a gruff nod, struggling for words. "It's been hard. The stroke."

"Oh, Daddy." I hugged him then, and he wrapped me tight. "You're still strong, still important. You always have been."

He'd patted my shoulder, uncomfortable with all the emotion. "Fine then. You run a tight kitchen. Now get to it. Lunch crowd's coming."

And that was that.

Sully's voice pulls me back. "Only makes sense," he says. "Nobody packs the place like Sorrow here."

"And you taught her everything she knows, didn't you?" Marlene pats his arm. "Though it's a wonder Bear didn't see what was going on under his nose. What a shock about Dabney."

"I guess Damien will get his shot at Simmons Timber sooner rather than later," I say. "His dad can't run the company from prison, can he?"

"Prison?" the Kidd sisters gasp together.

"Just what we need," Laura mutters. "Another Simmons male on the throne."

I defend him instantly. "Don't count Damien out. There's a good guy in there—he'll find his way out."

"Speaking of changes…" Marlene's gaze drifts across the grass to her grandson spreading a picnic blanket for him and his date. "Did you hear? Craig's headed to Great Lakes after graduation. Joined the Navy. Says he's tired of being land-locked." She sighs.

"It's a good life." Sully tucks her closer, ignoring Pearl and Ruby's scandalized looks at his open affection. "He's ready, Marlene. He's a man."

She pats his hand, grateful. Those two make a great couple.

I glance at Laura to share a look, but her eyes are narrowed in that scary way I recognize. Here we go.

"Where's your boyfriend?" she asks.

Boyfriend. The word doesn't fit anymore—it's too small for what Billy is. This morning he caught my hand as I rushed past, pulled me back, and pressed a kiss to my temple without a word. That simple gesture was all it took to ground me again, his steady warmth already woven into my days.

We haven't been together long, not in the scheme of things, but what we have is built, not imagined. Solid. Even without him here, I feel anchored. Aware of him, certain of us—like our hearts are connected no matter where he is.

Something flutters beneath my ribs. Anticipation I can't name.

But I only shrug. "Once he saw the booths were all up and running, he said he had some quick department business to take care of."

I don't find out exactly what that pressing business is until later that afternoon.

Chapter Forty-Five

Billy

I HATE LEAVING Sorrow on her big day, but it's only for a little while, and it's necessary.

I've got a ring to pick up in Silver City.

I cut the timing close, but I want everything perfect—perfect size, perfect fit—when I give it to her. And man, this ring is just right.

I knew it the moment I saw it in the jewelry store window. An antique diamond, circled by tiny sapphires in an engraved platinum setting. Delicate and exquisite, but solid, too. Not flashy. Not pretentious. A classic.

Just like Sorrow.

As the namesake and great-great-great-granddaughter of the original Sorrow Crabtree, she's been asked to join the other women in their period dresses for the late-afternoon supper show. Plenty of townsfolk have gotten into it, dressing like pioneers and prospectors from the gold rush days. Everyone's drifted from the picnic grounds into the hall for the music and saloon dance numbers the elder Sorrow might've performed herself.

Little does the audience know they're about to get an even better show.

Unable to resist her enthusiasm in the days leading up to the festival, I found an old-time sheriff's costume online. And

I'll admit, I feel like a badass clinking around in my new spurs.

We've talked around marriage enough that I'm pretty sure I'll find a willing partner. Lately, though, I've been avoiding the subject—not because I'm unsure, but because I want to keep the surprise.

My smile is wide as I watch her laugh and fake her way through the dance-hall steps. For someone so hardwired for responsibility and family, she knows how to experience joy. The pleasure she takes in her cooking is just the start. She embraces life with an easy, natural immediacy that's helped me step back into my own life. Back into my own heart.

The number ends, and for a moment I lose her in the milling, cheering crowd. A sharp pang hits me when I spot her again at the edge of the stage. The buzz of the audience tunnels out. She's the reason I'm here, happily wearing this silly costume with a diamond ring in my pocket.

I watch her, everything in me settling just from the sight of her. Someone in the crowd shouts something, and she smiles down, caught in a three-way conversation with June Harlan at the piano. Sorrow is openhearted, fiercely loyal, stubborn in the best way, quick to laugh. Everyone loves her. How I get to be the one she comes home to is beyond me.

And she really is the one. My heart is clear on that. Maybe, deep down, I sensed it from the start. After Keri died, I thought the well inside me had dried up for good. But Sorrow brought it back—quietly, steadily—just by being in my life.

She's the gift I never expected: a second chapter. A love more profound because I understand now how rare, how precious it really is.

I can't wait another second. I move toward her, parting the crowd, the clink of my spurs widening my grin.

I hop onto the stage and take her hand. The room hushes.

She beams. "Hey, stranger! There you are. I've been wondering—"

I drop to one knee. The crowd gasps, and her words stop.

An elderly voice calls, "I knew it!"—one of the Kidd sisters, probably Pearl. Laughter follows, cheers rising behind it.

I barely hear any of them. All I see is Sorrow. The room goes quiet.

I look up at her, flushed from dancing, blond waves slipping loose to frame her face. She's a vision.

Her eyes meet mine—bewildered, thrilled. I can see her breath catch against the tight bodice of her dress.

Something in my chest loosens. She'll say yes. I know it. I know *us*.

Calm and sure, I squeeze her hands and clear my throat. "Sorrow Ann Bailey, would you do me the honor of becoming my wife?"

Whoops and whistles explode through the hall. I hear Bear somewhere boasting that he's got a lawman in the family now.

She laughs and cries, nodding hard, her eyes serious but her expression bright. Radiant. Joyful. So perfectly her. "Yes, yes," she says. "Yes."

That word reverberates straight through me. I'd planned to be discreet—being the town sheriff and all—but I can't help myself. I stand and kiss her.

The crowd erupts again.

My next words are just for her. She's always longed to see the world, and I need her to know she's free to chase every dream. I'd follow her anywhere. Home is wherever she is. "We can go anywhere," I tell her. "Live anywhere. I'd even go back to the city, if you wanted. You name it."

She cups my cheek, her touch electric, her blue-green eyes locked on mine. The last ache inside me melts away. "We'll travel," she says. "But I always want to come home with you. To Sierra Falls."

Sorrow

THE CROWD SWIRLS AROUND US, but I barely hear them. Billy slides the ring onto my finger—antique platinum, a diamond circled by tiny sapphires—and it fits like it was always meant to be there.

I look up at him, this man who showed up in my life when I wasn't looking. Who saw me clearly when I couldn't see myself. Who made something true feel inevitable.

His eyes are bright. Hopeful. A little nervous, even now.

I rise on my toes and kiss him again, slower this time. *Mine,* I think. *Ours.*

Behind us, someone wolf-whistles. Dad's voice booms something about champagne. The piano starts up again, and the hall erupts into noise and laughter and life.

But right here, in this small circle of two, everything is quiet. Everything is certain.

I'm home.

Read on for a sample of *What Love Desires,*
book two in the Sierra Falls series. Pre-order now!

Laura

My eyes track up the ladder and land on one of the tightest posteriors I've ever seen. My brain blanks. I'd come here furious —an entire speech rehearsed on the drive over. But apparently one magnificent male tush is enough to wipe my thoughts clean.

The ladder squeaks as the man shifts and looks down, and I catch the ruggedly handsome face attached to said magnificence.

Every muscle in my body locks. A Jessup. I'm allergic to Jessups.

Eddie Jessup, to be precise—the worst of the bunch.

He grins. "Can I help you?"

My morning hadn't started like this. It'd been great, actually, helping my family handle the breakfast rush. Business is booming. Visitors to Big Bear Lodge are up, diners are piling into the tavern, and I'm riding high as the new manager overseeing it all.

For months I've thrown myself into the work. Ever since my sister found those gold-rush letters, I've used my experience and Bay Area contacts to generate press. We've attracted a handful of tweedy historian types, which means even more visitors and more momentum for our family lodge.

But not if Eddie Jessup and his cursed Jessup Brothers Construction are doing what I heard they're doing.

It's a clear June day. I shield my eyes against the glare as he climbs down the ladder. I'm definitely *not* noticing the way his white T-shirt clings in places under the hot sun.

"You got something to say, or did you just come to ogle?"

That snaps me out of it. "I have better things to do than ogle you, Eddie Jessup."

He laughs—easy, confident—which only makes my cheeks heat. I glance down at my phone like I suddenly need to check a text.

He hops off the last rungs, dusts off his hands, and smiles at me. "Well, darlin'? To what do I owe the honor?"

This particular Jessup has been tormenting me since middle school—teasing, coaxing, challenging. Back then, I was counting the days until I could bolt from Sierra Falls. Somehow, Eddie sensed it and doubled down. A habit he's never outgrown.

But I have. Big-time.

I'm Jessup-proof now. I'm a college-educated, formerly successful Silicon Valley marketing professional who moved home as a full-grown woman for perspective. I'm definitely not in search of a man—Jessup or otherwise. I swore off dating, along with the fast-paced city life and the ex-fiancé I don't miss. I'm here to figure out what I want, what makes me happy.

I plant my hands on my hips. "I'm not your darlin'."

He gives me an assessing look. "More's the pity."

I fight the urge to adjust my shirt under that stare. "So don't call me that."

"Yes, ma'am." He taps the brim of his ballcap with infuriating solemnity. Before I can tell him not to ma'am me either, he adds, "So what brings a fine, not-your-darlin' city girl like you to a construction site? Because I can see it all over that pretty face—you've got something to say."

Fine. Pretty. I refuse to react. Eddie probably tosses compliments like that at every woman within ten miles. And I do have something to say... if only my brain would cooperate.

My rehearsed arguments finally resurface. "What are you doing here?"

He puts on an innocent look. "Fixing a storm drain."

"I can see that. I mean what are you doing..." I sweep my arm at the abandoned house and surrounding ranch property. "Here."

"Ah." For once, he looks serious. "You heard the news."

"Yeah, I heard about your Golden Slumbers Ranchlandia."

He laughs. "It's Sleepy Hills Resort and Spa."

"Whatever." I wave a hand. "Sounds like a cemetery. Fitting, since you're about to bury the Bailey family business."

"We have no intention of burying your business." His tone is annoyingly calm. "It'll be good for the whole town. Fairview Properties contracted us. We'll buy supplies local, from Tom's hardware. We'll hire local. And those workers will go eat at your tavern. Money coming in all around."

I tap my chin. "And the big winner? Fairview. They roll into town, build their giant resort, and mow down anything in their path." Including my family's lodge. "What's next? A Hilton?"

"Easy, Laura. I'm not the bad guy here."

His soothing tone only irritates me more. I jab a finger into his chest. "How about we kick the Kidd sisters out and turn their house into a Holiday Inn?"

"Nobody was kicked out. Those dot-com folks abandoned this place for a swanky Sausalito condo years ago. It'll be good to fix it up." He takes my finger, gives it a gentle squeeze. "Look, Laura. I run a small business. We take the jobs we get, just like everyone else." His hand is warm, callused, and aggravatingly gentle.

I pull free. "What about *our* business? The lodge can't compete with this." I glare at the ranch house—a rambling one-story with sagging beams and likely ancient wiring. "It's a dump, by the way."

"Nothing the Jessup boys can't fix."

"I hope you get overrun by raccoons."

"Don't get any ideas." He steps behind me, hands settling lightly on my shoulders as he looks out at the property with me. "See the size? Smaller than a typical hotel. Fairview wants a boutique spa. High-end. The kind of people who like to think they hike but wouldn't know a day pack from a day planner." He squeezes my shoulders. "But your lodge is authentic. Tourists love that. You'll be fine."

I stiffen and step out of his reach. The last time a man told me *you'll be fine*, I lost my job. "Eternal Slumbers here could put us under and you know it."

Eddie's expression shifts, thoughtful in a way I don't trust. "What do you want me to do?"

"I want you to get back in that ridiculous vehicle of yours, call Fairview, and send them packing. Let them menace some other small town while you crawl back under whatever rock you came from."

Instead of rising to the bait, he gives me an exasperating smile. "Not a fan of the pickup, huh?"

"You're compensating."

"Look, Laura. I'm sorry. Really. But if we hadn't been hired, someone else would have. At least this way I'm here, in your corner. I can make sure we build something good."

I fist my hands at my hips. "Something good? The only good thing would be canceling the whole project."

"I promise you, this will help business." He steps closer, lowering his voice. "Hey, I wanted to talk to you about something else, too."

My hackles go up. When a man says that, it's never good. "What?"

"You and me..." He hesitates.

My heart kicks. "There is no you and me, Eddie Jessup."

"We grew up together. And we'll be seeing a lot of each other while this place goes up. I thought maybe we could—"

"*Maybe* nothing. You know why? This." I sweep my arm at the house. "The you and me thing? Not happening."

"We have history, Laura."

I huff a laugh. "And that history tells me to keep my distance." I shake my head. "You've been under my skin since we were twelve. Whatever you've got in mind? It's not going to happen."

His gaze heats. "That sounds like a challenge."

"It's a fact." I step back. "You want a challenge? Convince Fairview to build somewhere else. Otherwise, leave me alone."

I spin on my heel and head for my car. His low chuckle follows.

"See you around, Laura Bailey."

I don't look back. I get in, slam the door, and pull away. In the rearview mirror, he stands with his hands in his pockets, that infuriating grin still plastered on his face.

Eddie Jessup is going to be a problem. I can feel it.

And the worst part? Some traitorous part of me is looking forward to it.

Pre-order *What Love Desires* now!

<u>**Highland Heroes**</u>

Time Travel Romance

Master of the Highlands

Sword of the Highlands

Warrior of the Highlands

Lord of the Highlands

<u>**The Pressing Dark**</u>

Young Adult Time Travel Romance

Across the Pressing Dark

Beyond the Bounds

Ballad of a Bonnie Rogue

<u>**Novellas**</u>

The Drowning Sea

About the Author

Veronica Wolff is an award-winning, bestselling author who likes monsters, fight scenes, and first kisses. Sometimes all at the same time. She lived everywhere from Texas to Hawaii to India before settling in Northern California, where she shares a home with her husband and her black cat familiar, Josie. She writes across several genres, including Scottish historical romance, time travel, contemporary romance, and young adult. She may or may not have a top-secret alter ego named Ron Wolff, who publishes gonzo sci-fi thrillers.

Veronica Wolff
Where you'll find me:
https://veronicawolff.com
https://veronicawolff.com/newsletter/
https://www.goodreads.com/author/show/1140298.
Veronica_Wolff

instagram.com/veronicawolff
facebook.com/VeronicaWolffFanPage
bookbub.com/authors/veronica-wolff
amazon.com/Veronica-Wolff/e/B001ILMBMK
bsky.app/profile/veronicawolff.bsky.social